EIGHT

MYSTERY WRITERS

YOU SHOULD BE READING

NOW

Lisa Alber
Kathleen Cosgrove
Michael Guillebeau
Chris Knopf
Jessie Bishop Powell
Larissa Reinhart
Jaden Terrell
Lisa Wysocky

Edited by

Michael Guillebeau

Stacy Pethel

Madison Press

River of Glass, originally published by The Permanent Press. Copyright 2014 by Jaden Terrell. Cover by Lon Kirschner.

"Searching for Bubba," copyright 2015 by Lisa Wysocky.

The Fame Equation: A Cat Enright Equestrian Mystery, originally published by Cool Titles. Copyright 2015 by Lisa Wysocky.

Publisher's Note: This is a work of fiction. Names, characters, places, and incidents are a product of the authors' imaginations. Locales and public names are sometimes used for atmospheric purposes. Any resemblance to actual people, living or dead, or to businesses, companies, events, institutions, or locales is completely coincidental.

Cover design by Charlie Wetherington.

Eight Mystery Writers You Should be Reading Now/ Edited by Michael Guillebeau. —1st ed.
ISBN 978-0-9972055-1-0

TABLE OF CONTENTS

INTRODUCTION

It's easy to find a book; it's hard to find *the* book, that new author who sets your life on fire.

That's why we put this collection together. This book gives you an easy way to sample a group of eight up-and-coming mystery writers who you may not have heard of, but who critics and award committees have noticed. We've assembled eight very different styles to let you sample a wide array of stories and find new voices you might have trouble finding on your own.

We have hard-boiled detectives, and we have crime-solving animals. We have deeply flawed characters, and we have cute youngsters. We have damaged women, kick-ass women, noble women and mean women, sometimes in the same character. We have tough guys in spades, and we have funny in spades.

Each writer contributed a story, a sample chapter from a book, and an interview. Because of our variety, there's sure to be something here you'll love, and maybe love for life.

So come on in for a taste. Here's our menu:

<u>Lisa Alber</u>–*Mystery with a smattering of psychological suspense and tons of atmosphere. Beautifully written, complex stories set in the Irish countryside.*

Reminiscent of Erin Hart, Julia Spencer-Fleming, and Susan Hill. Rosebud Award and Pushcart Prize Nominee.

<u>Kathleen Cosgrove</u>–*Florida weird with a middle-aged woman returning home. Kick-ass funny.*

<u>Michael Guillebeau</u>–*Broken war hero has to navigate the oddballs and save the girl to get back to the bar he's been hiding in. Reminiscent of Elmore Leonard and Carl Hiaasen. Silver Falchion Finalist, and Library Journal Mystery Debut of the Month.*

<u>Chris Knopf</u>–*Hardboiled in the Hamptons. Ex-boxer Sam Acquillo is a noir descendent of Travis McGee and Spencer, and one of my favorite characters. Nero award winner.*

<u>Jessie Bishop Powell</u>—*Cozy noir mysteries that embrace the genre's extremes. In The Marriage at the Rue Morgue, police suspect an orangutan of murder. Primatologists Noel Rue and Lance Lakeland have to save the ape and still find time to get married. Sounds light, but Powell's stuff is as intense as it is funny.*

<u>Larissa Reinhart</u>—*If you like Janet Evanovich's Stephanie Plum, you need to read Reinhart's Cherry Tucker. A damaged artist with twice the depth, twice the funny of Plum and set in small-town Georgia. I dare you to put this down. Daphne du Maurier Finalist*

Jaden Terrell—*Hardboiled hero with a soft heart. Nashville PI Jared McKean has enough emotional issues to carry a book by himself, and then Terrell throws him into big issues like human trafficking. Shamus Award Finalist.*

Lisa Wysocky—*Multiple awards for Lisa's books about a horse trainer with a smart horse who helps her solve crimes. One of the most realistic and loving use of animals in mystery. Winner of American Horse Publication Awards, and the IBPA Benjamin Franklin Awards.*

We invite you to see what looks good, and take a bite for yourself. If you find something you like, our chefs will be happy to give you a full meal.

And we all deliver.

FOREWORD

What are you reading? It's a question as personal and compelling as any we ask. And it's irresistible. New acquaintance or old pal, we're curious and eager—and a little hushed as we await the answer. Maybe the title we're about to hear will be our best book of the year! There's always the possibility, the intrigue, the moment of revelation.

If it's a book we've already read—ah. Then yes, we get a different kind of connection. Yes, I loved it too, we say, and proceed to compare notes on the fictional world that—through the magic of words—we two real people have entered together.

But ah, that mention of a *new* title.

Oh, I've never heard of that one, we say, our eyes widening with the prospect.

Oh, yes, our fellow reader explains. It won the—fill in the blank here—award, or got a star from *Library Journal*, or is on the new list of nominations for the Pushcart prize. Or, they say, I heard about it from someone I trust—a librarian, a friend, another writer, a bookseller. Or a reviewer I respect. Oline, maybe, or Hallie or Joe or Jon or Lesa or Jeff or Kris.

Aha! We say. That sounds terrific. And we wonder—how did we miss it?

For any number of reasons, right? Gone are the days of the leisurely stroll in the neighborhood bookstore, the class assignments, even, for some, the book club. Our schedules and our pressures, the Internet and the economy have conspired, sometimes, to keep us carefully apprised of all the books we'd hear about anyway—but not the secret treasures just waiting to be found.

These eight authors, talented all, would love to entice you to sample their mystery wares. Isn't it thoughtful of them to make it so easy to find your next unputdownable read?

So now? Do what you love the most in life: turn the page.

HANK PHILLIPPI RYAN is on-air investigative reporter for Boston's NBC affiliate, winning 33 EMMYs and dozens more journalism honors. Bestselling author of eight mysteries, Ryan's won five Agathas, two Anthonys, two Macavitys, the Daphne, and Mary Higgins Clark Award. Her TRUTH BE TOLD won the 2015 Agatha, and she edited the 2015 Agatha-winning non-

10

fiction anthology WRITES OF PASSAGE. Critics call her "a superb and gifted story-teller." A founder of MWA University, Hank was 2013 president of Sisters in Crime. Her newest book is WHAT YOU SEE, a Library Journal Best of 2015.

http://www.HankPhillippiRyan.com

LISA ALBER

Lisa Alber spent many, many years writing before her debut novel, *Kilmoon*, was published and nominated for the Rosebud Award for Best First Novel. Along the way, she graduated from Berkeley with a degree in economics, worked in international finance while living in Ecuador and Brazil, and moved to New York City to change her career to book publishing.

She finally got her break after working with *New York Times* bestselling novelist Elizabeth George in three writing workshops. Ms. George invited Lisa to apply for a writing grant from the Elizabeth George Foundation. Lisa won a grant that allowed her to quit her day-job for a year so that she could devote full energies to her fiction. What a year! She completed the manuscript for *Kilmoon* and started writing her second novel, *Whispers in the Mist* (Midnight Ink, August 2016).

In addition, Ms. George invited Lisa to write a short story for the *Two of the Deadliest* anthology (HarperCollins), which includes such notables as Laura Lippman, Dana Stabenow, and Patricia Smiley. Specifically, Ms. George thought of Lisa for inclusion in an "Introducing. . ." section to spotlight up-and-coming writers.

Nowadays, Lisa lives in Oregon with a spunky Chihuahua mix, an accident-prone cat, and her trusty laptop. She likes photography, red wine, and scary movies. She's at work on her third novel, tentatively titled *Touch of Death* (Midnight Ink Books, August 2017).

Lisa wanted to address you in her own words:

Dear Readers,

Thank you for picking up Eight Mystery Writers You Should be Reading Now. *We writers, we love readers. We do. And I'm tickled to be part of this project, getting to address myself directly to you.*

We're unapologetically tooting our horns to entice you, the almighty book lover, to share in what we do. You love to read, and we writers were all readers before we started writing. So we get it. In addition, I love interacting with readers, and I admit to the thrill of receiving kind words such as these:

Kilmoon *has captivated me and transported me to the land of my ancestors. It won't relinquish its grip! Thank you.*

Isn't that sweet? It fills my heart with quiet joy to know that my writing spoke to this reader. It's like magic.

I often get asked why I write. I write because it's in my heart to do so. Writing is who I am. It's how I process the world and my life. And then there's the question: Why write mystery rather than, say, romance or science fiction? For as long as I can remember, I've been asking "why." As in, why do people act the way they do, especially when they're being bad? Crime comes with a psychological context. I love exploring the roots of crime in my fictional world.

Also, the ultimate mystery of human existence is death itself. It's the fact of life we all share. What happens to us after we let loose our mortal coils? I have no answers. Exploring these themes through storytelling is my way of pondering the big eternal questions.

I hope you like my excerpts and also the interview. My series takes place in County Clare, Ireland. The stories are traditional in many ways; you'll discover the final solution at the end of the books with twists along the way. But they're also what might be called "psychological suspense" because I love delving into the whydunit aspect of the crime as much as the whodunit.

Please feel free to look me up on Facebook and Twitter. I look forward to hearing from you!

Happy reading!

Lisa Alber, December 2015

P.S. Just for this book, I included a deleted scene, too!

EXCERPT

Kilmoon, A County Clare Mystery

"Brooding, gothic overtones haunt Lisa Alber's polished, atmospheric debut. Romance, mysticism, and the verdant Irish countryside all contribute to making *Kilmoon* a marvelous, suspenseful read."

—Julia Spencer-Fleming, *New York Times* and *USA Today* bestselling author of *Through the Evil Days*

"This first in Alber's new County Clare Mystery series is utterly poetic ... The author's prose and lush descriptions of the Irish countryside nicely complement this dark, broody and very intricate mystery."

—RT Book Reviews (four stars)

"In her moody debut, Alber skillfully uses many shades of gray to draw complex characters who discover how cruel love can be."

—Kirkus Reviews

"Newcomer Lisa Alber's stirring debut *Kilmoon* ... exudes Irish countryside atmosphere. The murder plot is solved neatly and the door is open for Merrit's further adventures."

—Library Journal

"Lisa Alber's assured debut paints Lisfenora, County Clare, at the height of the local matchmaking festival, when the ordinarily sleepy village is crammed with revelers, cadgers, and con men galore. Amid mysteries and mayhem, Alber captures the heartfelt ache in all of us, the deep need for connection, and a true sense of purpose."
—Erin Hart, Anthony and Agatha-nominated author of *The Book of Killowen*

You can order *Kilmoon* from online retailers or through your local booksellers.

June 28, 2008

Northern California

Merrit McCallum rolled a plastic vial between her palms so that the liquid morphine sloshed against the sides. Red and viscous—like blood—the liquid coated the plastic on the inside of the vial while her slick palms left smudges on the outside. She was tempted to squirt the opiate down her own throat rather than contend with Andrew, who waited her out from his rolling bed. She no longer called him *father*.

If only he would shut up, but no, his whispered voice penetrated the leaden exhaustion that she had succumbed to weeks ago. "You know you want to," he said.

She turned away from Andrew's shrunken almost-corpse to gaze at a large framed photograph that hung above the fireplace mantel. A mist-enshrouded church stood among Celtic crosses. It was a nothing of a place, a moldering heap of rocks so old that without the crosses, it could be any artifact left to crumble in the North Atlantic rains. Andrew had insisted on hanging the image on this prime section of walled real estate. Merrit's mom, meanwhile, had banished it to the coat closet during Andrew's frequent business trips. All Merrit knew was that her parents had met in a village near the church. In Ireland.

She stared at the picture in an attempt to drown herself in the imagined sounds of whipping winds and pounding rains. It didn't work. Andrew's voice irritated like the fly that bounced against the window. The fly, like Andrew, didn't mean anything by its incessant buzzing. The fly, like Andrew, was nothing but a miserable prisoner inside this morgue of a house. Both of them irritant buzzes, no more, no less.

Just a buzz, she told herself. Don't let him get to you.

"I'm in excruciating pain," he said. "You hear me?"

She dropped the oral syringe onto the swiveling bedside table, now parked near the Barcalounger and far away from Andrew's bird-claw fingers. "It's too soon for another dose."

"Check my nightstand," he said. "You can read your mom's notebook for yourself. Then you'll see."

Notebook? What notebook? He'd never mentioned a notebook before. Or maybe he had. No, surely she wasn't so out of it that she'd forgotten something as important as words written in her mother's hand.

Merrit wished she could steady her voice, but it wobbled out of her, giving her away. "I don't understand what you're getting at. I'll see what?"

"Oh, you know."

But she didn't know anything except that Andrew exuded more energy now than he'd shown for weeks. Despite the morphine, he held her gaze with the steadiness of a combatant on the battlefield.

Merrit pressed trembling hands together and struggled to maintain her poker face. If only she could think straight. If only she hadn't been stupid enough to assume she could care for Andrew on her own. She'd forgotten why she'd insisted. Something about duty, or devotion, or loyalty. Now, six months after returning home to help him, her efforts felt pointless.

She fumbled for the cell phone that she'd left on the mantel, knocking over her inhaler in the process. It rolled under the Barcalounger. A worm of tension squeezed Merrit's lungs as she pressed in the hospice phone number. Unfortunately, sunlight barely lightened the eastern horizon. She'd have to leave a message with the answering service. She steadied her voice, requested a hospice visit, and hung up.

Merrit listened with her back still facing Andrew. She didn't need to see him to know the cracks of bitterness that etched his face. He'd been awake all night, restless and demanding, and with a strange light in his eye. She sniffed against the oppressive odor of illness in the stuffy room and eyed the knitting needles sticking out of a ball of yarn. For a while the new hobby had helped her cope. She'd even gifted Andrew with her first afghan, which now lay in a discarded heap beneath the bed.

"This pain," he said. "It's torture."

Slowly, she turned around. The glow from the bedside lamp illuminated his shiny head, which stood out of the murk like a floating skull. She knew about his pain. The hospice folks had explained it all, and it was horrible to witness. Yet, he didn't seem to be in that much pain right now. She stepped forward. And then again. Until she stood next to him. She reached out to adjust his pillow. Andrew's hand latched onto her arm. Merrit steeled herself

not to flinch at the dried-up boniness of his fingers pressed
against her skin.

"You're a coward," he said. "But then why should I be
surprised. Runs in *your* family."

"What are you saying? Why now?"

"All those years your mother kept up the pretense that she
loved me, not him," he said.

Patting her chest, Merrit retreated to the Barcalounger once
again. She dropped to her knees and felt around under the chair for
her inhaler. She pushed at the chair, but it was already wedged into
the corner of the room. Worse still, she didn't have the strength to
maneuver it over the edge of the rug and away from the wall.

Breathing hard, her brain fuzzy with exhaustion and
distress, Merrit staggered to her feet. Andrew's insidious, creeping,
rasping voice kept at her. His lips smirked. They pulsed, they pursed,
they stretched around more words.

"Your mother was a lying whore."

No.

"She screwed a goddamned hippie freak—an *Irish* hippie
freak—and said it didn't matter. Nothing but a mistake."

No. No.

Merrit grabbed the morphine syringe. She managed to
gasp, "Just to sleep for a bit. Until the hospice nurse arrives."

"You're so weak. Look at you. Poor baby can't breathe."

Merrit leaned against the lounger, panting. White bubbles
floated across her vision. She lifted the syringe and depressed the

plunger the tiniest bit. One bitter drop of morphine landed on her tongue. Andrew's hand spasmed toward her and fell back. His voice wheedled up a notch, its incessant buzz pitched high.

"Your fault she died," he said.

NO.

Merrit acknowledged the truth of the matter: Andrew had never loved her, and he never would no matter how hard she tried to be the perfect daughter. Sobbing, beyond caring, just wanting to survive this moment, she dripped another smidgen of morphine onto her tongue. Calm down, lungs, please.

"If not for you, she'd still be alive."

NO NO.

White hot despair and guilt coursed through her, so molten that anger seeped in around its edges. She pictured her mom striding away from her, hurrying away really, because she'd wanted to flee her spiteful child. Merrit opened her mouth, but nothing came out except a painful wheeze.

"You should never have been born. A mistake."

NO NO NO.

Merrit clenched the morphine syringe, shaking. The fly still buzzed, louder than ever. Her vision narrowed into a dark tunnel through which all she saw was Andrew's caved-in face. His hateful face.

"The man your precious mom fucked right before she fucked me back in 1975? He never wanted you either. Ask him yourself. After you read the notebook."

Her head exploded. "Shut up!" she screamed.

*****

The white hot rage subsided and Merrit's vision cleared. She blinked, disoriented and shaky with leftover adrenaline. It took her a moment to realize that she still held the syringe. She gaped down at the plastic vial—now empty—and then at Andrew's self-satisfied rictus of a smile, at his eyes focused on nothing. Depleted to her very core, she sank to the ground and let the syringe roll off her palm. The haunting image of the church gazed down at her as it always had, but now it also beckoned her. Come home to Ireland, it seemed to say. Find out the truth.

A trickle of longing surprised her. Yes, she'd discover the truth that had simmered beneath the facade of her parents' marriage, which was the truth that defined Merrit's very existence. Her mom died long ago, leaving Merrit alone with Andrew. Now Andrew was dead, leaving her—what?

Guilty. Lost. Possibly irredeemable.

She stared at the empty syringe lying beside her on the rug. The truth. From her real father.

Part I

Friday, August 29th – Sunday, August 31st

"Better well-intentioned duplicity than truth's fallout."
—Liam the Matchmaker

Liam Donellan's journal

Ah Kevin, as you know, we Irish, closet superstition mongers all,
find solace and hope in imagining faeries, in calling upon the spirits of the
long departed in moments of stress, in deifying the woman who gave birth to
Jesus. Whether the wood sprite at home in the local thicket or the Holy Virgin,
we Irish, we tend to prefer our myths to daily realities. Hence, the fame of the
Matchmaker of Lisfenora. Me.

In the '70s free-lovers traveled here in hopes of a good shag during
the matchmaking festival. And you'd best believe I was the shag king who
scoffed when a stranger proclaimed that my swagger masked kindness, the
proof of which was my talent for creating happily-ever-afters. Matchmaking is
the best part of me, true, but only a part of a flawed whole.

Here's what she said, this stranger: "You have something, whether
it's an amazing knowledge of human nature or an uncanny sixth sense, I don't
know. What do you call this ability of yours?"

She was an American journalist, you see, and she wanted a
rational explanation for my success rate. So I said, "There are math and music
prodigies, no one doubts that, so why not a—" and here I stopped for I didn't
know what to call myself. A gut-instinct virtuoso? An intuition whiz? Bloody
hell, an empath—that soulless word used in science fiction?

"Call me charmed for it," I said.

Chapter 1

For the seventh day in a row, Merrit sat on a plaza bench in Lisfenora, County Clare, Ireland. She sat with back straight and sure against the bench, and with bare legs stretched out and crossed at the ankle. Unlike most tourists—especially her fellow Americans— she wore flip-flops instead of sturdy walking sandals, and a skirt instead of hiking shorts. Day after day, she appeared to be waiting for someone. While she waited, she jabbed her knitting needles through blue yarn hard enough to skewer the poor sheep to death.

One of the locals, Marcus Tully, lounged beside Merrit with hands settled over his crotch. A fresh, unopened flask perched next to him. As usual, Merrit had invaded his self-assigned bench in the plaza with its centerpiece statue depicting an illustrious O'Brien of generations past. Fuchsia-lined walkways radiated from the statue like bicycle spokes. Sunlight cast a mellow glow onto colorful gift shops and pubs that pushed up against the sidewalks. All of it was bathed in an Irish heat, milky and cocoon-like compared with August in California.

Merrit stopped knitting to stretch out her fingers and gaze around the village. She reminded herself to be grateful that her journey had brought her to Lisfenora rather than to one of the nondescript villages she'd driven through after her red-eye flight.

Lisfenora was only thirty-five miles from the Shannon International Airport, yet she'd imagined she was driving into the outback, Irish style. Drystone walls snaked for miles over the hillsides, delineating emptiness rather than relieving it. One-horse— or maybe that would be one-pub—villages rose out of the early morning mists and slid away as the green expanses took over again. The roads narrowed, and Merrit hugged the embankments as she drove, unsure of herself because of the left-handed road rules. She gripped the steering wheel and scraped along the hedgerows, predicting head-on collisions every time a car barreled toward her from the opposite direction.

Two hours after leaving the airport she had arrived in Lisfenora jet-lagged and frazzled, but also intact despite the scratches marring her rental car's paint job. One glimpse at Lisfenora and she'd heaved a soul-unburdening sigh. Charming, yes, and lively, and obviously historic. It was a far cry from the claustrophobia and trauma she'd left behind in California.

Lovely, all of it, and she'd absorbed everything from the *failte* welcome mats to the old-fashioned name boards and cheery shop fronts, trying to imagine what her mom had felt when she'd first seen the village. The fact that her mom had looked upon the same stained glass transom windows had amazed Merrit most of all.

Unfortunately, after a week, her amazement had long since faded. She was here for a purpose, after all, and her purpose had led her to pester every local she'd met to no avail. She'd given up cajoling information out of Marcus days ago.

"I'm after warning you not to waste your time," he'd said. "Liam's address and phone number are off limits to tourists. You'll have to wait for the matchmaking festival to start and stand in line with the rest of the love-starved wankers."

The problem was that Merrit wasn't just any tourist, was she? She'd bet Marcus would lead her to Liam the Matchmaker if she revealed she was Liam's long-lost biological daughter. But this knowledge was hers and hers alone.

Well, almost hers alone. Anxiety constricted her chest as she fumbled her knitting. She counted back the stitches along the shorter edge of the afghan and continued on with the trim that she'd begun earlier in the day.

"Yonder Ivan, one of God's own victims," Marcus said as a short man with jutting Adam's apple and red Albert Einstein hair rounded a street corner and disappeared from view.

Merrit waited, hoping for more, then shrugged away the knot in her stomach, or rather, tried to, but the same tension that disturbed her sleep prevented her from relaxing now. "I wouldn't call Ivan a victim. He seems savvy in his own way."

"And how would you be knowing that?"

"I've met him. At the Internet café."

Marcus's grunt came along with a wrist flick. He drank with athletic gulps as if his body needed replenishing—and fast. The silver vessel settled back onto his lap, discreetly covered by his hands. Merrit thought he'd doze, but he surprised her.

"I'm a bloody ghost for all I'm noticed." He nodded to himself. "Sozzled I may be, but I'm not deaf or blind. Oh, and here comes that Lonnie the Lovely. Bloody piece of shite. Who's minding the café while Ivan is at his lunch?"

Marcus sank into grumbles as Lonnie came abreast of them from the direction of the hotel that lined one side of the plaza. Merrit averted her gaze, trying to keep her needles clicking in steady fashion. Her knuckles turned white with the effort.

"Marcus, you manky old git," Lonnie said, "made your move on Merrit yet? Get on with you or I will."

"You'd like to try, wouldn't you then. Push yourself on her. That's your way, you damned—"

"Watch yourself, old man." Lonnie turned toward Merrit, smiling as if Marcus didn't exist. "Pleasure to see you again."

Lonnie in his tight Euro-jeans and linen dress shirt bowed to Merrit and strolled off in the direction of Internet Café, which he owned.

"You stay away from him," Marcus said. "He's a shifty sort."

Too late. Since Merrit's arrival, Lonnie had aimed himself at her like a money-seeking homing device. Within twenty-four hours of meeting her, he'd boasted of knowing that she was Liam's bastard daughter—and of knowing a few other things besides. What he might know about her had caused her lungs to spasm. She'd peppered him with the obvious questions. How could you possibly know I'm Liam's daughter? What *other things* do you mean? Other things about me, or about Liam, or both?

Unfortunately, Lonnie had only smiled and shrugged. "I'll let you dangle for a while longer. More interesting that way."

Slimebag.

Lonnie could sabotage her fresh start with a fresh parent. What a depressing, not to mention infuriating, thought. This was why she couldn't sleep, and why she sat here knitting an afghan when she could be out exploring the ancient sites her mom had visited thirty years ago, especially the church that had haunted Merrit from its position on the living room wall. Merrit longed to feel Atlantic winds chapping her cheeks and scouring out the ache that had shackled her since long before Andrew's death.

Instead, here she loitered, vigilant despite Marcus's insistence that before the festival started she'd sooner see a leprechaun than see Liam. She loathed the idea of Liam learning about her from a nasty piece of work called Lonnie O'Brien. Yes, he was one of those O'Briens, descended from the founding father himself to hear Lonnie tell it. And he was quite the talker when it suited him. She imagined gossip about her circulating the pubs, which was to say the village. Lonnie could say anything, and she'd had enough public speculation aimed in her direction to last the rest of her life. This was a good enough reason for her to pay Lonnie cash in exchange for his silence. For now.

She dropped her needles and slouched like Marcus. Meeting Liam wasn't supposed to be this difficult. She couldn't have predicted villagers circling the wagons around their celebrity, this matchmaker who'd put Lisfenora on the map, who'd managed to turn an annual festival into an event known to lovelorn singles all over Europe and North America. Unfortunately, the longer her quest took, the more apprehensive she became. The possibility of rejection loomed larger than she had expected now that she was actually in Ireland.

"Look there, will you?" Marcus said, interrupting Merrit's thoughts. "Now you'll be seeing how beloved is your Lonnie. That's Danny Ahern."

Marcus had brightened at the sight of the man named Danny, a detective sergeant, Marcus said. Perhaps this detective sergeant with the careworn facial stubble and graceful hands could help her out with her Lonnie problem.

"See there?" Marcus said.

Indeed, Danny had stiffened at the sight of Lonnie and then plastered a neutral—some might call it professional—smile on his face. The two men stood at the edge of the plaza near a row of parked cars, Lonnie doing all the talking and Danny all the nodding. After a moment, Lonnie walked on and Danny grimaced in Marcus's direction. "Cheers, Marcus," he called. "Have to get on, but you'll take care not to annoy our Lonnie, will you? Seems to think your presence might be throwing off his business."

"Piss poor shite I call that!"

A smile sparkled for the barest moment before Danny tossed up a wave and departed.

"Village life," Marcus said, yawning. "After a time, you'll recognize all its muck, sitting here. Not that Lisfenora's muck is special in that regard. That Danny's a good one though. A lifesaver to me, that's the truth. And like a second son to Liam, I might add. Quite the threesome, them."

Second son?

"The matchmaker has a son?" Merrit said.

"Indeed. Kevin. But he's not much about the village since last year's festival. Been keeping himself scarce you might say. As anyone might expect, truth be told."

Merrit waited, but once again Marcus lapsed into silence. That was the problem with Marcus—just when he started to open up, he stopped talking. Still. A son, a brother. Maybe she could get to know Liam's son first. She imagined a man similar to her, but younger—yes, surely several years younger—with reddish brown hair and a small bone structure. She'd always wanted a brother. How she used to pester her mom to have a baby, little knowing that her mom could no longer bear children after her own birth.

Her mom had loved children.

Marcus's head tilted onto his shoulder. His eyelids fluttered, and Merrit leaned closer, breathing in the smell of mint toothpaste and gin fumes. The bags under his eyes looked heavier today, swollen with bluish half circles. As ever, sitting next to him comforted yet pained her. She was drawn to his kindly father-figure presence, and it was this, precisely, that caused her heart to clutch with worry about his welfare. Marcus, a widower for many years now, had admitted to a daughter dead to him, yet he also appeared in clean slacks and button-down shirt. Thankfully, someone helped him out, and this someone probably provided the mint toothpaste, too. Unfortunately, Marcus's patron didn't bother about Marcus's tatty sneakers painted with green and yellow stripes—some teenager's idea of a fun time while Marcus snoozed, so he said.

"Marcus?"

He harrumphed.

"Tonight I'll finish this afghan for you. It's the least I can do in exchange for invading your space all the time. You're my first friend here, you know."

"Off with you then. I'm that wrecked."

"OK, but I'm coming back later with food. I insist you eat something."

Merrit rolled up the afghan and tucked it under her arm. Despite Marcus's terse shrug, she spied the beginnings of a smile stretching his lips. He'd never toss aside one of her afghans like so much garbage, leaving her to wonder why she'd bothered.

Chapter 2

Merrit walked down one of the plaza's paved spokes, hoping to catch sight of Danny, the detective sergeant. From what Marcus had said, Danny was an honorary member of Liam's family. She could introduce herself, start a conversation, bring up Liam. She could try, anyhow.

The plaza sat like a bump at the top of the T-juncture where Burren Street ended at what the locals called the *noncoastal road*, which was to say that in either direction it meandered toward the coast through other noncoastal villages with other plazas. Turning right once she reached the noncoastal, Merrit headed toward the village church, which wasn't breathtaking—hardly St. Patrick's Cathedral—but in a certain light, like now when softened through clouds, the nineteenth-century walls reflected a peaceful yellowish glow.

The detective sergeant had disappeared into the throngs of tourists who strolled along in a carefree way, no doubt anticipating their future love connections. Merrit squeezed through a gaggle of Germans and pardoned herself past two Englishmen until she was forced to slow down behind a gang of women who turned out to be none other than Lonnie the Lovely's mother and sisters. Just her luck.

She backtracked but not fast enough to avoid catching the matriarch's eye through their reflections in a pharmacy window.

"Well, here you are," Mrs. O'Brien said.

The women held fast, and the people stream parted around them. They gazed at Merrit expectantly, so she raised her shoulders with what she hoped was friendly confusion. In reality, she longed to duck into the pharmacy.

"I was after telling my girls that you plan to be here for a while."

Mrs. O'Brien's girls looked to be pushing their forties. In the rush of introductions and floral cologne, Merrit didn't let on that she knew them by name already: Mariela, Eloisa, Constanza. Why the Spanish names? she'd asked, to which Marcus had replied that Mrs. O'Brien fancied herself descended from Spanish high society— *aristocrats*, not deckhands, mind you—who had sailed to Eire and stayed. According to him, there was a reason they were all single, and that reason was their ghastly mother, who'd nag the devil out of hell itself. Merrit had avoided the O'Brien women because of Marcus's warning. "The mouths on them, you wouldn't believe. Gather flies, the lot of them. You'd better be sure Mrs. O'Brien will take an interest in you."

As if to prove his point, Mrs. O'Brien said, "You're staying in Mrs. Sheedy's upstairs flat for the month. She's the sort to watch over you, but she's hardly in a position to help you meet people. In fact, I have a brilliant idea."

Merrit had a nasty feeling about Mrs. O'Brien's so-called brilliant idea and tried to exit stage left, right, or backwards, but she couldn't because the daughters had her surrounded.

"I've got a prescription waiting," she said.

"We must visit my son," Mrs. O'Brien said. "He'll be the one to introduce you to the nicer elements of Lisfenora. You don't mind my saying that you ought to keep better company, and our lad, he's charming. I'm sure you've seen his business headquarters, the flagship as they say. Such an odd word really. Flagship. What could it possibly mean?"

Merrit caught herself patting her chest against tension gathering around her lungs. She drew in a deep breath as the women pushed her forward. "I need to run into the pharmacy," she tried again, but by then they had arrived at the Internet café.

"'Alloo," Mrs. O'Brien called as she opened the door.

Ivan sat behind the counter. At the sight of the women, he tugged on an earlobe and bolted into his workshop, but not without first aiming a tentative smile in their direction.

"The Russians are such a cowardly lot," Mrs. O'Brien said.

"He's Belarusian of Russian descent," said one of the daughters from behind Merrit. Which daughter, she couldn't tell. They all sounded the same to her. "Do the favor of getting it straight if you're going to malign him."

"Oh, do stop. Belarus, Russia, it's all the same. He speaks Russian and that's enough for me."

The powerful momentum of the O'Brien women propelled Merrit across the room, around the service counter, and into Lonnie's office. His monitor faced away from the door, but even so, he clicked his mouse once before stepping around the desk to greet them. "And what's this?"

"I implore you to rescue Merrit here from that Marcus," Mrs. O'Brien said.

Lonnie relaxed. A smile popped into place. "Just Merrit's luck to have met us then." He turned to Merrit. "As I recall, you're here for family research. Any luck?"

"What you'd expect." She matched his bland smile with one of her own. "No help at all, some people. In fact, some people aren't worth knowing."

"This is my point exactly," Mrs. O'Brien said. "People worth knowing. Remind me, Merrit—your surname?"

Merrit hesitated, glancing at Lonnie, then said, "Chase."

"Solid name but no Chases in this area. Unless you're here to look up your mother's lineage?"

Lonnie grinned. He knew well enough that Chase *was* her mom's lineage and that Merrit had officially changed her last name. Merrit rubbed her fatigue-laden eyelids. To think, she'd first entered this shop because she was having trouble with her wireless connection. Lonnie had suggested she leave her laptop for a few hours. His man Ivan would figure it out, he said, but just then he was busy. Lonnie's offer seemed kind at the time, but now she puzzled over how he knew within two minutes of meeting her that he'd find something interesting on her laptop's hard drive. She'd left laptops with technicians plenty of times and thought nothing of it.

"Well?" Mrs. O'Brien prodded. "Your mother's surname?"

Merrit spoke up against the daughters' side chatter. "My mom's side is well-documented back to the eighteen hundreds. They came over from County Cork, and every last family member emigrated."

"Oh. Cork. Now, where was I?" Mrs. O'Brien clapped her hands within inches of Lonnie's face. "Are you listening? Merrit must be your date to Liam's birthday party. How else is she going to meet the people who matter in Lisfenora?"

"What birthday party?" Merrit said.

"Quite the annual event for us, Liam being Liam. And best yet, this year his birthday falls on a Saturday. Tomorrow night, mind you. Over at the Plough and Trough. You'll have fun, I have no doubts, especially with my Lonnie to escort you."

Lonnie spluttered into a laugh, causing Mrs. O'Brien to aim an uncertain blink in his direction. "I don't know why this should be so funny. Everyone will be there."

"Of course," Lonnie said. "I had it in mind to get to know Merrit better anyhow."

Mrs. O'Brien patted Lonnie's cheek. "That's grand. You will escort Merrit."

Within seconds, the O'Brien women were gone. The electronic snore of dozing computers filtered into Lonnie's office. He fingered a thin braid that hung to his shoulder. Merrit longed to take scissors to the puerile affectation. Instead, she said, "Your mom's a real piece of work."

"And lucky fecking me." He settled himself on the edge of the desk. "Actually, this is a fascinating development. Mustn't disappoint Mother, mind, or she'll give me a bollocking for sure. What time shall I pick you up for the party?"

Merrit swallowed hard against galloping nerves inside her chest. This was exactly what she didn't want. Being railroaded. Not to mention the dubious distinction of being Lonnie's "date."

"Thank you," she said, "but I'll go on my own."

"Private party, only locals and their dates allowed. Old Liam's one stipulation, and even *you* won't get past the barricade." He held up a hand before she could protest. "Believe me, you won't. However, if you come with me, I'll announce you to Liam myself."

"You wouldn't dare."

He grinned. "Wouldn't I?"

"I'll introduce myself to Liam on my terms, not yours. And definitely not in front of the whole village."

"You and I both know you're itching to go."

She stared at him, loathing him for being correct. She was more than itching to go—compelled would be more like it. At the very least, she longed to observe Liam the Matchmaker from afar, to get a sense of whether he'd welcome or reject her.

"How much is it worth to you to ensure I keep my mouth shut during the party?" Lonnie said.

Merrit had considered scuttling back to California rather than deal with Lonnie, but that would have been yet one more sign of her weakness. Some might have called Andrew's end a death with dignity. But she knew different. Powerless against a tidal wave of fury and despair and exhaustion, she'd snapped. Now she had to live with the horrid truth of it: she was capable of taking a human life. Lonnie might or might not know something about the darkness that lurked within her. He might or might not decide to reveal her darkness to her real father just because he could.

"You are such a—" Merrit yanked her wallet out of her purse, then the cash out of her wallet. She threw the wad at him. "I'll go to the party with you, but you'd better keep your mouth shut about me."

Lonnie's smile turned gleeful just before he bellowed. "Ivan, fetch us coffee, will you?"

"Oh, that's right," she said, "we're such good friends. Screw you."

"Why so uptight?" he called after her. "You could probably do with a good shagging after all that."

*****

Ten minutes later, Merrit reclined on her bed clutching a battered spiral-bound notebook with a psychedelic rainbow and "September 1975" on the cover. She'd found it in Andrew's nightstand just like he'd said. After reading it, her shock had been so profound that she'd barely survived the next weeks of funeral arrangements and legal turmoil. She was better now. She hoped. At the very least, she wasn't using her inhaler every ten seconds anymore.

She fingered the notebook's tattered cover. Above the rainbow, her mom's precise block lettering spelled out "Ireland Article." Within the notebook, the pages revealed scribbles, cross-outs, and journaling that bore witness to her mom's increasing distraction back in 1975. Julia Chase had started out earnestly enough with initial research for her first big travel-writing assignment. Quite a coup for a woman, given the times, but the travel piece went unfinished due to the source of Julia's distraction. None other than Liam the Matchmaker. A man her mom had called *Liam the Lion*.

One sentence always filled Merrit with sadness. *I'm a coward, that's what I am, and all I can do is pack my bags because I hate myself for loving the man ...*

Merrit's life, her mom's life—how different they would have been if Liam had fought for her mom. But he hadn't, and Merrit had to know why. Since childhood, she'd yearned to fill the void where the unsaid and the murky festered beneath her mom's smiles. Merrit couldn't recall when she'd realized that her mom was a woman who hid her unhappiness well most of the time. Nor could Merrit recapture the moment she first noticed that Andrew treated her like a houseguest who'd overstayed her welcome, only that it hadn't mattered until after her mom's death. All she knew was that the answers lingered along Lisfenora's cobbled lanes, along which Liam had walked arm-in-arm with her mom.

SNEAK PEEK EXCERPT:

Whispers In The Mist, A County Clare Mystery #2

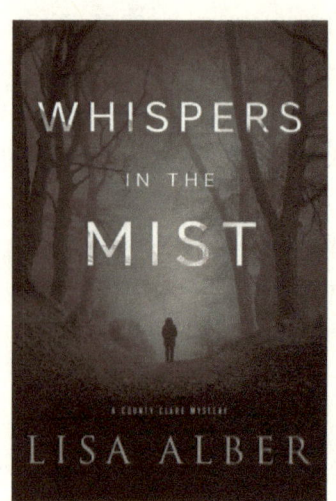

Author Note: As I write this introduction, I'm putting the finishing touches on *Whispers in the Mist*, which will be published in August 2016 by Midnight Ink Books. So what you're seeing here is an almost-ready-for-publication version of Chapter 1. Fun stuff! You're seeing it before anyone else! This novel continues the stories of Merrit Chase and Detective Sergeant Danny Ahern from *Kilmoon*. As we left Danny in *Kilmoon*, his personal life was in turmoil. Now we see him a year later in Chapter 1. I've included the prelude that sets the tone for the novel.

You can order <u>*Whispers in the Mist*</u> from online retailers or through your local booksellers.

*****

There was always a voice within the fog, from ancient times its wet hiss could cajole, could fool an innocent into the Grey Man's grasp. The Grey Man brought death, every one knew that. Locals in Lisfenora village, County Clare, had always known what haunted the fogs that rolled in off the Atlantic.

So it went without saying that on a Wednesday afternoon, mid-September, locals marked the day Grey Man spread its moist shroud over sheep, rock walls, and pocked limestone along the Irish coastline. Local lore about the dark faerie that oozed its way onto land when the fog rolled in sent children to their mammy's beds in fright for their lives. In the fogs that lay thick over the land anyone might catch a glimpse of a figure with cloak made of swirling mists. It might arrive anytime to cling to the land with sinister tendrils, waiting for the right moment to snatch an innocent soul into its gloom.

Later, the most superstitious of the locals claimed to have felt a tingle along their spines and a few hairs risen on their necks.

And later still, all of them would ponder the grey man within their midst.

******

Chapter 1

2009

A breeze buffeted dank mist against Danny Ahern, sinking a chill deep into his bones where regret had already started to calcify. Standing at the threshold of the house into which he had carried his bride and later their wee ones, he wavered, closing his eyes. This, the scene of the slow, corrosive death of his marriage.

On a silent exhalation, he opened his eyes and pushed open the front door to the sound of wailing from one of the bedrooms and screeching from the kitchen. Mandy ran into the living room, her gaze clouded with panic.

"Mam!" She skidded to a halt upon seeing Danny. "Da, you're here!"

"You bet I am. Every day, all the time."

Mandy had called Danny to inform him that her ride to school had cancelled and Petey was acting scared and Ellen had rolled over instead of getting out of bed.

One of Ellen's bad days, in other words. They might both be to blame for the failed marriage, but he was the culprit for Ellen's current mood. He'd moved out a year ago, and he was certain Ellen remembered the date as well as he did. September 8th, 2008. After two long years of turmoil and anger and waning patience on both their sides, he'd finally admitted that he was the reason she wasn't healing. His very presence rubbed her the wrong way, intensifying her guilt over their youngest daughter's death. Beth had fallen from a jungle gym—an accident—but the extended emotional aftermath had worn out their marriage.

September wasn't a good month for either of them. Beth had died in September.

"I'll drive you to school, sweetie." His son's wailing still echoed from the back of the house. "Why's Petey crying?"

Mandy leaned against him. "He had a nightmare and went to bed with mam. He won't come out of her room."

Jesus, the look in his daughter's eyes. She was only nine years old, for Christ's sake. Her gaze shouldn't be dulled by worry and fear that she was doing everything wrong. He knew the feeling well, but she must not end up stuck on that sorry path.

"You did everything right," he said. "Just perfect."

Her chin wobbled. His heart breaking, Danny knelt and hugged her to his chest.

"Are you feeling bad?" he said.

She nodded against his shoulder. "My tummy hurts."

"That's no good," he said. "In fact, that's a fat bloody wad of cowshite."

"Da," she sighed, but she smiled as she raised her head. "That didn't even make sense."

Danny carried his daughter back to the kitchen, poured cereal, milk, and orange juice, and told her to brush her hair. He found Petey standing beside the windows in Ellen's bedroom, hiccupping on snotty breath and peeking outside from between the edges of the closed curtains. Ellen sat on the bed with her head resting on raised knees. Danny picked up Petey and carried him out of the room. His initial sadness gave way to concern when he felt Petey's feverish forehead.

"You get to stay home from school today, little man. How do you like that?"

Petey landed in his own bed in a jumble of limbs, his hair stuck to the sweat on his forehead. Danny swiped at the reddish-brown hair that his children had inherited from Ellen and tucked Petey's lanky limbs—Danny's contribution to the gene pool—under the covers.

"I'll be safe at home, won't I?" Petey said.

"Of course you will. Mandy said you had a nightmare—?"

Petey grabbed his stuffed flamingo. "Because yesterday I saw *him*. You know."

Danny didn't know but he nodded, keeping his expression neutral.

"He came out of the fog right in front of our house. He had a big cape like you see the baddies wear on the telly, and he was dragging someone behind him. Sucking her up. She tried to run away, I saw her, but then he held out his hand and his evil Grey Man powers made her come back to him. But when she came back she was all curled up like her stomach hurt."

Danny sat on the edge of the bed, inhaling the sweet scent of child sweat and trying to come up with a comforting response. Petey, at five, was prone to nightmarish fancies on the best of days— and today wasn't one of those.

Petey gazed up at him, imploring him to believe that he'd seen Grey Man, the predatory faery that haunted the fogs that rolled in off the Atlantic.

"Did you see a swallow?" Danny said. "Swallows always follow Grey Man when he's lurking about."

Petey shook his head. "There was too much mist."

"That's true. Here's what I think. I think that Grey Man passed our house without stopping for a reason, and that reason is because he knows I'm a Detective Sergeant, and I'll capture him and I'll throw him in jail."

Petey rolled away. "But you don't live here anymore."

Danny rolled him back over and kissed his forehead.

"Grey Man knows I'm around, just a few miles away. He knows I protect everyone in this house. Now, how about you think about the great day you'll have doing a bunk from school?"

Petey semi-settled, Danny checked on Mandy in the kitchen, and then returned to Ellen. He exhaled hard in an attempt to dislodge the knot that always affixed itself to his rib cage when it came to his wife. The bedroom smelled fusty, like too many unbathed skin cells settled on every surface. Danny flung back the curtains so that the rings clanged against the curtain rod.

Ellen lifted her head. Dark circles dragged down the skin beneath her eyes. Her hair lay tangled around her shoulders rather than in its usual sleep-braid. "I know," she said.

"Have you been taking your meds?"

She waved a dismissive hand. "Leave it. I had a bad night, that's all. I'm awake now, and I'll see to the kids. I'm fine."

"You're sure? I could—"

"I said." She tossed a pillow in his direction. "I'm fine."

This was the way of it between them now. Petty jolts of annoyance at every turn.

"I'll take Mandy to school," Danny said, "and I told Petey he could stay home—"

Ellen sighed.

"—and that's not a problem, right?"

Ellen rose and closed the bathroom door behind her with a decided click. Not quite a slam, but enough to let Danny know she'd read something in his tone that he should have kept to himself.

"I'll come the usual time tonight," he said through the closed door. Normally, he visited each evening to tuck the children into bed. His favorite time of day, in fact. Reading stories returned them to their sunnier days as a family. He was determined to maintain as many of their old routines as possible. Patience and perseverance could work wonders. He knew this well enough from his police work.

For now, there was nothing for it but to kiss his son goodbye and bundle Mandy into his ailing Peugeot. The car ground to life with a sputter and a gurgle. Ellen had been better the last three or four months, but her improvement didn't come without relapses.

The fog had thickened in the 30 minutes he'd been inside the house, bringing with it the scent of the ocean. Drystone walls along the side of the road lurked like a monster race of serpents, petrified but ready to return to life. Danny's mother used to tell him all manner of old tales about serpents, changlings, sprites, and especially Grey Man, the dark faery who festered off shore waiting for its chance to ooze inland, visible to anyone who could see beyond the fog of their limited vision.

Danny turned onto the lane toward Lisfenora and Mandy's school.

"Da?" Mandy tapped his thigh. "I think maybe Petey did see Grey Man. On our lane."

"Believe me, sweetie, Grey Man hasn't come calling. Not to worry."

Five minutes later, Danny's mobile *briiing*ed and Mandy held it up to his ear while he drove. He'd spoken too soon.

DELETED SCENE FROM *WHISPERS IN THE MIST*

Author Note: I don't know about you, but I'm always curious about authors' processes. So, I thought I'd share a deleted scene from *Whispers in the Mist*. This is what a first draft looks like—for me anyhow—which is to say it hasn't seen the light of a professional edit or copyedit. This scene is interesting for a look-see because it shows the relationship between my two protagonists, Merrit and Danny, which I'd call awkward at best.

In the end, I deleted this scene because it was redundant. I show their relationship in plenty of other scenes that also move the plot forward better than this scene does. Sometimes I write scenes that I later think of as exploratory because they help me get to know what's going on with the characters. There's a saying among fiction writers: Kill your darlings. So, yes, in the end, I needed to hack this exploratory scene out of the manuscript.

P.S. Liam is Merrit's newfound father, whom she met for the first time in *Kilmoon*.

*****

Merrit threw off the covers and sat up in bed. Most nights, Merrit slept well in Liam's guest room. Its masculine simplicity comforted her: the solid navy bedspread and tallboy dresser, the unadorned window with a pair of shutters for privacy, the unstained floorboards and rust-colored area rug beside the bed. She hadn't imprinted herself on the room yet. The pile of jewelry on top of the dresser

didn't count, nor did the shoes lined up along one wall. She had
an idea for an afghan she might knit for the bed, but she was in no
hurry. She didn't want to jinx herself by becoming too comfortable.

She reached above her head and pulled down an old robe
that she'd slung over one of the bed's corner posts. Liam had lent her
the robe, and it fell across her shoulders like a friendly arm. The area
rug tickled the arches of her feet when she stood; the cool
floorboards caused her toes to curl a moment later. Steeling herself,
she opened the casement window. A blast of clammy air gripped her
torso. She eased the window open just enough to reach out and push
the shutters open onto a night made pewter by fog. She let the swirl
of fresh air clear her senses as she gazed out into nothingness.

Liam was like the foggy night, she thought. Beyond the
surface haze of him hid everything. There was a point to these
thoughts that kept Merrit awake, and it was more than rehashing
Liam's quixotic personality. It was more than trying to come to grips
with her need for a father figure. But she was too tired to figure
herself out at the moment.

She closed the window and shuffled to the dresser to pull
out a pair of wool socks. After slipping them on, she eased the
bedroom door open. A warm glow threaded its way into her room
from the nightlight stationed in the hall bathroom next door. The
living room and dining area opened up to her under the gaze of a
reading lamp that Liam left on through the night. He didn't sleep
much. He'd fixed himself a cup of tea while she was tossing and

turning. She transferred the cup into the kitchen sink and returned to the living room to hover like a wraith. Indecisive, restless, worried.

Instead of demanding that Dermot explain his accusation, she'd pushed her way out of the pub in a blind panic that her lungs would seize up like they did. Damn them. Damn her weakness, her outsider status, her isolation. Liam was wonderful, but she needed friends of her own. Alan should have stuck up for Merrit instead of making that snide remark about the identity of her father.

"Get a grip," she whispered to herself.

After all her tossing and turning, the grandfather clock only said 11:30 p.m. Merrit moved to the pile of shoes near the front door. She pulled on boots, then rifled around the antique coat rack for a suitable coat to throw over her robe. She chose a parka that hung almost to her knees. It was so huge it would barely keep out the cold, but no matter. She couldn't sit with Dermot's words bouncing around her head a moment longer. Like it or not, Detective Sergeant Danny Ahern was the only person she could confide in at this point.

Outside, she turned right onto a track that led her toward a porch light that shone weakly through the fog. A prickly feeling climbed up and down her spine, which could stem from paranoia about lurkers with paint or from nerves at initiating a conversation with Danny.

She stopped in mid-stride and raised her face to the invisible sky in hopes she would catch of sign. Knock on his door, or not?

A nearby slither caught Merrit off guard and she whirled around. Out of the fog trotted Liam's cat, Burt, yammering for companionship. It shot toward Merrit with tail straight up, and in a game of chase veered around her toward the cottage that Danny lived in these days. Acquiescing, Merrit stalked after the cat, who flitted in and out of the fog banks, enticing her forward with a few rolls in the dirt and come-hither looks. By the time Merrit grabbed the purring creature up, the cottage had solidified through the fog. Danny's crappy Peugeot rested at a cocky angle, half on the grass. Lamplight illuminated the curtains.

Her first knock barely whispered over the wood on the front door, yet it swung open a second later. Burt jumped out of Merrit's arms and into the cottage. Danny peered after the cat with a blank expression, blinking like a turtle coming out of its shell. Still gazing over his shoulder, he said, "No meddling on this one, so you might as well go away now."

What she'd been about to say fled Merrit's head. "I—what?"

She stepped out of the glare of the porch light to get a better look at Danny. His hair hadn't been cut in awhile and it stood up in tufts. Some of her nervousness abated as she took in his flannel pajamas in a green tartan plaid. He'd misbuttoned the pajama top.

"What could you possibly want?" he said.

"The cat, for one." Merrit hoped her sentence hadn't ended on a questioning note. She stepped under his arm braced against the doorframe. "Here, Burt," she cooed.

Behind her, Danny grunted the door closed. "If you must," he said.

She'd never been inside the cottage, so she took her time peering into the dark corners for the cat. Liam had modernized the old whitewashed building that much was obvious, but it still retained a slightly claustrophobic 19th century feel within its shoebox structure. Liam had told her that he'd raised Kevin in this cottage. It was hard to believe that two such large personalities had once fit here. Even Danny, with his—for the most part anyhow—less demonstrative demeanor cramped the space.

Ignoring Danny's mess of clothes and papers, Merrit bypassed a threadbare sectional sofa with blankets thrown over it. Inset shelves lined with books rose up to the ceiling and a series of wood-turned bowls lined the mantel. The kitchen was a little more roomy with spare white counters and cheerful buttery yellow walls. It was a long skinny room that ran the length of the backside of the cottage. Merrit imagined that it soaked up all available sunlight. It was also warmer than the living room, which was why Burt had gravitated there.

At one end of the room, a pile of reports and photos covered a drop-leaf table. Before Danny could block her view, Merrit caught sight of a close-up shot of a boy's face with half-lidded gaze aimed at nothing. Swallowing, she stepped toward the oven in front of which Burt sat cleaning herself.

"Your oven's on." She cleared her throat. "Did you know your oven is on?"

"It's a handy space heater." Danny stepped up behind her. "Got the cat now?"

"It's nice that Liam took in a lost cat. Gave it a home."

"Liam was always good with strays," Danny said on a dry note.

"The tourists who come for the festival are strays too, I guess. In their own way. But strays aren't so easy."

"No?" Danny turned to a dirty saucepan and started in on hand-scrubbing the remnants of what looked to be cocoa.

She crouched near Burt, her face burning more from embarrassment than the oven's heat. She shouldn't have come, and, worse still, now that she was here, she was rambling like an idiot.

"Take Burt, for example. Sometimes she's in the house going neurotic as if she doesn't believe she deserves her new, stable life. She'll purr one second and lash out the next. Liam's got a few scratches on his hands, but he doesn't seem to mind. He's learning the cat's rhythms. I noticed that the cat is also learning Liam's. It's a slow process, I guess, two beings getting used to each other."

Danny's silence was too loud. In one of her flashes of instinct, she understood that her presence pained him, literally pained him.

"I know Liam appreciates the cat for its company," she said.

"Strays are good that way, as Liam should well know anyhow. Some people collect them." He turned around, catching Merrit off guard. "After all, look at us, his current strays."

"Yes, it's good of him to let you use the old cottage."

Danny closed his eyes for a second, and when they opened Merrit saw his pupils contract. He had a steady gaze, with eyes melting brown as the cocoa. The warmth was in there, Merrit knew, but Danny cloaked it well.

She crouched to gather Burt toward her again, more than ready to leave Danny alone. She wasn't sure why'd she come anymore. When she looked up, he was standing at the table shuffling through his paperwork.

"This news will be in the papers anyhow," he said, "so how about you take a step closer to satisfy your curiosity and be done with it."

Merrit recalled what he'd said the moment she entered the cottage. About the meddling. So, he'd assumed she'd caught wind of his latest case and was visiting him to pry, just like she'd pried her way into village life and into his life, he was no doubt thinking.

"That's not why I dropped by," she said.

"Oh?"

"Never mind. I'll figure it out myself."

With a last glance at the photos of the deceased boy who still had the pretty androgyny of youth, Merrit retreated through the kitchen and living room to the front door. Burt struggled in her arms, but Merrit held her tight and didn't bothering closing the door after herself. She knew well enough by the silence in the kitchen that Danny would follow after her to ensure that she'd departed.

INTERVIEW

Michael Guillebeau: Let's begin with *Kilmoon*. You begin the novel with a rather harrowing death's bed scene. What inspired this scene in particular, and *Kilmoon* in general?
Lisa Alber: Oh boy, yes—that scene. It's a toughie! But it so sets the stage for Merrit and the mysteries to come. At the time, I was grieving my own dad's passing (from cancer). He was at home under hospice care, and when I visited him, I found odd, little things incredibly sad—like the way the swing table squealed when we moved it so he could reach his food and water. The liquid morphine was real and red, and it freaked me out, just the fact of it. It was only later in the writing process that I realized I was processing my relationship with my father through the father-daughter themes that run through the novel. Of course, in *Kilmoon* they're far darker than anything from my life. Thank goodness!

For *Kilmoon* in general, two places in Lisdoonvarna, County Clare, Ireland, sparked my imagination: The Matchmaker Bar and an early Christian ruin called Kilmoon Church. The Matchmaker Bar represents my fictional village's annual matchmaking festival and Kilmoon Church represents secrets long buried. Together they grounded me in place and set my thoughts churning about a matchmaker with a dark past.

MG: Yes, Liam, Merrit's father, is a celebrated matchmaker. I had wondered how you came up with that idea.

LA: An actual matchmaking festival that's held each year in September? Oh, it exists all right!

My fictional matchmaking festival is a hyped-up version of the real thing in the sense of it being internationally known and full of foreigners. Although, in recent years it has grown. It's got its own website and is the largest matchmaking festival in Europe. Here's the website if you're curious: http://www.matchmakerireland.com/.

There's a bona fide matchmaker. His name is Willie Daly, and he's a local celebrity. Everyone knows him, where he lives, and what he's up to. I had a chance to ask him questions, but I didn't base my fictional matchmaker on him because in this case reality needed a boost.

Let it be known that Liam the Matchmaker isn't a cozy kind of character. I don't write cozy mysteries. And I don't write romantic suspense either despite the matchmaking aspect. I was attracted to the juxtaposition of a dark reality lurking beneath a happily-ever-after façade.

MG: Which brings up the next question: What kind of reader do you think would be interested in your novels?
LA: It's safe to say that my stories are a tad dark, psychologically complex, and atmospheric. There's a lot going on with all the characters—definitely an ensemble cast. So if you like your mysteries to be more than the mystery plots themselves, definitely give my County Clare series at try!

If you detest swearing in your novels, then I offer a humble warning. (I'd add a smile emoticon here, but I don't think we can do that, can we?) I love the way the Irish swear; they're wonderfully inventive. And swearing is the norm, so, yes, I include some colorful language.

Authors that come to mind that I like and that I'd aspire to are: Sophie Hannah, Deborah Crombie, Julia Spencer-Fleming, Tana French, Susan Hill, Erin Hart, Carol Goodman, just to name a few. Early Minette Walters and Elizabeth George (my mentor!) too.

MG: Your locale is very evocative—sometimes dreamy, sometimes harsh. How did you settle on County Clare for the location of your series? Did you spend much time there?

LA: You might say I accidentally ended up in County Clare. I traveled to Clare for the first time to visit an ecological area called the Burren, which is a vast area of limestone leftover from the Ice Age. I'd read about it in a memoir. I planted myself in a random B&B near the Burren—in Lisdoonvarna, as luck would have it. While there, I discovered that Lisdoon (as the locals sometimes call it) hosts an annual matchmaking festival. I visited the area three times for novel research.

I found the landscape both harsh and dreamy. The Burren has a harsh appearance, that's for sure, and the winds that come in off the Atlantic can be dismal. On the other hand, on mild days, the rolling green hills with their drystone walls are peaceful and otherworldly—like the landscape hasn't changed in a thousand years.

MG: *Kilmoon* is your first novel. What was the most surprising thing, for you, about the publication process?

LA: After all the editing, copyediting, and proofing you can still find errors and typos. I was reading the galley proofs for the second—not first, but *second*—time when I found a locked door that should have been unlocked and a woman standing in front of a house rather than a church. Those errors had been there since the beginning!

Let's not talk about typos. I can hope that none remain in the final version. I can hope!

MG: And now, tell us a little about your second novel, *Whispers in the Mist*. As you mentioned with the excerpt, you decided to center this novel on Detective Sergeant Danny Ahern. Why?

LA: When I first started writing *Kilmoon*, Danny didn't exist. Then one day, he appeared in a scene. Then ten thousand written words later, I realized that he was the secondary protagonist after Merrit and had a boatload of problems of his own. By the time I finished writing *Kilmoon*, I loved the guy and wanted to know what's next for him. So *Whispers in the Mist* continues that train of thought. (Of course, Merrit's story continues too.)

MG: Merrit and Danny are certainly fully realized characters. How many books are planned in the County Clare Mystery series? Plus, what's the most fun part about writing a series? What's the most challenging?

LA: I originally thought this might be a trilogy because there's a natural end that could occur. In fact, because I was (am, still) a newbie author and wasn't thinking in terms of writing a series at the time, I painted myself into a corner by the end of *Kilmoon*. A fact about one of my characters implies a natural end point to the series. However, I've been thinking hard, and I've discovered a way to wriggle out of it. In fact, I'm writing that novel now! I've tentatively titled the third novel in the series, *Touch of Death*. (The publisher has last dibs on the title, so it will probably change.)

I have a basic idea for the fourth novel also. After that, I'm not sure, but I think the world I'm building has enough in it to last for a while—I hope!

Most fun? Returning to Ireland both in real life for research and in my imagination. It's a little like returning home. Most challenging? Balancing how much context from the previous books to include. Readers need to understand what's going on—I'd like my novels to be readable as standalones—without giving away too many spoilers from the previous books. That's a tricky proposition.

MG: I was going to ask you, "What's next?" You've already mentioned your third novel, *Touch of Death*.

60

LA: I'm writing the first draft in the midst of revision work for *Whispers in the Mist*. Whew! But it's going well. In addition to continuing Danny's and Merrit's stories, one of the minor characters in *Whispers* takes center stage in *Touch of Death*. His name is Nathan Tate, so look out for him in *Whispers*!

KATHLEEN COSGROVE

Kathleen is a humor and fiction writer living in Nashville Tennessee. Her Maggie Finn novels, *Engulfed* and *Entangled* are comedic mysteries set in Florida's southwest coast. She is currently working on the third novel in the series, *Entrapped*. Her short stories appear in several anthologies and magazines. Her collection of Sam Heart shorts, a send-up of the Dashiell Hammett Sam Spade novels, will be available on audio by late 2017. She writes and performs her humorous memoirs in different venues in the Nashville area and those will be available as a collection called, "The View From Under My Desk," by 2017.

SHORT STORY

Sam Heart and the Case of the Pinned-Up Knickers.

I was sitting at my desk, cleaning the gum from my shoe and watching the 5:06 pull into Union station right at 6:30 when the sound of footsteps on pavement told me I'd better grab the Colt 38 and check the barrel. Most of the time what's on the other side of that door is trouble, and I mean with a capitol T and that rhymes with P and that stands for trouble. I don't look for it, but it looks for me, and usually finds me too, here, at my desk, in my office.

You see, I'm a dick, a private investigator, a gumshoe, a flatfoot, a sherlock, a bizzy, a tracer, a snoop, a shamus. My name is Sam Heart, but the folks around here call me Sam. When I say around here I mean Nashville, the home of bright lights and shattered dreams, beautiful music and ugly...well, some ugly things too.

What I could see from the other side of the glass was definitely *not* ugly. She had a shape like a real shapely dame and it was clear from her tight dress that she wasn't packing. I put the Colt back in the drawer and called out, "Door's open sweetheart, come on in."

She was even more beautiful than her silhouette, full red lips, an hourglass figure and silky golden hair that looked like gold silk.

"What can I do for you Miz...?"

"You can get me one of whatever it is you're drinking," she pointed to the glass of gin in my hand. "And put some ice in it. I like my gin cold and my men hot, if you get my drift." She grinned like the cat that swallowed a little yellow bird. I was tempted to grab her and kiss her, but she looked like more trouble than a big sack of trouble.

"So doll, how'd you get that blood all over your dress, you shoot someone?"

"Say, what kind of detective are you anyway?" she asked. "I'm the one that got shot. See the hole in my chest where my inside stuff should be?"

"All you broads think you're so clever, but I've seen it all before; you shoot your lover, put a hole in your chest and call yourself the victim."

"But I *am* the victim," she said, starting to cry.

"Here," I handed her my handkerchief, "blow your nose and spill your guts."

"But I have no guts, can't you see? I'm dead, and when I say dead I mean not living, deceased, a corpse, a used to be an alive person. Didn't you notice I came *through* the door instead of opening it?"

The broad was making sense now, but I still didn't get her angle.

"What do you want from me? Looks like you need an undertaker, not a PI, a dick, a gumshoe, a..."

She broke in with more crying, "It's not me who needs the help, it's too late for me." She finished her drink and handed me the glass, "More please."

She downed the next one like a man...like a man that drinks gin, and then she walked slowly over to the window. "I used to love to ride the trains, they're so connected to each other," she said

She turned back to look at me, "It's Little Johnny Knickers, you know, the guy who plays guitar and sings over at the Opry, he's famous. They're blaming it on him. The cops have got him locked up tighter than a guy in jail. He didn't do it, I know, I was there."

"Well, if he didn't kill you, than who did?"

"If I knew that, I wouldn't be here, asking you for help. You see," she stopped and looked at the cigarette in my hand, "you gonna keep those all to yourself?"

I lit one and gave it to her. She inhaled. I couldn't take my eyes off of her, watching that smoke pour out of her like smoke from a thing that's burning.

"Go ahead," I told her. "You were gonna tell me how you don't know who shot you."

"I don't know who shot me." She dragged hard on the Camel. "It was dark, and the shooter was wearing a hat and coat."

"This is 1943 doll; everyone wears a hat and coat, even in August."

"You see, Little Johnny and I were in the bushes and this... person in the coat walks up and just shoots me. Little Johnny's knickers were up in a tree where I threw them, just playful like. Anyway, there wasn't time for him to get them down before the cops got there. I was laying there, on the ground, watchin' him trying to shinny up there and get them. I was saying, 'Run Little Johnny, run, don't worry about your knickers now'.

But he just kept jumping and grabbing and saying, 'Shit, this is gonna be real bad for my career.' But anyways, he couldn't get a good foot hold, you know how that is.

By the time the cops got there, I was too dead to say anything, so they put the cuffs on Little Johnny and took him off... without his knickers."

"Ok, so the two of you were havin' a roll in the hay when..."

"No, not hay, bushes, or a hedge, or maybe even a flower bed, but not..."

"Never mind all that, tell me about the shooter. Could he have been the blackmailer?"

"How did you know...?"

"Doll, there's always a blackmailer."

"Well, someone's been getting backstage at the Opry and pinning notes on his knickers," she said, making smoke rings from the hole in her chest.

Then she walked over and picked the 38 off of the desk and pointed it at me. "Is this a gun in my hand, or are you just happy to see me?"

"Put that down and come with me."

"Where are we going?"

"To the Opry, it's show time."

*****

The cabbie that brought her to my office was waiting for us at the curb.

"I hope you don't mind," she said, "the only cab I could get was this dead guy."

"Hey, how many times do I gotta tell you, I ain't dead?" he yelled out the window.

"Sure you are honey, don't you feel a breeze where the back of your head should be?" she asked him.

She whispered to me, "Look at the size of that hole in his head, you could hang drapes in there."

"You're right, but in this town, the last thing you need to drive is a brain."

*****

68

The Opry is a mixed bag of rhinestones and cheap whisky; of dames with soft voices and stiff hair; of men with cowboy hats and big city type things.

Little Johnny's dressing room was now being used by Mrs. Maybelle Carter and her three girls. They looked innocent enough, but I smelled a rat, or maybe it was Old Spice. I knocked on the open door.

"What can I do for you PI?" she asked. "Why don't you take off your beige trench coat and wide brimmed hat and have a seat?"

"Thanks," I said. It sure looks like you made yourself real comfortable in Little Johnny's dressing room."

"Say, are you accusing me of blackmailing Little Johnny so there would be a red herring into the investigation of the murder of his girlfriend and then murdering his girlfriend and letting him take the blame for it so that I could have this dressing room?"

"You're real sharp for a dame, a doll, a skirt..."

"But I love Little Johnny like a brother. He promised that one day I can even perform on stage 'stead of just playing my guitar back here, in the dressing room and sewing sequins on his under drawers."

"You seen anything suspicious since you been here, in Little Johnny's dressing room?"

"You don't believe anyone here at the Opry could be a murderer do you?" Mrs. Maybelle asked. Why, we're just plain folk who like to sing, play guitar, go to church, read our bible, drink our own home made whiskey, beat our wives, put things in our hair to make it look like something other than hair and cheat when there's a good song in it."

"That's right," said the oldest girl, little Junie, who was dressing her dolls all in black. "Everyone here is real nice to us, except for that lady who comes in here and puts notes on Little Johnny Knickers' knickers, she was rude."

I could see that I broke this kid good. She was ready to spill her guts and I was ready to catch 'em.

"Tell me everything you know kid and I promise the feds will go easy on you."

"The feds?" she started crying

"Why, you don't suspect little Junie of doing anything wrong, do you?" asked Maybelle.

"In this town, every man with a guitar across his back and song lyrics on a matchbook is a suspect." I said. "Every woman with a tune on her lips and an agent in her bed is a suspect. Every..."

"Ok, I'll tell you," yelled out little Junie. "It was Miss Bitsy, the one who owns the bar back behind here. She gave me the notes and a nickel and told me to pin them on, but I didn't kill anyone, honest. Don't make me go to prison."

"You're not goin' to prison. Just keep your nose clean and steer clear of drunks. Here, clean your nose."

*****

Our cabbie took us around the corner to Bitsy's Fuschia Lounge.

Every bar stool in the joint was filled with people sitting at the bar. Someone on the stage was yodeling, so I shot him in the foot. I needed to get everyone's attention and that guy was askin' for it.

"Someone go get me Miss Bitsy." I said

"I'm standin' right here in front of you PI"

I had to look down to see her. She was three feet if you didn't count the hair, four if you did.

My ghost dame was standin' at the bar, hustling cocktails from a guy with a stab wound. The place was crawling with dead drunks. "Hey," I shouted to her, "This dame look like the shooter?"

"Who the hell are you talkin' too?" Bitsy asked, "Are you off your nut or somethin'?"

"Oh, didn't I tell you?" my client said, "No one else can see me, just you and other dead people. Can we stay a while? I think the drowned guy over there is giving me the look over."

I looked back down at Bitsy, "Don't try to change the subject. I know it was you that was blackmailing Little Johnny. The kid you paid to do your dirty work sang like a canary that tells on people."

"Are you saying Little Johnny and me were lovers?" asked Bitsy. "That we used to roll around in the costume trunk and play 'hide the choo-choo in the tunnel'? That I found out that he was two-timing me with that floozy of a tramp of a floozy and ratted her out to her husband? That I'd been planning it all along and that's why I let the kid pin the notes on the knickers, so a PI would come along and think Johnny was being blackmailed?"

"Sounds like you covered all the angles Bitsy, all but one."

"What is it PI, dick, shamus, flatfoot, snoop...?"

"You're holding the murder weapon in your hand."

"Damn it, you're smarter than you look, PI."

"And you're wearing Little Johnny's knickers."

"I thought you said there was only one thing."

"And the coat and hat you wore the night of the murder."

"OK, OK, you got me."

"And the guy on stage is holding up a sign says he saw you do it."

"Are you still talkin' or am I gonna have to call the cops on myself?"

*****

I was sitting at my desk, scraping gum from my shoe when I heard footsteps on the stairs.

"Come on in sweetheart, door's open."

It was a red head, and I have always been a sucker for red heads, especially when they've got red hair.

"What can I do for ya', good lookin'?"

"You can help me find my killer," she said.

EXCERPT

Engulfed

"I couldn't stop laughing and couldn't put it down. Engulfed is a great read full of a cast of characters that any Florida town would recognize. From a cop born again as a hippie complete with a halfway house full of unusual taco dip, to a nursing home with bodies falling everywhere, to a senator with an unusual hobby to a middle aged heroine whose life has never been so exciting, this book is a funny, fantastic, free for all of twists with its own Yoda in the form of a seagull named Sherlock Holmes. I loved it and can't wait to read it again! - Amazon Reviewer Susan B

CHAPTER THREE

Edison invented the electric lamp in 1879. He also invented the talking doll in 1886, but that's beside the point. The point is, if we've had electric lamps for 130 years and had wind and rain for at least that long, it should stand to reason we would have come up with a way to make electricity work even when it's windy and rainy.

I knew these Edisonian tidbits from the little Thomas Edison brochure I found lying on the kitchen counter in my parents' home. It seemed Thomas Edison lived and worked, and thought about talking dolls just a few miles north of here in Ft. Myers.

There were all kinds of little touristy brochures my mother left for me, which I was reading, by candle light, to remind myself that this is a nice state, a friendly state, a happy state, a state that tourists pay lots of money to come visit. It's a place that's just fine for my parents to live out their golden years. I had to remind myself of these things because right then it felt as though I were living in one of the nine circles of hell.

Hurricane Fanny. What a stupid name for a hurricane. If you wore a T-shirt that said *I Survived Hurricane Fanny*, people would think you'd won it in a mud wrestling contest.

I was surrounded by all the supplies the helpful man at Home Depot advised I get. There was duct tape, bleach, batteries, canned food, bottled water, first aid kit, candles, flashlight, and a bottle of wine. Ok, the wine was actually my idea.

Cut off from the world save my little battery operated TV, I was second guessing my decision to stay here instead of going to one of those hurricane shelters. After convincing myself earlier that one could be just as easily blown away there, as at home, that logic now no longer appeared as sound and the idea of cots and port-a-potties didn't seem so bad after all.

Three hours after the storm started Fanny was in her full glory. The wind made roaring, window rattling sounds, hail was hitting the windows and there was lots of lightning. By lots, I mean the sky was almost continually lit. In fact, it was the only illumination I could see besides an occasional flashlight beam from the house behind mine. There was one exception though, and that was the intermittent large blast of greenish blue brilliant light, with its accompanying ear splitting crack and boom. These were, in fact, Mr. Edison's great-grandchildren exploding as wires come lose and hit the ground. I was not quite sure if one of those monsters of power was outside my parents' home. That's not one of those things you look for when you're negotiating a sales price from your crooked real estate agent and simultaneously toying with the idea of feeding her to an alligator.

I had learned from the lawn guy that the alligators here were free to wander around Florida hunting our poodles and de-clawed cats and he took it upon himself to warn me about all the creatures lurking just outside my door waiting to bite, chew, claw, and sting or eat me. "Great," I'd said, "my parents are living in a jungle, isn't that swell?"

The power went out after the first 12 raindrops fell so there was no air-conditioning and the house had become a fifteen hundred square foot sauna. I was sweating profusely and at some point, regardless of what might happen, I cracked open a window.

I wandered from room to room, unconsciously turning on light switches and wishing I had bought unscented candles; the house smelled like a new age shop.

Staring at the patio doors, I was afraid something, or God forbid, some*one* would come crashing through them. The very concerned man on the TV was talking about how I should have boarded those up, as if he could see into my home. "A little late for that now," I yelled at the TV, "Thanks for the heads up, Home Depot guy."

Going back out for boards was out of the question so I emptied and flattened packing boxes, taped them to the doors and windows and stood guard. I was reminded of a scene from a Winnie the Pooh book I read to my granddaughter. Pooh stayed up all night marching back and forth, in his little Pooh house, with his little pop gun, protecting hearth and home from Heffalumps and Woozles. That was me. "Stay away you Heffalumps and Woozles, I've got duct tape and I'm not afraid to use it."

The sustained wind speed, according to the news reports, was eighty five miles per hour but occasional gusts were much stronger, tearing tiles from roofs and uprooting trees, one of which went down in the neighbor's yard and put a hole in their roof. I was very glad they were away in a regular state that God was *not* smiting, instead of being pinned under a large coconut palm in their bed.

With every sound, I'd held my breath, imagining a tree falling into the living room and somehow impaling me into my mother's pink sofa. There would be blood stains that I'm sure even she, the self proclaimed Queen of Laundry, would be unable to remove. The first aid kit looked ridiculous in the face of tree impalement, but at least I had the wine. It was good; it was a Pinot Grigio, even warm, those go down well.

Another flash of lightning and I could see how many screens there were left on the patio; just one, holding on by 3 molecules, flapping in the wind.

The little TV was my only company, and I was fascinated watching this poor weatherman in his bright yellow parka, standing out in the storm, warning us to stay indoors. Street lights were whipping wildly around him attached by only one cable, and he kept listing to the right. The rain was hitting his little baby face with such a force that I was sure he'd be pock marked for life. A large black garbage can went flying over his head and nearly hit him. He should go back inside, I thought, and wondered how much he was getting paid to stand out there. I was guessing it was not a lot and hoped he had a flask stashed inside that parka.

I kept pacing through the house, which was nothing like the home in Brooklyn that I grew up in. First of all, this place was much bigger with a lot more windows. Everything was decorated in pastel pinks and blues and there were pictures of the ocean and sail boats and pelicans on the walls.

"Who are these people who live here?" I said out loud to no one, "And what have they done to my parents; my born and raised two blocks from Prospect Park parents?"

Along the entire back of the house large sliding glass doors opened from the living room to the patio.

In Brooklyn, everyone sits out front; in Florida, everyone sits out back. Patios are big here and the stores make a killing selling people all kinds of furniture to go in them. Umbrellas for tables are more plentiful than cannolis in Italy. If I lived here though, and had this swimming pool, I'm certain it would be no time at all before I too joined the tanned and unsociable set and put furniture in the back of my house.

I got a pad and paper and amused myself thinking of creative curse words and derogatory anagrams I could make with the name Florida, and also to come up with equally creative excuses I could use to *not* visit my folks here in the future. I loved them, and wanted to see them, just not here.

"Do your worst, Florida!" I hollered, "I can take it. Hurricane shermicane, you're not so tough, but sweet Jesus, it's hot. It's soooooo damned hot!"

I got a helping of semi- liquid ice cream from the freezer and held the bowl to my forehead for a minute before eating, or more accurately drinking, it down.

The worst of the storm appeared to finally be over and Fanny was making her soggy way out of here, leaving us all to locate our missing patio furniture and stray pets.

I had sweated away twelve pounds and immediately put them back on by eating all the ice cream in the freezer. I used up all the batteries in my little TV and burned down all the fragrant candles, and was, fortunately, not killed by either flying bodies or tree limbs.

I figured I'd try to sleep a bit, and in the morning, when this chapter out of the Old Testament was over, maybe I'd be lucky and wake up in Oz or Kansas, or even Jersey, anywhere but here.

SAMPLE CHAPTER

Entangled

"I haven't enjoyed a mystery like this one in a long time. Granted, being from southern Florida was an extra enticement for me, but even if I wasn't, the ambiance created by Ms. Cosgrove puts you in the gorgeous and muggy thick of it. Fast-paced, plot and character driven (which is hard to do), intriguing, and filled with twists and turns, the well-written story covers environmental issues, as well as our protagonist, Maggie, being older, lonely, and funny at often ill-advised times. The action scenes are wonderfully vivid. The reader is put right there. You can't help but fall in love with the lagoon, the dolphins, the scooter, but I'm starting to give the plot away. Read Entangled for a colorful journey to Florida, several real belly laughs, and a whacking good mystery." –

Heather Haven, Award Winning Author of the Alvarez Family
Murder Mysteries

Chapter 1

The instructions the boat captain gave me for the use of the knife
were vague, but I felt better having it in case I needed to cut myself
free, were I to be pulled through the Gulf of Mexico by my catch, a la
Captain Ahab.

Deep sea fishing can be fun as long as someone else baits
the line, holds the pole for you until you get a bite, and then hauls in
the catch when your arms get tired. Thus was the experience for the
four bikini clad co-eds who had also booked this charter.

I, on the other hand, have not worn a bikini since Jimmy
Carter was president. Today I was sporting a *Ben and Jerry's* ball cap,
an oversized Yankees jersey that once belonged to my ex-husband,
and seven or eight layers of sunscreen.

Captain Billy of *Billy's Big Boats* was regaling the young
ladies with his tale of once captaining the actor who played the blind
guy in *Star Trek*, when I was almost jerked out of my chair. In truth, I
was strapped in, but the belt nearly sawed me in half.

"Billy?" I yelled over to him. "Something's pulling here!"

Billy glanced over disinterestedly and said, "Good, good,
hold the line."

My feet could get no traction sliding in seawater and
fish scales on a boat that was only slightly more seaworthy than a '58
Buick sealed with duct tape.

"Billy? I might need a hand here."

Billy did not hear me over the giggling, his own as well as
the girls'.

The pull on my arms and hands was becoming painful but I
was not about to let go; my pride wouldn't allow it. Those girls were
young and beautiful and...young, but I was the one going to haul in
a...I don't know, a tuna or a giant squid.

I was like Spencer Tracy, in *The Old Man and the Sea*. I began
speaking to it using a Cuban accent. "Fish, I love you and respect you
very much, but I will kill you dead before this day ends."

Sweat poured into my eyes and onto my sunglasses giving
everything a blurry, distant look, so I could not see if the fish was
jumping, swimming away, or charging me.

Then *Billy's Big Boat* leaned hard to the port side as my catch
stopped there, momentarily anchoring us. Two of the young ladies
fell conveniently onto Billy who also fell, not so conveniently, into
the bucket of chum.

The girls, now covered in minnows and shrimp, began to
scream. Billy, scrambling to his feet, tripping over buckets and
skidding in water, was stringing curses together so creatively that
under different circumstances I would have applauded. Then he and
his crewmen managed to pull in my catch which turned out to be not

as I had suspected, a gigantic fish, but a net filled with several medium-sized fish and three average-sized dead guys.

Captain Billy called the marine police and one of his men sedated our hysterical debutantes with Rum and Diet Coke. Someone found a pirate flag under a seat cushion and laid it across the men's faces, but their bloated bodies were still visible to anyone brave enough to look. I tried, in the interest of journalism, because I was, in fact, a journalist, to inspect them a bit closer. An object that resembled a kind of whistle worn by gym coaches hung around the neck of one of the corpses. After kneeling down to get a better look and inhaling the accompanying putrid odor, my body decided throwing up over the side of the boat was the more appropriate action.

We arrived at shore before we ran out of alcohol and I out of patience. Everyone seemed more annoyed that their trip was so abruptly interrupted than the fact that there were three men on the deck with their eyeballs missing.

*****

On dry land answering questions from one of the uniformed officers, I said, "So, a triple murder, bet that's a call you don't get too often."

I had no idea if the men were murdered or merely drowned but I was baiting him, so to speak.

"Huh? What?" he asked, looking forlornly at his fellow officers who were assigned the task of questioning the girls from the boat who had been much too busy shrieking and saying, "Oh my

God," to be bothered pulling t-shirts over their skimpy tops. The regularly scheduled late afternoon storm clouds were moving in from the west and the gusting wind that preceded them gave the women an even sexier hair-blown look. It had all the makings of a Playboy photo shoot, but with corpses.

He ignored my question and asked, "Why were you on the boat today?"

"I did a trade-off with Billy."

He raised an eyebrow and before the smirk could fully form on his lips I said, "Don't *even* go there. We traded for ad space on my website."

I had no desire to speak to this man another minute. I wanted to talk to my only friend on the force; Rose.

Rose Shelton is the Fort Myers' police department's rising star. She's more accurate with a gun than Clint Eastwood, smart, ambitious, fun, and one of the most beautiful women I know.

"Is Officer Shelton coming? I'd like to talk to her if she's here. No offense, but we're friends."

"That figures," he said without looking up. He wrote something on his notepad and I stood on my toes and craned my neck in an effort to read it. "No, Shelton's working another case," he said, turning the pad away. "Did you know the deceased?"

"I'm the one that hooked them and reeled them in, but other than that, no."

He looked at me, not so much as if intimidated by my amazing dead body retrieval skills, but more incredulously, like I had sprouted antlers.

"Yes, yes, I know," I said, "I'm not sure I believe it myself and I was there. So, are we done? Because if we are, I'd like to go speak to those gentlemen over there."

He nodded and I proceeded to where the bodies were being loaded.

A woman I noticed as head of forensics was near the coroner's van. I almost didn't recognize her in the white coverall suit that made her look as though she were transporting plutonium.

"Hello," I called to her in my practiced, non-intimidating yet firm voice.

She turned and said, "Oh, it's you. That figures."

"Hi Miranda, nice to see you too," I said. "Why are you, you know, doing this?" I turned my head into the back of the van.

Miranda was my version of an arch enemy, but I needed her so I didn't take her attitude personally; I pretended she was merely socially awkward. I smiled broadly to help her feel less so.

"Don't touch anything," she said. "You're not supposed to be here anyway."

"A little late for that, I'm the one that reeled them in."

She raised her right eyebrow, that being a skill, by the way, I'd never been able to master.

"Ok, so, I had some help reeling them in, but it was me that hooked them and helped open the net..."

She interrupted, "Yeah, why'd you do that? I thought you were experienced enough by now to know better than to tamper with evidence." I could see sweat pouring from under her cap, running onto her paper mask; she looked hot and miserable. I gave her some slack.

"They were bodies, I mean, they...well, maybe I could have...I don't know...I had to..."

"What, you thought you could do a little CPR maybe? Because it seems to me that a smart *blogger* like you would have sense enough to, I don't know, figure out when a body's been floating in the ocean for a few days."

She was right, I knew better.

I had firsthand experience investigating some fairly nasty criminals when I arrived in Florida a little more than a year ago. Now I write a crime-scene blog and sell ad space for it, which pays nearly nothing, but sometimes I can trade for stuff like this trip today. A police scanner that I found used on Craigslist, a Vespa, internet access, and the willingness, a calling even, to be annoying were all I needed to start my own little career in journalism. This was the *being annoying* part.

"So," I said, "they've been dead a few days? They've been in the water that whole time?"

She walked away but I stayed on her like a border collie, "How come forensics is messing with the bodies before the autopsy? What was that whistle thing?"

She stopped, turned to look at me like I had confessed to the Lindbergh kidnapping and said, "I'm sure you didn't take anything from any of the bodies. Even *you're* not that stupid."

"A, I'm not stupid, thank you, and B, of course I didn't take anything. Why? What's missing? The whistle thingy?"

She turned and walked back to the group of men in coroner gear and when I tried to follow, she said, "That's as far as you go Mizz Finn, if you've given your statement already, you can leave the area."

"It's ok, I know these social interactions make you uncomfortable," I called to her retreating form.

Interview

Michael Guillebeau: Kathleen, you're known as a comedy writer first, and mystery novelist second. Is that how you see yourself?

Kathleen Cosgrove: That would be a fairly good description of my writing and also how my mind works. I always look to see how any situation can be made funny, and it almost always can. I enjoy making people laugh and it seems I have a gift for that, as opposed to say, well, any other talent really. I've tried a lot of ways to express myself creatively, but it wasn't until I wrote *Engulfed* that I realized I had a bit of a knack for the absurd in writing. I had a lot of imaginary friends when I was little because, quite honestly, the real kids wouldn't play with me. I was hard-of-hearing, had to wear an eye patch for amblyopia, and was so socially awkward I could make Boo Radley seem like Cary Grant. It was then I created a rich fantasy life full of larger than life characters that eventually paid off, although that wouldn't happen for decades.

MG: What made you decide to sit down and write *Engulfed*?

KC: I was reading one of Janet Evanovitch's Stephanie Plum novels. They are a blast to read, very funny, with a whole cast of quirky characters. The main character is in her early thirties as are most of the other main characters. There are richly drawn recurring characters who are older, including her mother, who is probably about the age I was when I was reading it. The mother's role in the novel is to worry about her daughter's marital status and the tenderness of the pot roast. I wanted a world where her mother, and all women of a certain age, left the house and began having adventures of their own. I decided if I couldn't read it anywhere, I'd write it. I wanted a story where Baby Boomers were still out there having fun, mixing it up, even making bad decisions or saving the day, having sex, smoking pot, being the hero or villain, but most of all, being relevant. Jessica Fletcher was an older amateur sleuth, but I could never see her back stage at a drag show, which is where I put my own Maggie Finn in *Engulfed*.

MG: What should your readers expect when they pick up one of your Maggie Finn novels, *Engulfed* or *Entangled*?
KC: I expect those readers to be ready for an escape from the ordinary. My novels are lighthearted, fun, easy reads, perfect for a beach bag. If they can embrace the absurd, to be willing to take a ride with a boat load of eccentric but lovable characters, well, it's a murder mystery so they're not *all* lovable.

I had a reader write and tell me that reading *Engulfed* gave her the first laugh she'd had since tragedy had struck her family. If I never get another review, I can live with just that. It made the whole labor of writing it worthwhile.

MG: What book makes you feel good, one that you've read over and over?

KC: *To Say Nothing of the Dog or How We Found the Bishop's Bird Stump* by Connie Willis. It's comic science fiction. The characters are so well drawn and perfectly believable in all their quirkiness that they become real by the end of the first chapter. I've read it three or four times and listened to the audio version about as many times. The first book I fell in love with was *How Green Was My Valley*, by Richard Llewellyn, the story of life in a Welsh mining village. I was probably nine years old and it was the book that taught me the magic books could do, transporting readers to different places and times. I became an obsessive reader after that one, spending lunch hours in the library looking for my next adventure.

MG: Is there a common thread that runs through your writing?

KC: That would probably be something along the lines of, 'It's never too late to be extraordinary.' I believe that *now* is the time to do what you may have feared trying, or didn't have the time or resources to do. Simply because it hasn't happened yet doesn't mean it can't happen still. I like the idea of reinventing oneself on an ongoing basis. That and 'redemption.' I've come to believe redemption is the most important component of any story or in life really. Not necessarily for the bad guy to see the error of his ways, but for the protagonist to have a moment when they realize they've grown into a better them, is a pivotal part of any great story to me. I grew up reading fairy tales and Beauty and the Beast was my favorite, probably for that reason. It's stayed with me.

MG: What have you written that you're most proud of?

KC: I'm pretty proud that I finished *Engulfed*. I'd written a couple novels before then, but never one that I felt was worthy of having other people read until *Engulfed*. Beyond that, an essay I wrote as kind of tribute to my mother and grandmothers. It's a humor piece that I've performed at various storytelling events, it's been published in a few places. It's been incredibly well received and it allows those amazing women to live on, to live on with laughter. It's how they would want to be remembered.

MG: Are you working on a third Maggie Finn novel?

KC: I'm outlining one now. I'm traveling to Miami, Florida for 'research.' It may take several visits for me to get everything I need for it. I'm making the Seminole Casinos down there a focal point, so naturally I have to visit one or several.

MG: It sounds like rough work, are you filling those gaps between tanning and slot machines with anything else?

KC: You left out the Tiki Bars and yes, I am. I'm putting together an anthology of essays I'm calling, *The View From Under My Desk*. I grew up in the *Duck and Cover* years and most of the stories are from that era or how growing up in that era formed us Baby Boomers. It is, of course, a comic look at those decades between then and now. I'm giving them a test drive by performing them at storytelling venues to see what lines get the biggest laughs and which ones fall flat. The storytelling audiences of Nashville have become my content editors. I hope to have it completed by early 2017. If I wait too long, I'll have to start including stories about STDs in retirement villages and no one wants to read about that, or maybe they do. No, I'll for sure be done by 2017, probably.

MICHAEL GUILLEBEAU

Michael Guillebeau's first book, *Josh Whoever* (Five Star Mysteries, 2013) was a finalist for the 2014 Silver Falchion Award for Best First Novel: Literary Suspense, and received a starred review in *Library Journal*, and was named a Debut Mystery of the Month by *Library Journal*. His second book, *A Study In Detail* (Five Star Mysteries, 2015) received the following praise from the Midwest Book Review: "Recommended for romance and mystery readers seeking something different... fresh, original and witty." Guillebeau has published over twenty short stories, including three in Ellery Queen's Mystery Magazine.

Michael Guillebeau lives in Madison, Alabama and Panama City Beach, Florida. You can find him at www.michaelguillebeau.com.

Short Story

The Man In The Moon

(Mike's Notes: This story was first published in *Ellery Queen's Mystery Magazine* in May, 2011, and it is probably still my favorite story that I've written because it is, at heart, a love story between a father and a very special daughter and about how that love can transcend even some of the biggest issues in life. I've got a daughter who's that special. I hope you enjoy this story half as much as Mary and I do.)

Mom and the man were sitting on my bed when I woke up in the middle of the night. He was older than I expected, his hair short and grey now, not jet black and long like I remembered. But the eyes were the same: pale clear blue but sad. Mom says I have his eyes but I don't know. I read a description in a story once that I think fits my eyes. Dead fish eyes. When I look into my own eyes I see nothing, no emotion.

"Carrie, do you remember your Dad?" said Mom, her arm around his shoulder.

"Hi, Daddy," I said. I should have said more, but I didn't know what.

"Hi, Carrie," he said. I couldn't remember him ever calling me Carrie; it was always "Princess," or "Pumpkin." But, as I said, it had been a long time.

He laid his hand on my shoulder and I tried not to flinch, but I think I did, a little. I had passed the point a long time ago where I could feel a man's hand on me without suspicion, and I'd spent those years in between fighting back at every little challenge since I'd last seen him. I guess I was older than he realized, still curled up under the blanket with my body hidden and just my head sticking out for him to see. I relaxed and felt something warm and basic and barely remembered flow through the connection between his hand and my shoulder.

"Carrie, I've come to tell you a story. Remember when you were little, how you wouldn't go to sleep until I told you a story? Couldn't just read you a book, had to be a story I made up."

I was surprised that I did remember. I had forgotten what it was like then, lying in bed in frilly pink sheets, miniature ponies on the wall, safe because this smiling giant was there to protect me. And more, the first taste of little girl-woman power, knowing the giant would do whatever I asked, stop the world and tell me a story, slay a dragon or two, if only I asked and added the magic word, "Daddy."

"I've got one now I've been working on a long time, just for you. I know you're already sleeping, but can I tell it to you now?"

I started to tell him to go to hell, then I wanted to jump out of the covers, hop up and have the big man catch me like a feather and carry me off to sleep. I wanted to say, "Please, please, please" in a little girl voice again. Instead, I just said, "Yes, Daddy," and that was enough for him.

"This is a story about the man in the moon. Once upon a time, a long, long time ago, when the moon was just a plain white ball, there was a boy named Lobo. He was a very ordinary boy, happy doing ordinary things. He ran errands for the shopkeepers in the village. He listened to stories from the wise old men, and he loved the stories. He never felt he was in the stories, though, because he never wanted to be anywhere but where he was.

"So his days were filled up, and his days went by as days should: not just using days as building blocks to some great future, but loving each day for itself. He was lucky, but didn't know it.

"Then one day his world changed, and changed in the best way that a world can change: he fell in love. And it happened in a single moment. He was carrying a box of vegetables from a farmer to a shop in the village and he looked up and saw a great procession of noblemen and knights. Because he was polite, he stopped and sat the box down to wait while the procession passed.

"He had seen many processions before and honestly, had never been impressed. Other people would bow down before the noblemen and explain to him that the nobles were better than them.

"But it never looked that way to him. He knew that, in his own village, the mayor sometimes acted like he was better than the shopkeepers, and shopkeepers acted like they were better than the beggars. But he knew that sometimes the beggars had the best stories, and the mayor often had nothing but empty words.

"So he figured it must be the same in the castle, that people were all alike, that noblemen were just people with money, knights just men in shiny suits. So he stopped and waited for the procession to go by, just as he would have waited for the man carrying manure from the fields to go by."

"Where?" I couldn't keep quiet; the story was missing a critical element of a Daddy story. "The village has to have a name, Daddy."

He smiled and looked at me like he had always looked at me, like I had just said the wisest and most wonderful thing in the world and he couldn't wait to see what I would say next. He blinked his eyes and looked away.

"Herewin," he said, slowly. "There were two towns with the same name, one on the left, one on the right. This one was on the right. So they called it Right Herewin. How's that?"

"That's good. Puts us in the story."

"Yeah," he said. "Want to be in the story."

"OK. So Lobo was waiting for the procession to go by, like every other procession, but this one had something different. In the middle of the procession, when he wasn't expecting anything, his life changed forever. He saw the princess. And she was the most beautiful thing he had ever seen, with beautiful long blonde hair and the bluest eyes, eyes so blue he felt like someone had captured the sky on the warmest summer day and put the whole sky in her eyes.

"He thought she was a miracle, wondered for a crazy minute if she was just a world unto herself, if the people in that world had her eyes for a sky every day, and he wanted to be in that world, even though he knew that was silly.

"And there was more: he could tell by looking at her that she was kind, and not just the sort of kindness that sits back and wishes the world were better, the sort of kindness that demands the best and makes it happen.

"And he didn't know if he was falling in love with her beauty, or falling in love with her kindness. But he knew he was in love, and always would be."

"No," I said, and I sat up now. "You can't just do that. You can't just make her kind because you want her to be kind. You got to show me something, make it real."

Daddy smiled. "When you were little, I thought you always demanded details to drag out bedtime. It took me a long time to realize you wanted things right, and got mad when they weren't."

"I don't just want a story. I want a Daddy story." I didn't know where that line came from, but it came out of my mouth.

"Yeah. That's what you used to tell me. I used to practice stories hoping I could get through without hearing that line. The few times I did, I thought I'd feel proud, but I just felt wasted because it made the story go by too fast. So here we are, back where we were."

And we looked at each other for a minute and I saw what he had become and still was, and he saw what I had become and always would be. He sighed, looked away and continued.

"All right, so there was this cat. Cat's name was Alley, cause she lived in the alley by the shops and lived on scraps. She was sort of Lobo's cat, sort of her own cat, but she was old, too old to move fast. She was also stubborn. She decided then that she wanted to cross the street, and no procession was going to get in her way.

"So here she came, moving about as fast as a snail, head up, not giving the procession even one look. She almost got stepped on by the knight's horse, the knight not even trying to avoid her. Nobleman was worse. He tried to make his horse step on her, hurt the cat just because the cat was too little to hurt him back.

"Alley avoided the nobleman's horse somehow, but here came the princess's carriage, gigantic, the size of a house. Alley's dead for sure. But the princess stands up, and out of this delicate little princess comes the biggest voice Lobo had ever heard. 'Stop!' she yells. 'Stop now.'

"And the voice shakes the shops and stops the procession instantly, the horses frozen in mid-stride and the noblemen all going nowhere now, all from the giant voice from the little girl.

"And Alley, taking her time, sashays across the street without so much as a thank you to the princess who saved her life. When Alley was safely across the street, the princess, in a little girl voice again now, said, 'You may proceed,' and they did, the noblemen and the knights pretending that they had never been bossed around by a little girl for the sake of a worthless old cat."

Daddy looked at me. "Better?"

"Daddy story, now," I said. I got back under the covers, snuggled up to Daddy's leg, and waited.

"OK, so now Lobo's in love. Now he wants something he can't have. Every day, he sees those eyes. Every day, he looks up at the sky and it's not blue enough. But he's just a poor boy, what can he do, he can't even get in the castle. Then one day a courier rides into town. You know what a courier is, right, kind of like CNN before there was TV?"

"Of course I know what a courier is. They often travelled together with minstrels and jesters. Provided news and entertainment. Not just like CNN. More like television before there was television. Or vaudeville. Or modern theater. Or..."

"Yeah, yeah, I get it," said Daddy, again with that admiring look. Two of those looks in one night; best night I can remember.

"Anyway, if I can be allowed to continue, the courier blares his trumpet, don't really know why but that's what couriers do. Nails up this notice. There is going to be a competition for the hand of the princess. Whoever brings the princess the most magical thing, on noon in two days time, wins the hand of the princess. That's what the notice says: most magical thing, not best or most expensive, but most magic. Also, you have to go through a certain door, door will only open for one minute at noon and then, boom, slam shut. There's probably a lot of legalese at the bottom of the notice, but we're going to skip that in the interest of moving the story along.

"So now Lobo doesn't know what to do, he's in a tizzy. On the one hand, he's terrified. If someone else finds the magic thing, the princess is lost forever. He just doesn't think he can live with that. On the other hand, he's got a chance, a real chance for the first time. If he can come up with a magic thing, he can win the princess and live happily ever after.

"So he doesn't know what to do. Thinks about it all day, just pacing around, probably drinking coffee all the time, would be smoking a cigarette, but he's a good boy and doesn't smoke cigarettes. Got nothing.

"All his friends are poor, too. The shopkeepers, the beggars, the farmers, they'd help him if they could, but what's he going to do, take a chunk of cheese or maybe a pair of work boots up to the castle, say, 'Here, Princess, it's magic cheese. Got lactobacillus, good for the digestion.' Don't think so.

"So everyone in the village is trying to help, but, still he's got nothing. He's up all night, thinking, getting nowhere. But the next day another boy comes to him with an idea. This boy's name is Larcenious. Not really a friend, but an acquaintance. An acquaintance is like a friend that you don't really trust. Larcenious says, 'I know how to break into the workshop of the wizard. All sorts of magic there. Wizard would probably never miss it if we went in there and took something."

"Larcenious?" I mumbled. My body was half-asleep, more relaxed than it had been in a long time. But my brain was hanging on every word, and this one was wrong. "Kind of heavy handed, don't you think, guy named after the Latin and Old French root, 'larcin,' meaning to steal. Can't he be 'Fred' or maybe 'Lefty' if you're going for a Damon Runyon tone?"

"No," Daddy said and I opened my eyes and saw that Daddy was tight-lipped, tense at this part of the story. "I'm telling the story. I've heard of Latin, too.

"So Lobo is torn. Doesn't trust Larcenious, don't care if you don't like the name, that's his name and that's that. Doesn't trust him, but maybe this is a way out of the tizzy. Lobo's never taken anything that wasn't his in his life, not even an apple when he was carrying boxes of apples from the orchard early in the morning and hadn't eaten. But he wanted the princess. See, that was his flaw. Not the princess, wasn't her fault for being wonderful. Not because he loved the princess, that's a good thing, too. But the wanting to have something, to possess it rather than just to love it and see where the love will take you on it's own, that's what was wrong.

"Maybe it was the coffee, too. Maybe if he hadn't been up all night, brain wired on caffeine, maybe he'd have said no. But he didn't. He said yes. A million times later, in his mind, he'd think about it and say, 'No, I only want what's mine,' but this time, the time that counted, he thought long and hard and wrong and said, 'Yes.'

"So that night, the night before the door to the castle would open, he went with Larcenious to the wizard's lair, which is where wizards live and work."

He looked over at Mom. Mom was getting impatient. "So, anyway, they break in and steal this magic crown. I'm going to skip a part here, magic things in the wizard's workshop, scary things that Lobo had to fight. Important part, but that's really a boy's story anyway, with dragon's blood and stuff a little girl doesn't need to hear about anyway." He looked over at Mom and she nodded, still holding him around his shoulder.

"But the crown was wonderful, the most magic thing in the wizard's lair, which was filled with magic things. The purest kind of gold you can get on earth is 24 karat gold. This was 24,000 karat gold, so pure it glowed. And it sang. Sang a beautiful song that only the person wearing the crown could hear. Lobo tried it on, thought, that's it, a song as beautiful as the princess, every time she puts it on she'll see how beautiful she is, and how much I love her. Good thoughts, if the crown was really his to give.

"So now he's at the castle, with the crown, ten minutes before noon. He's cleaned himself up—the tailor gave him a new set of clothes, sharp clothes, free, on account of all the good things he'd done for the tailor over the years.

"Lobo looks around, there's all these rich guys with great things, expensive presents, golden harps, perfume from Asia, stuff like that. They all look down on him, a poor boy standing there with a plain sack. But he smiles, knowing what he's got in the sack.

"So now it's noon, the great stone door screeches open, lot of noise because the door hadn't opened in a thousand years but it's open now and they're all fighting to get in, rich guys trying to shove him out of the way like he's nothing. Normally he'd let them go ahead, but this time he's fighting back. He's at the door, about to go in, on the verge of happily-ever-after, when he sees it.

"There's a cat sitting at the door. Same cat as before, Alley, always getting herself in trouble, but she's a cat, she doesn't care a bit. The door is closing, just a little, and Alley's stuck. He stops, plenty of time to help Alley and still get in. But she's stuck, really stuck this time. The cat that always gets in trouble may have done it this time. Only one thing to do. He puts the sack with the crown down, blocking the door, and it's slowing the door, but just a little.

"So he's pulling and pulling and Alley's looking up with that bored-cat look, not helping a bit. Finally, last second, he pulls Alley free, but the door crushes the crown and the door snaps shut. He's stuck on the outside, everything he wants on the inside, the thing he gave up his honesty for gone, just him and the mangy old cat on the outside. At that moment, he could probably have ripped the cat apart, had cat soup for dinner. Cat gets up, walks away like nothing happened.

"Lobo's sitting there on the cold stone, might as well be in a prison cell even if he's on the outside, and he starts to cry. First time he can remember, he starts to cry. He can't even tell you why, can't even tell you who he is anymore, just a crying man.

"Suddenly, there's this hand on his shoulder. I'll tell you something that's true, not part of this story, not part of any story. There's a certain spot, right on the shoulder, where people can connect and pass pure sunlight from one to another. Put your hand right there, like this, and light pours from you into them. It's true, even if scientists don't know it yet.

"So he feels that hand, feels that light, looks up into the bluest eyes he's ever seen and the princess, his princess now, is telling him, 'Kindness is the most magic thing," and they start to live happily ever after, right then, right at that moment. At least, that's the way it looked at that moment."

He was getting hard to understand. He was crying now, snuffling to keep his nose from running. Mom put her head on his shoulder and said, "That's enough for now. I need some of your time, too."

"What about the man in the moon?" I said.

"In the morning," Mom said, and they got up and left and it was just my room again. I lay there thinking.

I don't remember sleeping, but they were there when I woke up, sitting together on the side of the bed, so early it was still dark. Daddy had on the blue suit, the one I used to call his handsome suit. I could smell the clean promise of a fresh-ironed shirt.

"Morning, Carrie," he said.

"Morning, Daddy," I snuggled close to him and put my arm on his leg.

"Sorry to get you up so early, but we've got stuff to get done."

"Yeah," I said. "Lobo and the Princess are happily-ever-aftering, but you left it with an ominous tone."

I could see him smile, even in the dark room. "Ominous tone? Yeah, I guess I did.

"Well, anyway, Lobo and the princess are sitting there in the castle, you're right, they're in an ominous tone, but they're happy. They are in love, and it turns out that Lobo is a pretty good prince,

actually making things better for the ordinary people in the
kingdom instead of just the rich guys like most rulers do.

"Every day, he looks into those amazing blue eyes, blue eyes
just like yours, and he looks at the sky for comparison. Every day, he
sees those eyes have twice as much warmth as a summer day. He's a
lucky man, better than a lucky man because he knows he helped his
own luck, just a little.

"Good times. Old friends come from the village to see him.
He introduces them to the princess, and she's wonderful, treats them
like they were nobles, no, better because she knows they love Lobo
and she loves anyone who loves Lobo, because she loves Lobo. And
Lobo loves her.

"And that's all that ever matters. That's what you've got to
take from the story: the love is all that ever matters. Things happen,
can't control that, but the love is all that matters.

"Well, almost. Life goes on, outside of the heart, and
sometimes it's not good. One day a different villager comes to visit:
Larcenious.

Larcenious says, 'Hey, Lobo.'

Lobo says, 'It's Prince Lobo to you, now.'

Larcenious says, 'Yeah, well, I knew you when. Reminds me,
the wizard's been bugging me, wants to know whatever happened to
his magic crown. I gotta tell him, unless you can do me this one little
favor.'

"So Lobo does this one little favor. Then another. Then
another. Pretty soon, Larcenious is living in the castle, Princess

doesn't like it much because she can see he doesn't love Lobo, just likes the food in the castle. The favors turn into what they call illegal acts. Before you know it, Lobo's got two lives: the good life, in the day, with the princess, and a bad life at night, after the castle's asleep, when he and Larcenious sneak out and do bad things. Really bad things. Worse than you can imagine. You're just a little girl, I'm going to leave those parts out, but you know they're there.

"And it's ruining his good life, too. The princess knows something's wrong, so they fight a lot. He knows she's right, so he fights back harder, the way people do when they know they're wrong but can't face it. But he does face it, eventually. He sees that Larcenious is going to cost him everything that is good. So he tells Larcenious, take a hike, I'm done with you, do your worst.

"Well, that's just what Larcenious does, his worst. One day when things are back to normal, Lobo and the princess happy again, having fun ruling the kingdom wisely, the wizard shows up. And he doesn't just show up, he crashes through the big window in the castle, riding a fire-breathing dragon and everything.

"He looks at Lobo and says, 'You stole the most precious thing in the world from me. Now, I'm going to destroy the entire kingdom, and everything in it.'

"And Lobo stands up and says, 'I'm finished with lying. I stole your crown. I'm sorry, great wizard, and I know that doesn't change what I've done. But I know this, too: as valuable as that crown was, it was not the most precious thing in the world. Love is. The love I have for the princess, the way her love warms me like her magic blue eyes, even on days when I can't see her eyes. The love all the citizens in this land feel. It's greater than any crown, and it will endure, no matter what comes.

"'But I took your crown, and now the crown is destroyed and I can never give it back to you, and I know I can never make things right. But please, great wizard, it was my crime, and I, and I alone, should pay.'

"The wizard's heart is touched, but only a little.

"'I will spare the kingdom,' he says, 'but you have taken from me that which I held dearest. It is only just that I take from you that which you hold dearest.

"'I am banishing you from the presence of the princess forever. You will live your life a thousand miles away, and know that you will never touch her again.

"'But now, since you have been honest, I will grant you one small favor: you may choose where you will live, so long as it is at least a thousand miles away from the princess.'

"Lobo thought hard of all the wonderful places that people loved to go, but, without the princess, even the most glamorous place seemed miserable. An idea came to him.

"'Wise wizard, your punishment is just. I choose to live in the moon, always facing the princess. Every night, I will look down into her eyes and be warmed. Every night, she can look up into the sky and know that she is loved beyond measure. And everyone who looks at the moon can know that love is the only thing that is truly yours, the one thing that can never be taken from you.'"

Daddy paused, put his hand on mine, and said, "And that, Princess, is why there is a man in the moon."

Mom whispered something to him and he nodded. He looked away, out the window, nodded, said, "I've got to go now, Carrie. I know it's been a long time, but could you give me a hug before I go?"

I jumped up and tried to squeeze him so hard he couldn't leave.

"I love you, Princess," he said.

"I love you, Daddy," I said.

He told me to stay there when he left, but I got up and followed just behind him out onto the porch where the policemen were waiting. They put his hands behind his back and handcuffed him, reading some words that neither they nor he cared about.

I saw the side of his face, big Daddy smile, happy somehow, as he said to one of the men, "What're they going to do, execute me twice?" They turned him around all the way and he saw me standing there and I saw all of his faces from over the years: first, he was a stern parent, starting to fuss at me for disobeying him, then his face was angry at nothing and everything for a second, then he was just a man in love with a princess, trying hard not to cry as his fairy tale came true.

As he turned away, I saw the moon over his face, a half moon with half the face clear, the other half taken away by the night. It was the last time I saw my father, and the first time I saw the man in the moon.

EXCERPT

Josh Whoever

Library Journal Mystery Debut of Month Feb 2013

"...

VERDICT Guillebeau brings the emotional turmoil of his damaged protagonist to its peak while giving him good reasons to persevere. While the Russian mob, right-wing modern Confederates, and a paramilitary group might seem like overkill, the plot never wavers off-track, and the collection of oddball minor characters and surprise twists deepen an already strong story. An engrossing debut."

(Mike's Notes: *Josh* was my first book, and I'm still amazed at how it snuck up on me. First there was song, Steely Dan's *Here at the Western World*, about a guy spending all his time hanging in a run-down bar. At that time in my life, it looked like a pretty good way to live, so I couldn't stop thinking about how you'd actually do it. Thought about it until it became a short story. Months afterwards, I wondered what

Josh would do next. And next. Every day, the story kept writing itself until I had a book, and then Five Star Mysteries was kind enough to publish it. Thanks for taking the time to meet my friend Josh.)

Chapter 1

I only took this job to get fired, but now I stood here raising my hands in the air like any good citizen being robbed.

Two robbers had popped into the bank from nowhere. From inside my little bank teller window, I had no real view of them walking in the door but now they strutted around in white paper lab suits, looking like big bunny rabbits waving guns at random around the bank lobby.

The tall one did all the talking. "Open your cash drawers, put your hands in the air and shut up."

His eyes darted from teller to teller looking for a challenge. The young girl in front of him just stood there frozen. He waved his gun at the ceiling and let off a burst and the girl screamed and opened her drawer.

"This. Is. A. Robbery." He shouted each word loud and important, like he was hyping a band at a rock concert.

Like we needed a program to tell us what's going on here. Like I needed a program to tell me that my own future was over if they got away with this robbery.

The short one reached up with the barrel of his AK-47 and pushed away the video camera over the door so that it saw only the ceiling. They started at the far end and worked their way down the long row of tellers towards me.

I stood motionless and watched, curious about how they did this. I knew plenty about small-time scams, but I'd never seen a big-time bank robbery like this before.

The tall guy did all the talking but looked at the silent one for something. There: that was it. Silent shook his head, and Tall skipped a teller. Silent knew something; he skipped the tellers with dye packs.

I admired them for pulling this off, admired the details: the paper lab suits were a good touch. No one would remember anything about the robbers except the white suits with hoods. Probably buy them cheap at some med supply place; add a white ski mask and you can wear anything you like underneath.

Except for the shoes. Tall had flashy basketball kicks that demanded respect on the street, what you'd expect from a robber. But Silent had a pair of black Ferragamos, rich businessman shoes that cost three hundred dollars new, except his weren't new. The kind of guy who would buy these shoes wouldn't keep his shoes this long; he either had money or worked for guys with money and had to keep up. Either way, it stood out and it offended me. I was a pro in my own way. I respected pros. You've got to get the details right.

The two guys moved the same way: pro, but with a flaw. They looked casual, even random, but I could tell it was rehearsed. No one but me would remember that later, and that was good.

But the body language had a flaw. Tall moved like a
bank robber in a movie, all swagger and attitude, waving the gun
around and yelling at anything. Silent faded into the background and
that was good, too, but the pose was wrong. He hunched over and
shuffled like a kicked dog. This wasn't a man used to demanding
other people's money. Silent begged people for money every day and
hated doing it but had to pay the rent.

There, in a flash I had it. Silent's walk and Silent's shoes
belonged to Robert, the assistant manager of the bank. I watched him
get pushed around every day by the manager. Now Robert was
getting his payback.

See, that was the tell, the one detail that betrayed all your
hard work because it was too much a part of who you were for you to
even know it was there. I knew how to stay in character and keep the
game going until I got to the payoff. Even now, when I wanted to
grab the guys and tell them to start over, to come through the doors
this way or that, even now I just stood there impassively with my
hands in the air.

I wanted to tell them: be a pro. Be a pro, or be burned.

I reached over quick and took the dye pack from Kelly's
open drawer, one of the old style packs with a timer. Kelly smiled
weakly back at me, chewed her gum faster and looked away. I pressed
the timer button and put it in my own drawer.

Tall came to me and waved his gun. I smiled and scooped
up the cash and dye pack and shoveled them on top of the money in

the bag. I felt like saying, "sorry," to the big bunny rabbit, but the best I could do was apologize in my head.

Sorry, I thought, but I can't let San Francisco's finest look at the personnel records and ask me questions, the kind of questions these giant companies *should* ask before they hire someone but never do. Big dogs can't be bothered checking on the little guys who really make up their companies.

And that's why I hated these companies, hated so much of the world: be a pro, treat people and your job with respect, or get out.

Me? I got out.

Chapter 2

I stood in the bank and wondered what my next scam would be, hoping it would be easy again like the last one. Remembered sitting in the conference room of the big environmental company: just me, the company lawyer and the boss, all in jeans and shirts from all-natural materials to show how much they respected the earth. But they didn't respect the earth, didn't respect anything else either, including me, so there we were.

"So, do you prefer to be called Mr. Smooth Water, or Joshua?" said the lawyer, smiling, trying to be my friend so it would cost the company less.

"It's pronounced 'Ya-wa'." I folded my arms across my chest, trying hard to swell up with pride. "Joshua is just the white spelling. And Smooth Water is my formal Chippewa name from my mother's tribe. It should not be used by whites."

There. Let the lawyer know there's no friend of his here, and this would cost the company more. I could see him wondering, maybe this guy's native American, maybe not. I've got the kind of light-dark look that could be Hispanic, Middle Eastern, white, black, whatever I need. In any case, the lawyer couldn't challenge me on it. I also knew that this company had too much to hide for them to risk a big fight out in public.

"Thank you, Joshua," the lawyer said, pronouncing it "Ya-wa" like I asked, and smiling while he did it. I gave him no smile back, just sat there with my arms crossed like the picture of Sitting Bull, offended but impassive. "It's my understanding that Mr. Johnson here, acting in his position as your supervisor, has terminated you from your position here at California Green Industries. He believes he had cause, you believe he did not. Is that a fair statement of the situation?"

I glared at the lawyer and played out the part of a proud, offended man forced to describe a painful insult.

"I came to this company because it said it would help protect the land of my fathers, clean up the streams and take the white man's poisons out of the air. In the week I have been here, I have been insulted and shamed, despite doing my best."

"The jerk hasn't done a lick of work since the day he came in," said Johnson. He was having trouble sitting still. "He just sits on that cheap blanket drinking company coffee, explaining that each day is a sacred day of some kind or the other that won't let him do this job or that."

The lawyer held up his hand to Johnson, but they had given me an opening.

"Coffee is a sacred drink to my people. It is the water of life for me, the source of all movement. We have proudly shared it with the white man."

"I thought you people preferred something stronger," said Johnson, and the lawyer shook his head furiously but too late. The price had gone up.

"And now this racism," I said, "the true source of our problem here."

Johnson stood up. "The problem is you won't work. The problem is I've got a boatload of jobs that need to get done, and you're just dragging us down . . ." The lawyer held up his hand and interrupted.

"None of which you've documented, Mr. Johnson." He turned to me, his buddy, and smiled again. Amazing the problems that can be solved if we all just smile. Smile, and offer money. "Joshua, I think we all have the same interests here. We all want to see that the values shared by this company and your forefathers are not damaged by a pointless, bitter, public struggle. Clearly, we no longer have a position available for you at this company, but we want to treat you fairly. Would $2000 help you find a position more suited to your talents?"

We settled on $5000. Johnson was taken out of the room still screaming. Sometimes I got more, sometimes less, for a week or so's half-assed work at a company that would rather pay me off than fight publicly.

The scam worked best at companies that had something to hide, like this one that was taking money to clean up the environment but doing little more than generating publicity for itself. Mostly, I find companies already ripping off the public before I rip them off. Of course, sometimes just the fact that a company has money goes a long way to prove to me that the company is corrupt and needs to return some money to the community. And me.

So I strutted out the door with a check in hand, threw the sacred blanket in the trash by the big Fred Meyer store, dealt with the check, ran a few errands, and headed back to the Western World bar.

Mayor was behind the bar by himself. Three in the afternoon was too early to have a hired bartender, not to mention that Mayor was way too cheap to pay somebody to just sit behind his own bar and watch sports reruns, which is all Mayor ever does anyway. He looked up at me like I was just another channel on the old RCA.

"Thought I might not see you this time," he said. "Make a score, keep going someplace better. Become a citizen."

I looked at him and tried to smile. I hated seeing the disappointment rise in Mayor's eyes, knowing that I put it there. Mayor and the skinny girl who danced here were my only real links to the world. And, truth be told, this was the only world I could stand anymore.

"Hey, you know you'd miss me." But Mayor just stared, not willing to keep it light and make it easier on me.

"I've got twenty-five hundred." I pulled out a stack of bills without explaining the errands that had eaten up the other half. "How long will that carry me?"

Mayor stared a long time, and I thought for a minute that he might say no this time. But the money clock ran slow here; most drinks were paid for with wadded-up dollar bills and change counted slow from dirty pockets. A pile of crisp fifty dollar bills was rare, except from me. Mayor looked at the calendar, studied it like the football coach on the TV studying his playbook.

"Let's say the end of October. Same deal as always: sleep in the back room, sweep up at night, and drink only the cheap stuff, only enough to stay drunk. Eat from the lunch buffet, though you never eat much anyway. Don't cause trouble, though you never cause trouble. You can be everybody's buddy, but you can't buy them drinks 'cause you got no money and I ain't fronting you any.

"End of October, skinny girl and I will wake you up. Last two weeks, no booze, nothing but coffee and the buffet, sober up and go back, jack, do it again. Wheels turning round and round, find some scam or an actual job until you show up here again. Or not. Cash aside, won't break my heart if someday you get stuck in the real world and don't make it back here."

"Deal," I said, and shoved the bills across the bar. "Let's get started." Mayor reached under the bar and pulled out the plastic tumbler that was my cup and the gallon jug of the cheap stuff he used to top off the expensive-looking bottles behind the bar. No need for the pretense of a nice bottle. He filled the tumbler half full. No need for the pretense of dishing this out one shot at a time either. I looked at him and wished that I was one of those who got the good glasses with the tiny drinks. One of those that came in, had a couple of drinks, and toddled home to a happy wife and kids.

What bullshit. I picked up the glass and emptied it. I picked up my crushed and sad paper sack and headed to the back.

"Think I'll take my luggage to the Presidential Suite. I'll join you in the Main Ballroom for happy hour after I've freshened up."

"What do you do back there, anyway?" Mayor turned back to the TV.

"I'm a writer."

"Need any paper?"

"I don't write anything down."

*****

The next thing I remembered clearly was Mayor and the skinny girl shaking me awake at the end of October. The coffee cup in front of me looked like a swimming pool I was supposed to drink. Mayor just looked at me like I was another mess at the bar that Mayor had to clean up, but the skinny girl said to Mayor: "You don't know. I talked to a guy who knew him on the outside. He's somebody. Used to be somebody, anyway." I looked at her sweet, wasted face and wanted to thank her. Thank her, and tell her how wrong she was.

"He's a cork in a bottle," said Mayor. "And you're a professional heartbreak. Don't waste it on this one."

In a flash I remembered something else less clear: the skinny girl, sometime in the middle, holding my head, saying, "Oh Josh baby, oh Josh baby. You could do it for me, Josh baby." I couldn't remember if the words came during one of the times she had shown me a kindness, or just one of the times when I was too drunk to get to my room without help. But she said it, I was sure, and now I wondered what to do with it.

Chapter 3

I shook the memory of the Western World away and snatched my head back to the here and now in the bank. The robbers finished and told us all to lie down and face away from the door. Then they were gone and the bank was silent until the police crashed in like heroes here to save the day now that the day had walked out the door.

The detectives gave us all numbers, like we were in a deli waiting for a corned-beef sandwich, but instead we waited our turn to be brought into the conference room to have our formal police interview. My number was nine; they were on five. I was sweating and hoping the sweat wouldn't dissolve the little bits of glue that held my eyelids up to make me look more Chinese. Once they saw I was phony, or once they pulled my record and checked me out, then everything would all be over.

I shuffled humbly over to a detective standing around drinking free bank coffee and texting on a cell phone. Tried to tell him about the silent robber, nudge the detective into solving the crime before they pulled my record and talked to me. But no, the detective waved me back. Take your turn, sir, follow procedure, sir; we're not really interested in solving the crime, sir, just doing our jobs, sir.

I spotted the manager leaning on one of the desks in the middle of it all. He could have been watching guys mow his lawn for all the interest he showed.

"Mister—ah, sir?" I said to him.

"Romanov."

Christ, I thought. All I said to him was, "Romanov?"

The manager smiled at my surprise.

"Yeah, that Romanov. I run the bank for my father. He owns a lot of stuff."

Yeah, I thought, some of it's even legal. I hadn't known the Romanovs owned the bank. Now I wished I'd picked a different one.

Romanov looked up, squinted a minute, then it came to him.

"Joe Chan?" he said.

"Yes, sir." I answered to the name I'd put down on the application at the bank. "Though it's pronounced 'yow.' It's a traditional Chinese name, taken from my honorable grandfather who first came to this country seeking freedom. I'm honored that you know my name, sir."

Romanov shrugged. "Yeah. Dad believes I should know the employees. So I memorize names of new hires to impress him."

"Sir," I said, polite and deferential. "I've tried to talk to the detectives, but they seem to be busy. I believe I have information that might be helpful."

"So? What do you want me to do? Haul my ass over there; tell them Charlie Chan here has solved the case and saved the day? The bank's got insurance, son. Let it go."

"Sir, did you notice the way the silent robber walked? Now look at the assistant manager."

Romanov tried to look bored, but he looked at Robert at the other end of the bank and smiled.

"You weasel," he said, watching Robert. "Good for you. Finally grew a pair and stopped begging for it."

He turned back to me.

"Yeah, maybe," he said. "Cops already said they got one witness outside the bank. The witness saw a tall guy come out alone. Not wearing a white suit. Not carrying a bag. So they're looking inside already. Probably got him in their sights right now. I'll go tell them for you; you get the credit. You got good eyes."

A detective came out of the interview room and called out for number eight and I knew my time below the radar was running out. Romanov waved the detective over, snapping his fingers like he wanted another glass of water. I grabbed Romanov's sleeve but Romanov shook me off.

"Sir, it might be better to tell them you thought of this yourself," I said, "and leave me out."

The detective walked over and stood waiting for orders, knew he couldn't offend the manager. Didn't like being ordered around either, so he stood there, refusing to be the first to talk.

Romanov talked to the detective, not taking his eyes off me while he did. "Just wanted to know how the investigation's going."

The detective tried to smile politely but his mouth tightened into a narrow line. This rich jerk called him over for a personal status report?

"You'll know as soon as we do, sir." He drew "sir" out to about five syllables, and left.

"So." Romanov turned back to me. "You work in a bank where there's just been a robbery, but you want to stay below the cop's radar?"

I saw the detective looking for another witness, skipping number eight and coming for me. I saw Romanov looking at me and I needed a story and needed it right now.

"Yes, sir. I'm really a private investigator, sir, and don't need to attract the attention of the police. I only took this job because I need the money."

"Got a license you can show me?"

"No, sir, I'm kind of unofficial. That's why I'd prefer to stay anonymous."

"Yeah, I bet. Unlicensed private detective who can't pay the bills, and is afraid of the cops. Good luck with that. I think we'll just let the police do their job." He turned away and said back over his shoulder, "Good eye, just the same."

Nervous, screwed, no help anywhere. The detective was looking for me; somebody else in another room was pulling my application. I thought about running, a calculated risk sure to draw attention. Maybe if I could get through the door, maybe even get to another city, find another bar, maybe I could start over. It was more than I could handle just thinking about it.

Bang. There was an explosion in the assistant manager's office. The texting detective leaning in the office door looked in and saw red dye everywhere and a hole in the ceiling. He pulled his gun but there's no threat there, no one in the office, just an answer or the start of an answer anyway. The dye pack has gone off finally, stashed in the ceiling with the money and clothes and guns. Robert made a break for the door but everyone was on edge now and they wrestled him to the ground. Maybe running wasn't such a good idea.

They stopped bringing in witnesses. The detectives had an easy job now, and I had an easy out. Stay quiet and they'll send people home. Call in tomorrow too traumatized to come back to work. May even make some money here. I eased towards the door.

"Charlie Chan?" Romanov came up behind me. I thought about correcting him but decided, no, get this over with fast.

"Thinking about what you said."

I stared at him with a polite look on my face and my eyelids starting to sag and my feet already pointed to the door.

"You did pretty good back there. My family could use a detective, an unlicensed detective, do jobs other people can't."

The door looked good now. I needed to fail this job interview.

"What you charge?" asked Romanov.

"Five hundred dollars a day, plus expenses." There, that ought to do it. I had seen that on Mayor's TV, thought it was absurd. It sounded even more like a joke when it came out of my mouth. No straight citizen would pay that. But Romanov just looked back like I'd told him the price of a hamburger.

"Sounds about right. Look, my brother's got a twenty-three-year-old daughter who disappeared three days ago. Cops aren't interested, say she probably just ran off. Plus they don't like my brother too much. Or the rest of us Romanovs, for that matter. So my brother's got a couple of his guys looking into it, but they're bozos, plus they're not going to tell him anything he doesn't want to hear because they're afraid they'll get hurt cause that's what my brother does for my dad, hurts people.

"Come up with an address for her by the end of the week, and I'll pay your five hundred a day. Actually get my niece back home, and I'll double it."

He poked a business card at me.

"Deal with my brother's wife; it'll be better for you." He started to walk away and then came back. He smiled at me, a big Chamber of Commerce smile between partners.

"Enjoy your new job. Do a good job and there'll be more," he said.

Romanov stepped into me, nose to nose, and lowered his voice to a growl.

"Course, you don't do a good job for us, know this: we don't forget, and we don't forgive. My brother will come for you."

Interview

Kathleen Cosgrove: I first met Michael in 2014 at Killer
Nashville when we shared a panel on Oddball Characters.
Never, since the combining of bacon and chocolate in a
turkey, has the universe designed anything so chaotically
perfect. If you haven't read him yet, then stop *not* reading
him. Michael's ability to bring complex and off beat
characters to life in such a seemingly effortless way, and to
weave them into a story you can't put down, is a gift you
should no longer deny yourself.

KC: We've tried to put together a wide variety of stories in
this collection. What kind of reader should give your stuff
a shot?

MG: I grew up on John McDonald's Travis McGee and Robert
Parker's Spencer and anything by Donald Westlake or Elmore
Leonard or Ray Bradbury. I tend to write mystery and crime because
they stress characters, and not because I'm fascinated by solving
complicated murders or coming up with innovative ways to kill
people.

I tend to feel at home only with the oddballs of the world, and with the oddball view of life. Hafiz wrote about the beautiful, rowdy prisoners of life trying desperately to break out of their cages. If a character doesn't fit that description by the second or third chapter, I tend to get bored with them and not finish writing their books. Shows them.

I also like funny and like characters who are cynical and sarcastic. *Josh Whoever* is probably my funniest book, with *A Study in Detail* being a more gentle funny and *Play Nice* generally more tough than funny.

A warning: I like digressions. I write—and read—for fun. If I'm writing a great bunny rabbit scene (no, I don't have any of those) and I get fascinated with life in Kathmandu, well, my bunnies need to get ready to travel.

I also agree with T.S. Elliot (yes, that Elliot) that every mystery must be quest for the Holy Grail. Whether the characters know it or not.

KC: Tell us a little about how your writing has evolved?
MG: Growing up, I was the kid in the back of the room reading. I read everything in every genre. At different times, I got obsessed with Salinger, Bradbury, Ayn Rand (sorry, but it's true), Vonnegut and Ibsen.

Well, I read everything but mystery. Mysteries just seemed like puzzles, and not stories.

Then one day someone gave me a book about a non-detective who lived on a houseboat he'd won in a card game. I read every Travis McGee story written, at least three times. I was lucky enough to start the series while John McDonald was still alive. When I finished one of his books, I'd often read it over and over until the next one came out. Even now, if I wake up feeling lonely at 3 am, Travis and Meyer are the friends I turn to.

McGee led me to Spencer, and then Elmore Leonard and Donald Westlake and...

Oh, you wanted to know about my writing? Well, when I was in my twenties (I'm in my sixties now) I wanted to be a great writer so I wrote great important stories. I won some contests, got some praise, but made almost no money. As great as my stories undoubtedly were, no one—including me—really wanted to pay to read them. I had to give it up.

After forty or so years of writing software for NASA and DoD programs, I woke up one day with a story that I wanted to read that hadn't been written. So I wrote it. It led to another. In that first year, I wrote fifty stories, and sold ten.

One story kept bugging me after I'd published it. The story I'd written was about a guy who lived in the broom closet of a bar, hiding from a world that thought he was a hero when he knew he wasn't. In the process of running a small scam for beer money, he had to solve a bank robbery to protect his own identity so he could go back to the bar. The twist was that the bank was run by the Russian mob, who were impressed enough to hire him to find a missing relative. Find her, they said, and we'll make you rich and famous (not something he wanted). Don't, and we'll make you dead (even less so).

So the story ended there and the editors were happy enough to send me a (very small) check. But all the unanswered questions kept bugging me until it turned into my first book, *Josh Whoever*. Five Star Mysteries published the book and Library Journal named it a Mystery Debut of the Month.

And then Ellery Queen's Mystery Magazine published a story I wrote about a missing artist. And that turned into my second book, *A Study in Detail*.

And so it goes (bonus question: What author from the sixties (and more) peppered his books with that phrase? If you don't know, you're in for a treat when you discover him.)

KC: What do you want the world of your stories to feel like? Sad? Warm? Funny? Dark?

MG: I think the key word here is "feel." I'm not much on description (if you want great description, read James Lee Burke. The man can make a thunderstorm seem like an epic.) I'm more interested in how the world feels to my characters. I like damaged characters who often try to cover that through humor.

I think a lot of my stuff comes from an ingrained belief that life is a struggle between the world and the individual. The world is generally corrupt, even when it tries to be honest (think heavy-handed laws and religions and bureaucracies.) Individuals are often at their most noble when they think they've given up the struggle and are living on cynicism alone.

So I guess, at best, my world feels like a struggle, and a struggle where the only weapons we can rely on are bad jokes and an occasional magic, fragile connection to someone who's struggling with us.

I'd never thought about it till now, but I guess that's one thread that runs through all my stuff: We all feel like we're struggling alone, and that our struggle is meaningless and doomed. I want to hint to my readers that the world is full of other beautiful, rowdy prisoners fighting the good fight in the same loneliness that you are. And laughing about it.

KC: Which writers inspire you? Which writers do you think your books are like? Who do you wish they were like?

MG: Gosh, after dropping so many names on the last question, I'm not sure there are any left. I've actively studied Elmore Leonard and Carl Hiaasen to try to learn from them. One thing that I believe strongly is that each of these writers (and Bradbury, and Westlake and...) have the courage to follow the story, even if that means ignoring the plot.

Who are my stories like? I don't think my stories are even like each other. Smart writers establish a brand, so you know what you're getting when you buy, say, a Michael Connelly book. I've never been able to do that. A reviewer said *Josh Whoever* was like Leonard and Hiaasen. *A Study in Detail*, on the other hand, is almost romantic suspense. My third book, *Play Nice*, is kind of like an adult Noir Nancy Drew. Someday I'll figure out what I want to be when I grow up.

Who do I wish they were like? Donald Westlake. Or Leonard.

KC: **Tell me about one of your characters.**

MG: Stories are fun when the characters take over. I think that's true for readers, and it's sure as hell true for writing.

When I was writing my first book, *Josh Whoever*, I carefully outlined every chapter before I started. In about the third chapter, I had a woman who had one line. Didn't even have a name. But she refused to leave the stage, took over, and made everything better. After I finished the book, I realized that a woman like that had been living in my house for thirty years—and making everything better for me.

But that first day, I didn't make that connection. All I knew was that I had to have Marci (who now had a name.) So that afternoon, I redid the outline.

And that was how my writing day went for the rest of the book. Every afternoon, I'd rewrite the outline. Every morning, Josh and Marci would cheerfully rip the outline up and march off in their own direction.

But I got even with Marci.

CHRIS KNOPF

Chris has been writing himself out of trouble since he talked a teacher into accepting a short story in lieu of an essay, and an essay in lieu of a multiple choice exam. A college professor wrote a comment on a friend's paper that would have also applied to him: "You write well, which is good because you have very little command of the subject matter."

To support his fiction habit he started working for PR firms. That evolved into a career as an advertising copywriter and later a creative director at Mintz + Hoke, a marketing communications agency in Avon, CT, where he is now CEO.

His command of subject matter continues to be thin, but now more broadly based, having written technical papers for chemical engineering and bioscience companies, TV commercials for construction products, tire cleaners, banks and hospitals, radio spots for car dealers, yogurt and popsicles, and print ads for jet engines, medical insurance, valves, liquid chromatography, missiles, bicycles and casinos. To name a few.

His preferred environment involves a lot of saltwater, having summered as a youth on the Jersey Shore. He lives with his wife Mary Farrell in Connecticut and Southampton, NY, where he sets sail on the Little Peconic Bay.

SHORT STORY

The Best Is Yet To Come

When the boys got together at the Palatine Restaurant every month, the talk invariably went from comparing the greatest ballplayers of the Brooklyn Dodgers era to the current Yankees' lineup, to deciding which movie stars of today could have played Anita Ekberg's part in *La Dolce Vita*, to assessing the relative capabilities of past and present contract killers.

They didn't say the words contract killer, of course – or hitman, or trigger man – though discretion wasn't needed, given the Palatine's bug-free, wise-guy friendly environment.

"Joey Peaches, he's a clever son-of-a-bitch," said Tony "Two Step." "Does the close-in. Neat with the shiv."

"They say he's a surgeon," said Billy Panzano, aka Bogart. "You know, an actual doctor. Knows exactly where to slice and dice."

"Seems like a strange application of his professional skills."

"Maybe the surgeon business ain't so hot these days."

The Palatine was suitably dim and overstuffed with comfortable tables and chairs, with waiters in white coats and black bow ties and a piano player maintaining a discreet music bed under the murmur of voices and clinking tableware.

The boys, Two Step and Bogart, had been eating there for over twenty years, believing the owner's claim to the only authentic

Italian cuisine in Brooklyn, even though neither of them had ever been past Connecticut much less anywhere in Europe.

"I hear some Ruskie name of Petrov is comin' on strong," said Bogart.

The boys passed anxious looks across the table.

"You believe that?" Two Step asked.

"What's not to believe?" said Bogart. "Got his signature on a half dozen jobs just this year."

"You seen him do any of that?" Two Step asked.

Bogart allowed as how he hadn't.

"Nobody's seen him," he said.

"That's right," said Two Step. "Could be a bunch of different guys all pretending to be Petrov. Knowin' the Ruskies, they probably want to spread the fun around."

Though there was nothing funny about the Russian mob, which a look at the set of the boys' expressions would quickly confirm. Ever since the Italians lost their monopoly over the illicit trades of Greater New York, a lot of the joy had gone out of the business of narcotics, loan sharking, extortion and grand larceny, replaced by the creeping realization that their better days were all in the rearview mirror.

And most of the victims of Petrov's recent string of executions had an Italian last name.

"To hell with the Ruskies," said Two Step.

They toasted to that.

Despite being too far away to hear the conversation, and thus unaware of his affect, the piano player helped lift their spirits by launching into an ornate rendering of *New York, New York*. This prompted another toast and a snap of Two Step's fingers at the waiter to bring over another bottle of wine.

Soon after, the chef came out from the kitchen to ask how the pair liked the Spaghetti Bolognese. Both agreed it was prepared just the way mama would have done it, the ultimate compliment. The chef, flushed with modest self-satisfaction, shook their hands, saying *grazie*, though not exactly the way mama would have said it.

The piano player shifted into *That's Amore*, demonstrating again his instinctive sensitivity to the emotional climate of the occasion. The boys lifted their wine glasses to him in appreciation.

"We haven't talked about Louie Crackers," said Two Step, "the premier artist of all time."

Fond associations crossed their faces.

"Nobody had more style than Louie," said Bogart. "Come off a job, sit down to dinner right here in the Palatine, in a nice suit and tie. Fresh as a daisy."

"Got pretty quick service," said Two Step, getting a good laugh out of his associate.

"The special's on the house tonight, Mr. Crackers," said Bogart, producing even bigger laughs.

Some of the other patrons, drawn involuntarily to the sudden burst of gaiety, looked over at the boys' table, then quickly redirected their attention to their drinks and meals.

"Too bad about Louie's sudden exit from the living," said Two Step, dampening the tone if not the volume of their conversation.

"I saw him. That suit didn't look so great no more," said Bogart.

"No, listen," said Two Step. "Style is part of the point here. What's lacking today in our society is style. A manner of doing things. An attitude. What do them new people know?"

"Bupkis. You gotta have some knowledge about things to have style, am I right? If you don't know nothing, how you gonna know how to act?"

This supposition brought mutual agreement. Commentary ran to the sadly uneducated tide of Eastern European immigrants who had populated the ragged neighborhoods left behind by the Italians and Jews in Brooklyn, who'd made something of themselves and moved on up and out to places like Nassau County and the Upper East Side. Often leaving behind the same trades that had enriched the families of Two Step and Bogart.

On cue, the piano player slid into *The Way You Look Tonight*, causing Bogart to fix the knot of his tie with a theatrical flourish, a grin emphasizing the overbite that gave him his nickname.

"This is what I'm saying," Two Step went on. "You can't express a sense of style if you don't have a presence in the world. We all knew Louie. You'd recognize him on the street. This Petrov, who the hell is he? Tell me that?"

Bogart looked down at his Bolognese.

"No idea. Where's the professional pride?"

"Where're the balls, is what I'm thinkin'," said Two Step. "Afraid to show his face."

This was a new idea, that provoked a fresh line of commentary.

"You got something there," said Bogart. "This new style is all sneakin' and peekin', slippin' around corners in the middle of the night."

"Hiding among civilians."

The gentle waltzing rhythm of *Somewhere My Love* drifted over from the piano. The boys' pondered the significance.

"*Somewhere My Love?*" asked Bogart.

"Don't know the lyrics."

"It's about telling this broad you'll catch up with her some other time," said Bogart. "You know, 'later babe,'"

"Hasta la vista, baby?"

"That's Spanish. Then he'd be playing *La Bamba*," said Bogart, laughing more or less alone at his own joke. Though the reference gave rise to a discussion about New York's Latino population, with some appreciation for the cultural differences among the various nationalities.

"You can't be comparin' your standard Dominican with your standard Columbian," said Two Step. "And Cuban. They got this whole other thing."

"My sister married a Cuban," said Bogart. "Friggin' accountant. But okay, you know? Good to my sister and the kids."

"I know this Puerto Rican guy whose family's been here longer than mine. Can't speak a word of Spanish."

"Like your Italian?" Bogart asked.

"Hey, *fangul*," said Two Step. "How's that Italian for you?"

A young woman bussing tables caused further talk to hush while she cleared their dinner plates. Each of the boys politely moved to the side to give her room, allowing a chance to appraise her comely figure. Eye glances confirmed the consensus that she was worth the look.

When the woman left, Two Step said, "You think Francine would mind if I brought that one home with me?"

"Course not. Might like the domestic help."

While the boys took the next moment to visualize the impossible, the piano player provided *The Girl From Ipanema* as a soundtrack.

"Not exactly *La Bamba*," said Two Step.

"That's Bossa Nova," said Bogart. "It ain't the same thing."

"I didn't know we had a professor of music in our midst."

Bogart saluted his colleague and turned his attention to the dessert menu that the waiter had carefully placed on the table. Two Step rubbed his belly, as if assessing current capacity. Then he ordered a bottle of Grappa and glasses for two. When the drink was poured, they prepared for a toast.

"To style," said Two Step.

"May it triumph over the unstyled," said Bogart, leading to the first of several downed glasses of Grappa.

While the feelings at the table had moved toward brash booziness, the piano player, nearly unnoticed, had begun a medley of Tchaikovsky, beginning with Opus 20 from *Swan Lake*, the moodiness of which seemed to conflict with the boys' general humor. They sat quietly and listened.

"So, Bogart," said Two Step, "what the hell's that?"

"I think it's ballet," he said.

"Hate all that. Bunch of fairies jumpin' around the stage."

As if sensing some mild discord, the maître d' ghosted up to the table and asked if the gentlemen would care for after-dinner coffee, or perhaps another bottle of Grappa. Two Step said all-the-above, but to make his coffee an espresso. The other concurred on both counts.

The maître d' bowed and made his retreat, though Two Step called him back.

"Do me a favor and tell the piano player to pep it up a little," he said. "The classical stuff is rainin' on the party."

The maître d' nodded and headed for the piano. Neither at the table bothered to look, since they knew what would come next. Which in short order it did, in the form of *The Best Is Yet To Come*.

"Now you're talkin'," said Two Step. "Old Blue Eyes."

More toasts followed when the fresh bottle of Grappa arrived.

"Actually, it was Tony Bennett's song, not that anybody's counting," said Bogart.

"'Nother goomba, all that matters," said Two Step.

Thus the ambience was restored while the espresso and Grappa disappeared along with extravagant selections from the dessert tray, supplemented by special orders not seen on the menu. Once upon a time, the next round would have been cigars, but even the Palatine had been forced to bend to New York State's strict smoking ban.

Somewhere along the way, the music shifted yet again, with a nearly sub-audible delivery of *Speak Softly, Love*.

"Oh, no," said Two Step. "You're kidding me."

"Ain't that *The Godfather song*?" Bogart said, then started to laugh before saying, "I think he's trying to pay a compliment."

Both grinned at that, though Two Step got serious again.

"Okay, but he's gotta know this is not done in the Palatine Restaurant," he said.

Both agreed, though the accumulated effects of the meal had softened the force of their disapproval. Two Step snapped his fingers again at their waiter.

The man stood by the table while Two Step wrote something on a napkin. He told the waiter to bring it over to the piano player, then sat back to finish off his espresso.

"What'd you say?" Bogart finally asked, after some suspense had   built up at the table.

Two Step looked a little reluctant, but then said, "That song don't get played in here." Then he added, "And no more of that twinkle-toes crap."

Laughter bubbled between the two as Bogart pulled back to take some pressure off his inflated stomach. Two Step took notice and gave a little burp, which got another rise out of his friend.

The piano player's next song verified that the message had been delivered, though the selection was again a little mystifying, if not annoying.

"*Mack the Knife?*" asked Bogart. "What's up with this guy?"

The waiter approached with a folded napkin in his hand, which he gave to Two Step.

"What the hell's this?" he asked.

"A response from the piano player to your request, sir," said the waiter.

Two Step opened it up on the table.

Despite the breach of manners, the waiter couldn't resist reading the note over Two Step's shoulder. Not that Two Step noticed the affront, given what the note said, which took a few moments to completely absorb.

"Just need the music you boys want played at your funerals. Sincerely, Petrov."

EXCERPT

Cop Job

"*Cop Job* delivers not only smart and sassy characters, but a nifty narrative full of intriguing plot complications having to do with confidential informants and home town corruption. A Sam Acquillo novel is always more than well-wrought plot and character. Knopf has a fine eye for the quiet beauty of the East End, and he knows how to fashion a theme about the quirks of human nature that also allows for some timely, trenchant social criticism." –*Joan Baum*, NPR

Chapter One

I got there just in time to see the crane hoist Alfie Aldergreen out of Hawk Pond. He was still strapped in his motorized wheelchair. Grey green saltwater poured off his rigid body and cascaded over the chair's tubular chrome framing. His head was twisted back and his eyes were closed, thank God, though his tongue, a swollen purple mass, protruded through his lips, which were partly chewed away.

Dead bodies are never pretty.

The scene was lit like a night game at Yankee Stadium. Cops in uniforms and political people from the town milled around. Few had official functions to perform, but all tried hard to look as if they did. I saw Joe Sullivan in the middle of it all, a Southampton Town detective upon whose broad shoulders the burden of sorting through this dreary affair had already settled.

I was called there by Jackie Swaitkowski, a lawyer who worked for a philanthropic law firm specializing in hard-luck cases like Alfie's. I saw her standing near the crane, wearing a summer suit with a hem an inch or two above the entirely professional, clutching herself around the middle in a rigid pose of shock and sorrow.

When I tried to go to her, a patrol cop stopped me by sticking the butt end of a nightstick in my chest.

"Step back," he said "This is a secured area."

I looked down at the stick.

"I'm here with Attorney Swaitkowski," I said.

I looked over his shoulder and the cop followed my gaze. As luck would have it, Joe Sullivan and Jackie were deep in conversation. The cop dropped the stick and I brushed by, making a little more body contact than was probably necessary.

"Oh, Sam," said Jackie, as I approached.

I let her put her arms around me, and even gave her a slight squeeze. Sullivan just stood there and waited.

"What the hell happened?" I asked him.

"Your friend Hodges was fishing off the breakwater. When the tide went out, he saw the top of Alfie's head. It was almost sunset before he realized what it was."

"Any ideas?" I asked.

"Not yet," he said. "Jackie?"

She looked down at the ground and shook her head.

"He's been very agitated lately. Paranoid. More than usual," she said, looking up at me.

We were all aware of Alfie's mood swings. A regular presence along Main Street in Southampton Village, year-round, Alfie was known to have conversations with himself, or people no one else could see. He was usually happily engaged, often playing a very credible alto saxophone, though sometimes his face was lit with fear, and he'd stop passersby to warn them of impending catastrophe.

I'd spent a fair amount of time with the guy, sitting next to his chair on a park bench drinking coffee I'd bought for the two of us. One time I had to talk down an angry shopkeeper who thought Alfie had stolen some of her merchandise, when in fact one of his invisible companions had made it a gift. That's when I introduced him to Jackie, whose free legal services became a regular necessity.

"Not like suicidal or anything?" I asked.

Jackie looked around the area where we stood – a parking lot serving a boat launch adjacent to the harbor's breakwater.

"How far are we from the Village?" she asked. "Eight, ten miles? How would he even get here?"

"There were no wheelchair tracks leading up to the breakwater," said Sullivan, nodding toward a gravel-covered area cordoned off with yellow tape. "He'd have to fly to get there himself."

"Any other tracks?" I asked.

"Trucks, trailers, footprints everywhere. Nothing you could take an impression of. Not in gravel. We'll be back in the daylight for a closer look, but I wouldn't get your hopes up."

Alfie had a one-room apartment behind a small, freestanding art gallery a block from the center of Southampton Village. The gallery space changed hands every season, but the owner, Jimmy Watruss, let Alfie rent the back area for a small percentage of his disability check. Like Alfie, Jimmy was a veteran attached to a mechanized unit during the Second Iraq War. The only thing Alfie told me about his service was when the wizard Gandalf joined up with his platoon. Apparently, his fellow soldiers demurred when he set out across the desert to challenge the rising threat of Mordor.

Back stateside, the army shrinks set him up with a drug regimen, and after a few months of observation, sent him into the civilian world. The first thing Alfie did was buy an old Fiat S1955 Ducati motorcycle, which he drove into a bridge abutment trying to avoid a volcano that had suddenly erupted on the New Jersey Turnpike.

The VA put most of him back together, but there was no saving the bottom half of his spinal cord.

Alfie wore his DCU – short for desert camouflage uniform – every day, though he'd never let people draw him into a conversation about the war. I don't know how he ended up living in Southampton. I never asked, and even if I had, he probably wouldn't have remembered. I did get to see his apartment once, when the batteries in his chair ran out and I volunteered to push him back home. The room was spare and immaculately clean, his uniforms and modest belongings neatly stored in portable, olive drab metal closets.

*****

Paul Hodges, who lived aboard an old 48' Gulfstream motor sailor in the Hawk Pond Marina, emerged from a cluster of men watching the crane. I waved him over. In his late 60s, Hodges' arms were still strung with ropey muscles, the legacy of long years in commercial fishing, construction and slinging questionable sustenance at his restaurant in Sag Harbor. Never an attractive man, age had been unkind to his grey puffs of curly hair, and his face, which you might mistake for a less attractive version of Ernest Borgnine's.

"That poor son-of-a-bitch sure didn't catch his share of luck," he said.

Despite myself, my eyes were drawn to where Alfie sat in his DCUs, slumped over in his chair, his long brown hair stuck in sodden, forlorn strands across his face. He was guarded by two of

Sullivan's men so no one could touch the body before the medical examiner arrived. Not that anyone wanted to.

"I feel bad about this," said Hodges. "There he was the whole time I'm fishing. I thought his hair was seaweed. Sorry," he added, looking over at Jackie.

"You ever see him motoring around the marina?" Sullivan asked.

Hodges shook his head. "Never seen him anywhere but the Village. Never really knew the guy. Not like these two," he added, using his thumb to point at Jackie and me.

"Was he on his meds?" Sullivan asked Jackie.

"I don't know. I'm his lawyer, not his case worker. But I know who is. Esther Ferguson."

Sullivan looked at his notebook and wrote down her name. "I know Esther," he said. "Tough cookie."

Tough as in a cross between Joe Frazier and a rabid badger. She didn't like me, which placed her within a fairly crowded field. Her beef was my occasional intervention on behalf of Alfie, which offended her social worker prerogatives. I was offended that she didn't always do as good a job looking after her clients as she did upholding her exclusive right to their care.

So we were even.

"Alfie was murdered. That's the gist of it," I said.

"I could make a case for it being an accident, or suicide," said Sullivan. "But why?"

Sullivan had been a plainclothesman for about five years. Before that he was a patrol cop assigned to North Sea, the wooded, watery territory just north of Southampton Village. I lived in North Sea in a cottage off the Little Peconic Bay – when I wasn't staying on the *Carpe Mañana*, which was berthed next to Hodges in the Hawk Pond marina.

A Smart Car pulled into the parking lot and I knew the ME had arrived, based entirely on the weirdness of the vehicle.

Carlo Vendetti was a cheerful scarecrow of a guy with long, slippery black hair stuck out of his baseball cap, disguising the fact that the rest of his head was bald as a baby's ass. You'd say he had a weak chin, if he actually had a chin. With a beakish nose and black-rimmed glasses, Carlo was a right geek if there ever was one. That was okay with me. I got along fine with geeks.

"Sam the Man," he said, as he approached our little group. "Detective," he said to Sullivan. "And the most stunning defense attorney in the Eastern United States," he said to Jackie, taking her hand by the fingers and giving her knuckles a light kiss, much to her dismay.

"Hi, Carlo," she said, gently extracting her hand.

I didn't disagree with Carlo on Jackie's looks, I just never thought of her in that way. Too much of a tomboy, too frenetic and churned up with Catholic guilt and attention deficit disorder for my taste. I liked her better in the steady hands of her boyfriend, a guy about the size of a Sequoia with the equanimity and forbearance to match.

"Come with me, doctor," said Sullivan, placing a guiding hand on the ME's back. "Let me introduce you to Alfie Aldergreen."

Hodges tagged along. I waited until they were all out of earshot, then asked Jackie, "What do you think?"

She pushed a wad of kinky reddish blond hair back off her face, a gesture signaling equal parts confusion and distress.

"First I thought, 'Who'd want to kill a harmless, crazy guy in a wheelchair?'" she said. "But, of course, people like him get killed all the time just for being harmless and crazy."

"Did he say anything unusual last time you talked to him?" I asked.

"Like I told you, he was really worked up. He said a secret organization was out to get him. You know he was paranoid, but not that big on conspiracy theories. More focused on individuals. Conan the Barbarian comes to mind. Most would think crazy is crazy, but these folks have their themes. They usually don't deviate."

I'd spent enough time with Alfie to know that was true. His main thing was imaginary people, either inside his head or hanging around nearby. If you spent enough time with him, you could almost believe they were actually there.

"So, no ideas," I said.

She shook her head, hard enough to cause the brushed-away hair to fall back into her face. She swept it back.

"Nothing. Zilch. In a big city you might think sicko sadists preying on the disabled. But we don't have that sort of thing around here, do we?" she asked, hopefulness in her voice.

"We might," I said. "Who knows."

"There's a cheerful thought."

I pulled her over to where officialdom circled Alfie's dead body. Carlo Vendetti had Alfie's shirt open and was feeling around his inert chest, looking inside his mouth and probing his lower abdomen. I noticed Alfie's hands were wrinkled like an old lady's and there were red ligature marks on his forearms, just above where they'd been duct taped to the chair.

"I'll know a lot more when I get him on the table," Vendetti said to me, as if I had some official standing. "But since the water's still pretty cold for July, the body's in decent shape. There're no apparent wounds or contusions, no external bleeding, though there's saltwater in his nose and mouth."

"How do you know that?" asked Sullivan.

"I can smell it," said Carlo, holding up a gloved hand. All fought to keep the cringing under control. "Plus, his skin is blue, indicating oxygen starvation, and his limbs are secured with duct tape."

"So?" Jackie asked.

"So he drowned. Correct that, he *was* drowned, intentionally. Not conclusive until we do the lab work, but you asked."

An ambulance came shortly after that, and Carlo directed Sullivan and his men on how to get Alfie out of his chair and on to a gurney. The chair went into the back of a police SUV as evidence and the paramedics got in the front seat of the ambulance, since there was no need for life support.

I hung around until the area was clear of all but a single patrol car left to secure the crime scene, then dragged Jackie over to my boat where we could have a few drinks in the cockpit with Hodges and settle our nerves for the tough night's sleep ahead.

"Why do I get the most upset when bad things happen to people with the least intrinsic value to society?" Jackie asked, looking down into a plastic cup full of red wine.

"I'd tell you if I knew what intrinsic meant," said Hodges.

I swirled around my own cup, giving the ice cubes a chance to chill the vodka to the proper temperature.

"We've got to let Sullivan get to Esther before we do," I said to Jackie, "but that's where I'd start. I'd also go see Jimmy Watruss. He'll talk to me. I've done a lot of carpentry work for him over the years."

"So he likes you?" Jackie asked.

"Didn't say that. Just said he'd talk to me."

"I'll be fishing," said Hodges. "In the Little Peconic."

It wasn't all that late when I got back to my house. My dog Eddie was sitting on the lawn waiting for me, recognizing as he always did the sound of my old Pontiac rumbling up the street. As soon as I turned into the driveway, he jogged over to the parking area so he could try to climb into my lap when I opened the door. He never made it all the way in, and I never made it out without a small struggle. It didn't matter that we repeated this ritual several times a day. For him, at least, it was endlessly engaging.

"Such a pain in the ass," I said, gently shoving him back on to the grass, where he bounded off toward the cottage for the next stage in the process. I followed.

Amanda Anselma met me out on the lawn, which wasn't a surprise. She often drifted over to my house from next door and let herself in when I wasn't around. Eddie didn't mind, since she was a reliable source of Big Dog biscuits, a reward he officially didn't qualify for, being more of a mid-sized dog.

She also fed him aged brie and fresh grapes, biscotti and prosciutto, albeit in small doses, so maybe that had something to do with it as well.

"I hope everything's okay," she said, as I slipped my right arm around her and pulled her into me.

"It's not," I said, kissing her full on the lips. "I hope you weren't worried."

"I always worry. Everything could be fine, but why waste the emotion?"

"Somebody murdered Alfie Aldergreen," I said. "Dumped him in his chair off the breakwater on Hawk Pond. Hodges found him."

She pulled away from me so she could put her hand over her heart.

"That's horrible. Who did it?"

"No idea."

"I'm so sorry," she said. "I know how hard you tried to look after him."

"Sort of," I said. "Others did a lot more than me. Like Jackie. She's got that look on her face."

"The avenging angel?" she asked.

"Something like that."

We all went out to the sun porch, which was in its summer mode – windows off the screens, ceiling fan engaged, cool drinks in slippery wet glasses on the side tables. The Little Peconic Bay sending in the musical lap of tiny bay waves, the southwesterly breeze rippling the lawn, Eddie panting and slurping water from his bowl in the corner of the room.

"So what are you going to do?" Amanda asked.

"Find the bastards."

"Of course you are."

She chose that moment to thrust a slender, naked leg out from the silk robe she'd chosen to wear for the trip across our adjoining lawns. I got the not-overly-subtle message.

We hurried through the rest of our drinks and took it from there.

The phone rang at two in the morning. It was Jackie.

"How often do you listen to your voice mail messages?" she asked.

"I never listen to my voice mail messages," I said, once I was awake enough to talk.

"Me neither. Most of the time. But I saw the little light on the answering machine and thought, what the hell."

"And?"

"It's Alfie. Two days ago," she said.

I listened to some clunking sounds as Jackie put her cell phone within proximity of the answering machine.

"Jackie, Jesus Christ, they're going to kill me," said the tinny, yet unmistakable voice of Alfie Aldergreen, clearly agitated. "I mean, after all these battles with the forces of eternal darkness, I get wasted by some cop job? What the hell is up with that?"

Reproduced by permission of The Permanent Press

MG: Do you write naked?

CK: Who doesn't?

MG: Sorry I asked that. You write about some tough characters. Have you yourself ever been in trouble with the police?

CK: When I was a kid, a friend of mine and I thought it was fine to walk along the Schuylkill Expressway in Philadelphia with a BB gun. Explaining to my parents and the cop standing in our living room that our goal was shooting at stumps and rocks and not passing windshields was good training in extemporaneous narrative.

This also came in handy as a college student when I thought using a license plate found by the side of the road on an unregistered truck was a good idea. Turned out both the truck and the license plate were stolen property. I managed to get the Grand Theft Auto charge reduced to Incredibly Stupid, which carried a much more lenient sentence.

MG: Have you ever gotten into a bar fight?

CK: I went to grad school in London and my wife and I used to hang out at the same pub as the cast and writers of the Monty Python show. We knew nothing about Python at the time, just enjoyed those wacky men and women, whose privacy the other pub goers also honored, albeit adequately informed. One night, a drunk guy we'd never seen before got into an argument with one of the Python writers. The angrier the drunk got, the more cutting the writer's remarks – imagine a swordsman dispatching an opponent with a hundred tiny incisions. Having been in similar situations, I knew where this was going. I jumped in to pull them apart just as the fists started to fly, and nearly had a chair bashed over my head. I assisted the drunk to the door, obliging the writer who was a few steps behind, and who knows what happened outside. Only that the writer returned to the pub and bought us drinks for the rest of the night.

For a description of my experience with an all-out, bar room brawl in a saloon on the Jersey Shore, may I refer you to my book *Elysiana*. Only the names have been changed to keep me on the fiction shelves.

MG: When was the last time you found yourself in a situation you couldn't get out of?

CK: I'm not exactly answering the question, because I did get out of that situation, since otherwise I'd be dead. I was stepping off my sailboat one evening after getting her secured to the dock, and caught my foot on the standing rigging. I managed to get a hand on the dock ladder, but ended up slamming into the side of the dock, falling in the water and sliding into the dense muck under the boat. The next thing I remembered was sitting in the cockpit, soaking wet. I don't know how I got out of that situation, nor much of anything

else, since my memory was wiped clean by a mild concussion.
What I couldn't forget were two broken ribs, multiple abrasions and
a punctured lung. Makes me wonder how many passes I get from my
guardian angel.

MG: What do you want your tombstone to say?
CK: Trial and Error

MG: What secret talents do you have?
CK: I used to be able to touch my nose with my tongue, but some
dental work screwed that up. Though I can still wiggle my ears,
move my eye brows independently of one another, curl my tongue
and flip it upside down, and both flare and compress my nostrils. None
of these talents are a secret to my children and grandchildren.

**MG: Where is one place you want to visit you haven't been
before?**
CK: New Zealand. They got everything there. Snow-capped
mountains, rain forests, indigenous people with state-of-the-art
tattoos, the world's best sailors – by far – Hobbit theme parks and
kiwis, which are not a fruit, but rather tiny flightless birds. I want to
know why New Zealanders think so much of them.

**MG: If you could have an accent from anywhere in the
world, what would you choose?**

164

CK: I lived in England just long enough to contrive an accent that sounded convincingly legitimate to everyone but the English, who thought I was Australian. This was lots of fun, and came in handy whenever mobs on the Continent passed by carrying signs reading "Kill Americans". Unfortunately, six months home and I lost it. I'd like to have it back. An English accent compels American listeners to award you at least an extra 50 IQ points.

JESSIE BISHOP POWELL

Jessie Bishop Powell is originally from Ohio but now lives in Montgomery, Alabama, with her family. She considers herself a Midwesterner with distinctly Southern roots. When she isn't writing, she can be found grading college essays at a frenetic pace and begging her children to stop making rubber-band bracelets.

Her first novel *Divorce: A Love Story*, was published as an e-book by Throwaway Lines in 2011. Her debut mystery, *The Marriage at the Rue Morgue*, published by Five Star (a Division of Cengage, not a vanity press) came out in 2014, and its sequel *The Case of the Red-handed Rhesus* will be available in February 2016.

You can read more of Jessie's words at her blog *Jester Queen* http://jesterqueen.com. She's on Facebook as https://www.facebook.com/thejesterqueen, and she tweets, unsurprisingly, as @jesterqueen.

SHORT STORY:

The Tomato Paste Murder:

A Story in Soupçons

By Jessie Bishop Powell

Le Premier Soupçon

"Only Kevin could get killed with a can of tomato paste without being poisoned." The victim's Aunt Demelda honked into a handkerchief and tucked an escaping bra strap under her sleeve. Though her dress looked sedate enough from the back, her silver skirt stood at angles to her body in front, its pleats flaring away from her knees like the tines of an enormous fork. "I heard they couldn't get his cheeks to look human again," she added in a stage whisper.

"Mother, let's sit down." Demelda's daughter Virginia steered her aging parent away from an aghast stranger, some friend of Kevin's.

"Nonsense. I should be with Cressida." Demelda planted herself in the middle of the receiving line, completely halting its progress.

"She and Uncle Derek have this handled. Kevin is *their* son, you know."

"*Was*, dear."

"*Is* and always will be."

"Is that Robert Redford?" Demelda squinted across the room. "I think that's..."

"Kevin didn't know Robert Redford. I see Manny and Leigh, though. Let's say 'Hi' to them."

"Manny and Leigh don't know a thing."

Nonetheless, with a final yank, Virginia maneuvered her mother in the right direction. She tried to catch Manny's attention, but he and Leigh were trapped behind a man in Stetson hat.

As they crossed the room, Demelda identified four more celebrities, two of them accurately. Then a tall woman embraced Virginia from behind. "Augusta Flavius!" Demelda gushed. "I simply loved you in *From Tearoom to Trattoria*. You should have gotten an Oscar."

"You mean a Tony," Virginia squeaked. She squirmed around, bringing her eyes level with a row of gold busts of Caesar embroidered atop Augusta's red dress. "You played the role on Broadway, didn't you?"

"I'd forgotten all about *From Tearoom to Trattoria*," Augusta said, finally letting go. "You never told me you were Kevin's cousin, Virginia."

"When would I have had the opportunity to ..."

"His *favorite* cousin, Ms. Flavius," Demelda broke in. "No one on his father's side holds a candle."

"His *favorite* cousin," Augusta agreed. She cleared her throat. "I wonder," she said. She shifted from side to side, and all the Caesars undulated above her breasts.

When she didn't finish the sentence, Virginia broke the silence. "We don't have any control over the guest list for the *family* dinner." She put heavy emphasis on the word family, even though there were as many friends as relations coming to her aunt and uncle's house that evening.

"I'm invited," the woman said. "But will there be ... alcohol ... served with the meal?"

"Probably," said Virginia.

"Of course there will," said Demelda. "Cressida is bound to have those awful sweet wines. Riesling, Chenin Blanc, Malvasia—"

"You *aren't* the hostess, and you shouldn't be drinking on your medications, Mother."

Demelda ignored Virginia and continued to list sweet wines, shuddering each time, as if merely speaking the names turned her stomach sour. "Nothing *dry* to drink in my sister's house," she finally finished.

"I'd best send my apologies," Augusta said quickly, before Demelda could add more. "I'm a social drinker, you know, and events like this make it so hard to cut back."

"I'll let Aunt Cress and Uncle Derek know," said Virginia. She took her mother's arm once more, but the actress didn't leave, meaning Virginia couldn't make Demelda go either. "Was there something else?" she finally asked.

"No. Well, yes," said Augusta. "Is it true that you'll be replacing..."

"No," Virginia snapped before the question was finished. "I won't. Sorry to dash, but I see a couple I know." She pulled Demelda hard, but her efforts had no effect.

"You can't *dash* away from Augusta Flavius," Demelda chided her.

Virginia gritted her teeth and glared until Augusta ducked back into line. "Mother," she said, "I haven't exchanged more than five words with Manny and Leigh since this all started." She took a step back and landed on someone's toe. "I'm so sorry," she said.

It was the man in the Stetson. "No problem at all," he assured her. "I wanted to talk to you anyway."

"You did?"

Unlike Augusta Flavius, he wasn't slow in getting to the point. "That's a pretty sweet deal, taking over the KM Hour."

"But I'm not," said Virginia.

"Here's the thing. I've got a new album coming out. I know it's an awkward time to ask, but a slot on the Kevin McArthur ..."

"Mister ... Arizona Angus, right? It's ... nice to meet you. But I'm *not* taking over my cousin's show, no matter *who* told you otherwise." Virginia pursed her lips and looked at Demelda, who discovered some dust that needed to be brushed from her shoulder.

"Ah. Well." The man finally seemed to hear her. "If you find out who is..."

"I'll put in a good word, fine. L.E. Carmody is here somewhere. Maybe he'd hire you to do the job yourself. Mother, come *on*. I want to catch up with Manny and Leigh." Demelda didn't move, but Virginia's friends finally noticed her and eased into the space Arizona Angus vacated.

"You must learn to treat your stars with more respect if you're going—" began Demelda.

Virginia cut her off. "No. We are not discussing that."

"Has it been this way all afternoon?" asked Leigh.

"Almost," said Virginia.

"You have no idea what a *toll* Kevin's death is taking on us," Demelda announced.

"I can't even imagine!" Manny said.

"Poor thing," said Leigh. She patted Demelda's back but looked at Virginia. "Who could have been so angry? Kevin was the nicest person."

"He had his moments," said Demelda.

"Only with you, Mother," said Virginia.

"But bludgeoned to death by a can of soup!" Manny shuddered. "I never even knew him to *own* soup in cans. He and Carolyn cooked from scratch at our Saturday dinners, didn't they?"

"Yes, they were always in the kitchen when we were all there." Virginia agreed. "Since Kevin died, I've haven't eaten a meal without thinking about those dinners."

"We'll carry on in his name," said Leigh.

"But no soup. I couldn't stand to serve soup after this," added Manny.

"It wasn't soup that got him," said Demelda. "It was tomato paste."

"That makes more sense," said Manny. Leigh shot him a glare. "You know what I mean. He and Carolyn were so organic."

"Carolyn Routledge is a suspicious sort, if you ask me," said Demelda with a sniff.

"What? They're not accusing *Carolyn*, are they?" asked Leigh. "Last time I saw her, the wedding was all she could talk about!"

"Maybe he broke it off, " said Demelda. "If she's so innocent, why doesn't she step forward and clear her name?"

"Mother, lower your voice," Virginia pleaded, glancing over her shoulder to see if her Aunt Cressida and Uncle Derek had overheard the latest outburst. "As far as I know, they're still treating Carolyn's disappearance like a missing persons case," she told Leigh. To her mother, she scolded, "She vanished on the way *home*, you know. *After* she'd been notified."

"Surely she didn't drive herself did she?" asked Leigh. "All that way? Someone must have taken the keys away after news like that."

"Aunt Cress is the one who called her," Virginia explained. "Cress thinks Carolyn ran to the car in the middle of the conversation without telling a soul where she was going."

Demelda pounced. "That goes to prove my point. A *grieving* fiancée wouldn't ..."

"Mother, grief takes so many forms. You know that. Before then, people saw Carolyn all day at her reunion. She was three hours away when Kevin was ..." For a moment, Virginia's calm façade collapsed. Her face crumpled, and she muffled a sob in her palm.

"Here, here! I came prepared." Manny produced a tissue.

Virginia dabbed her eyes. "Thank you," she said. "I'm afraid something awful's happened to her as well. Some crazed fan who couldn't respect their privacy..."

Demelda grunted and blew her nose into her own already damp handkerchief. Her eyeliner was runny, testament to the weeping she'd done before they left the house, when Virginia had been the stoic one. "After everything that ... *hussy* has done to our family, I don't see how you can stand up for her. At least you can admit it's her fault the security system was switched off."

"No, I can't. She's completely right. They shouldn't have to live under scrutiny in their own home because Kevin hosted a talk show. And she hasn't done a *thing* to us!" Virginia briefly forgot her own injunction about lowered voices, and her words carried above the room's murmur. She cast a look of apology towards her aunt and uncle, but Cressida and Derek were engaged with a distant relation. They either ignored Virginia or genuinely didn't hear her.

"Clearly, they should have, or Kevin would still be alive," Demelda hissed before stalking away. With a helpless glance to her friends, Virginia followed.

La Deuxième Soupçon

Even the "limited" guest list for Derek and Cressida's catered buffet appeared to be too large. The tables in the backyard were overcrowded, and clumps of people milled around inside the McArthurs' house.

Leigh and Manny shuffled through the foyer, waiting for a seat. "Of all the things available in the kitchen, why choose a can of soup?" asked Manny. Leigh elbowed him and pointed to Virginia, who was leaning against a nearby wall. "Oh, I'm sorry," he said. "I didn't see you."

"It's fine," said Virginia. "I've been asking myself the same question."

"What have you done with Demelda?" he asked.

"She's fixing her mascara in the bathroom. I'm on guard to make sure she doesn't get loose when she comes out."

"Have you slept at all?" asked Leigh. "I wondered earlier, but you had to run off."

"Some," said Virginia. "But Mother's so paranoid. She had me up three times in the wee hours with her nightmares."

"Dreadful," said Manny. "Are there any real leads?"

"None that I've heard, but I've barely talked to Aunt Cress and Uncle Derek. I'm too busy shielding them from Mother and her wild theories. They may know more."

"What's this about Mother?" Demelda emerged but then looked at her hands. "Oh botheration," she said. "It's still on my fingers. You'll have to excuse me." She ducked back into the restroom.

"Mother..." Virginia began. "Never mind. It's pointless. Her hand washing is getting worse again, too."

"Did you hear they found Carolyn's car?" Leigh asked.

"The news was on every station I tried between the funeral home and here," said Virginia. "Last rest stop before town, right?"

"You'd think with all the people looking for her, someone would have noticed sooner," Manny said.

"One report said it didn't show up until day before yesterday," said Virginia. "And it wasn't identified until state troopers noticed it had violated the one-overnight-stay policy."

"I guarantee she's holed up in some cellar with her lover." Demelda had returned.

"Stop it, Mother."

"What can we do to help *you*?" Leigh asked Virginia. "You're carrying a lot of this load." She glanced ever so slightly towards Demelda.

A giant of a man in a lime-green paisley-patterned suit approached them. "So sorry for your loss," he said. He delivered a series of thumping pats to Manny's back. "Kev was the foundation of my network. I didn't realize how large his family was. No idea how we'll go on without him."

"Actually, we're his neighbors," said Manny.

"A lucky man to have that kind of relatives." Now the man pumped Leigh's hand.

Virginia saved her friends from another awkward reply. "Thank you, Mr. Carmody," she said. He mashed her fingers in a squeeze.

"You think about what I said on the phone," he told her.

"Please, don't ..." said Virginia. But he had walked away, already preoccupied with the next promotional opportunity.

"For the president of a television network, *he's* certainly rude," said Leigh, shaking out her arm.

"Probably thinks we should all be honored to stand in his airspace," said Manny.

"I assume you heard he asked *me* to carry on Kev's show?" said Virginia. "Of all the people. I've *co*-hosted two episodes, and he wanted *me*. Now *someone* has put it around that I've accepted the offer." Virginia glowered at her mother.

"It would be quite an honor," said Demelda.

"I turned him down. I'm a character actress."

"*I* told him to call back when she's had time to grieve. It's not often a forty-four year old woman has the chance to make her big break."

"The answer isn't going to change," said Virginia. "I have a wonderful career." She rubbed her temples and stared at the ground. This was clearly an old argument.

"At any rate, you've got no business saying you're mere *neighbors*," Demelda proclaimed. "Come sit with the family," she ordered Manny and Leigh. "We'll make room for you."

"We shouldn't..." Leigh began.

"Please, do," said Virginia. "For once, Mother and I agree about something. If Cress hadn't been overwhelmed with cousins, I know she'd have asked you to be a pallbearer, Manny. You were far closer to Kevin than some of these people who've been flying in.

Certainly closer than that *windbag*, and he's sure to squash
beside Cressida and Derek for the meal, unless he can crowd in
between them."

"In that case, we'll be glad to," said Leigh. She winked at
Virginia so fast that she might have been squeezing dust out of her
eye. Then she wrapped an arm around Demelda's bespangled
shoulder. "I know you're overwrought. As soon as everything is over
tomorrow, I want you to call your doctor," she said, as Virginia led
them to the backyard.

Le Troisième Soupçon

The crowd shrank for the funeral proper the next morning, but a
throng still gathered in the graveside tent. Virginia caught Manny's
arm as he and Leigh entered. "I have to speak," she whispered. "Can
you manage Mother when I go? Poor Aunt Cress deserves peace."

"Hell is murky!" Demelda wailed. Once more decked in full
regalia, she was seated as far away from Cressida and Derek as
Virginia could place her without actually moving her out of the
family section. The previous day's silver atrocity had been replaced
by a dress of black sequins with a jagged slash of red satin running
down the middle. She was holding forth to a small army of
mesmerized relatives, none of whom took much notice when
Virginia placed Manny and Leigh on either side of their temporary
queen.

"How are you today, Demelda?" Leigh asked. "Virginia says
you've been having nightmares."

Demelda sniffled. "What's to be done?" she asked.
Then she blinked at Leigh. "Oh," she said in a less theatrical tone.
"Hello. I don't see why they have us here at daybreak."

"Wasn't early morning Kevin's favorite time?" asked Leigh.

"Yes, well," Demelda humphed. She might have said more,
but the service started, and she immediately began wiping her eyes.

After the minister had spoken the final words and the first
handfuls of dirt had been cast on the coffin, another line formed
before Cressida and Derek. "I need to be with my sister," Demelda
told Virginia.

"Mother, no."

"Not until you've spoken with your therapist," Leigh said.
"And I mean right now. If you can't be calm, you'll make things
worse." Demelda had sobbed and shaken until Virginia all but force-
fed her two anti-anxiety pills. She seemed a little fuzzy now, if
quieter. She let Leigh draw her aside and even handed the younger
woman her purse to look for the phone.

"*You* need a break," Manny told Virginia. "And this tent is
stifling." He knifed a path through the crowd and led her towards the
rising sun.

"Thank you," Virginia said outside. She glanced at the
blockade keeping the media at bay then looked deliberately at Manny
instead. "What am I going to *do* with Mother? This morning, she had
a hissy fit, an absolute temper tantrum, because I couldn't find her
port-wine blouse and she had to wear black. As if wearing black to a
funeral was gauche."

"Leigh thinks it's her way of grieving," said Manny. "She's focused on the things she can blame on other people so she doesn't have to deal with her sorrow."

"She's going senile on me, Manny, or else headed for a nervous breakdown. She thinks Carolyn wanted to elope, sent a doppelganger to the reunion in her place, hid in the pantry, and sprang up to surprise Kevin. Only she didn't know the tomato ... paste, I suppose ... was in front of her. It flew out and crushed his skull. She finished the job to put him out of his misery, and now she's skipped the country."

"I don't think a *child* could fit in that pantry," said Manny. "Let alone a grown woman." On a street of mansions, Kevin and Carolyn owned a renovated bungalow

Leigh emerged, arms in the air. "Virginia, I'm sorry, I couldn't stop her. She's heading for Cressida."

"*You!*" Demelda screamed from inside. "*You're* the doppelganger."

"Oh, no. She *isn't*," said Virginia, cutting past Manny in her haste to re-enter the tent.

Demelda had forced her way to the front of the line, and now she clutched her sister's wig in one triumphant claw, holding it aloft like a newly discovered artifact. Cressida gaped at Demelda for a moment before burying her face in Derek's shoulder. He enfolded her in an embrace.

"Mother, give that *back*." Again, the throng gave way for Virginia.

"Look at her wig!" Demelda demanded. "It proves *everything.*"

"What does Aunt Cress's wig prove? Besides that she can't grow hair?" Virginia snatched the headpiece and handed it to her uncle.

"There's dried tomato paste in the hair!"

"Mother, I don't see how you can tell tomato paste from—" Virginia began.

"What did you say?" Cressida whirled away from her husband and seized Demelda's satin slash. Derek thrust the wig back at Virginia.

"Let me go you killer!" Demelda shrieked.

"What did you *say?*" Cressida repeated, as Demelda struggled not just against her sister's grip now, but also Derek's stronger arms.

"Isn't it obvious?" said Demelda. "That jealous harlot somehow tricked you into killing your own son, but you left the evidence in your wig. You didn't wash out the tomato paste!"

"There. You said it again," said Cressida. "*Who told you it was tomato paste?*"

Unexpectedly, Demelda faltered. "I ... I suppose it must have been Manny or Leigh," she said.

"No," said Virginia, still examining the wig as if it might actually be evidence of something. "*They* keep saying Kev was killed with a can of soup. *You* told *them* it was tomato paste."

"Well, I'm sure I heard it somewhere," said Demelda. "What does it matter?"

"What did he do to you?" Cressida sobbed. "What did Kevin *ever* do to you, Demelda? To you or to anyone?" She staggered away from her sister. Derek caught her.

"What's going on?" said Virginia. She tried to give the wig to Derek, but he let it fall.

"The press misreported the murder weapon," said Cressida. "Only a few people knew the truth. There's only one reason for your mother to be so certain Kevin was killed with tomato paste."

"Don't make this my fault," shouted Demelda, but her voice shook, and now she teetered in her high heels.

"It's the money, isn't it?" Cressida said. "You killed him because he'd have made Carolyn his heir when they married instead of Virginia. You *liked* him leaving everything to his favorite cousin. Don't you know he already changed his will?"

"Never mind the money... the money he hash now," slurred Demelda, her voice fading. "It's what he wash going to make when he went into film and overshadowed Virginia for good! *Thatsh* the real problem. This is about her *career*. Why should *he* be the famous one? I haven't worked all my life to make her a *character* actress. He simply would not see reason."

Demelda sagged against Virginia and groaned. "Oh oh oh!" she moaned, throwing a sequined arm around her daughter.

Virginia lowered her to the ground. "Mother, stop it. Is there a doctor?"

"Who would've thought the old man to have had so much *blood* in him?" wailed Demelda, her voice rising again for a moment before dropping to a whisper. "The evidench is all right there in the wig. The wig and the port wine . Maybe you can't see it, but everything leaves a trace. Every contact leaves . . ."

"What was in those pills I gave you?" Virginia demanded. "Was it really your anxiety medication?"

Demelda's eyes fluttered open. "No." she said. She arranged her free arm across her forehead before closing her lids again. "My sleeping pills. Been carrying them in the anxiety bottle so you wouldn't annoy me with questions."

"How many have you *taken*?"

"Been popping them like candy, and I still can't get decent rest. I simply can't believe ... all that blood... My God, it *is* Robert Redford."

La Quatrième Soupçon

"It's completely inadmissible in court," said Manny. "I don't care what Demelda knew about any tomato paste. No judge *I* know of would admit the confession of a seventy-year-old woman stoned on sleeping medication."

Virginia groaned. "I can't believe she switched the pills in her bottles. *Why?*" She punched in her door code and let them all in.

"Manny's right. She didn't do it," said Leigh.

"It's that blame thing," Manny agreed. "She's run out of other people to hold responsible, she's on a wicked bad trip, and she's accusing herself."

"Well thank you for staying with me at the hospital. Maybe having her stomach pumped will convince her not to do *that* again. If she gets to come home. She seemed to know so much."

"She certainly knows *something*," Leigh agreed. "But I doubt she has the physical strength to pound in somebody's face, especially not someone young and strong, like Kevin was."

"Can I get you something to drink," Virginia offered, "Or are you going home to turn in? I haven't seen this side of three a.m. in quite some time."

"Not much point in sleeping. I'll take coffee if you're brewing," said Leigh.

"Are you sure?"

"Of *course* we're sure," said Manny. "We're not leaving until we've torn this house apart looking for that damned port-wine shirt."

"I'm surprised the police don't already have a warrant. But about that ... I've been thinking. I'm not sure Mother even *owns*—"

"I *told* you," said Manny. "The lady doth protest her guilt too much, methinks."

"She was doing Lady Macbeth, not Hamlet's mother."

Manny waved Virginia off. "You're the actress. That's your job. I'm the lawyer, and I'm telling you, there isn't enough criminal evidence in Demelda's hysterics to cause even the media to take interest."

"That's true. They *were* notably absent. Do you want coffee?"

"Yes, please. Where should we start looking for this imaginary blou— Leigh! Get down! He has a gun!" Manny threw himself on the floor and the women instinctively followed suit.

"Who's there?" shouted Virginia.

"Get up, all of you. Hands where I can see them," bellowed L.E. Carmody, president of the Broadcasting Syndicate of America. He fired, and a vase exploded. "Up! Now! And throw me your phones." This time, he pinged a bullet off a decorative tureen dangerously close to Leigh.

Virginia, Manny, and Leigh stood. They surrendered their phones. "What are you doing here?" Virginia asked. "How did you get in?"

Carmody towered over them. Today he wore a powder blue shirt covered in orange musical notes with a hot pink BSA logo embroidered on the pocket. "Your mother was kind enough to leave the door and alarm codes in her purse," he said. "And you were all so distracted that I had plenty of time to find them. I was hoping for a mere house key. Now shut up, and let's negotiate this like civil people."

"You're shooting at things in *my* house, but you're asking *us* to be civil?"

Carmody blew up another vase by way of reply.

"Fine, we'll sit!" said Leigh.

"Can't we please go to the kitchen?" said Virginia. "If there's something to negotiate, let's do it over coffee. I have an idea of what you want, but I still can't understand *why*."

Carmody considered briefly, then waved the gun in the direction she had indicated. Virginia stumbled in the doorway, and Manny caught her. "Don't try anything," Carmody barked.

"Nothing!" said Virginia. "I fell. That's all. Watch your step. There's a loose baseboard." In the kitchen, she kept her hands visible and showed Carmody the inside of her cupboard with elaborate care.

"I don't need anything," he snapped, when she asked who wanted cream and sugar. "I've already helped myself."

"So I see," said Virginia. An empty bottle of Demelda's sauvignon blanc stood on the counter. Virginia picked it up and studied Carmody.

"Put that down!" he ordered her.

"Relax. I was trying to figure out if you're as much of a snob as Mother is. I've got a nice port if you drink sweet wines."

Carmody flinched as if Virginia was the one holding the gun. "Never mind the port! I know one of you tripped an alarm, and I need to decide whether I'm shooting you before the cops come roaring up."

"This is about Kevin's show, of course." said Virginia. She delivered three cups of black coffee.

"It is. It certainly is." With some hesitation, Carmody took one hand off his weapon long enough to pull a sheaf of documents out of his pocket. "Initial at all the highlights and sign the bottom of each page." He threw them on the table.

"Would you *sit*?" said Virginia. "At least *pretend* this is a real meeting."

"Fine, but I'm not giving away my leverage." Carmody lowered himself into a chair, which creaked under his weight.

"Wouldn't dream of asking. Do you have a pen, by the way, or do you want to march us all down to the office so I can find one?"

After another lengthy pause, Carmody again held the gun one-handed long enough to produce a neon pink BSA pen from his shirt pocket. "Now sign," he said.

Virginia picked the pen up but didn't write. "Please, tell me why you want *me*."

"Because you're the closest thing I can get to having Kevin back. If the Kevin McArthur Hour goes off the air, BSA is through. The big three are ready to suck me up."

"But did you *kill* Kevin? I need to know before I can even read this."

"What do *you* think? He was my *star*. Why the hell would I kill my star? But that doesn't mean I'm not ready to shoot you if you don't *all* develop a vested interest in keeping your mouths shut about tonight. I know what *you* can give me. What have your friends got to offer?"

Virginia gripped the table edge with her free hand. "I'm *not* Kevin, Mr. Carmody. He drew stories out of his guests by knowing how to turn himself off. He became invisible when they sat down beside him. I can't vanish like that. I'm too much like my mother. When I'm in a piece, I'm *in* it. You've seen how different the KM episodes I co-hosted were from all the rest.

"My roles may be small, but people always remember them. I've been in the theater and heard the guy down the aisle say, 'Virginia Irwin played her? I had no idea she was in this! I shouldn't be surprised, though, because I couldn't look away from the screen when she was on.' He *couldn't look away* when my stereotyped, clumsy maid was on the screen."

Carmody started to interrupt, but Virginia smacked the table for silence. "Look at me. You're the one who wanted to go fast," she snapped. "If I'm taking over this program, we have to play to my strengths, or you'll still lose your network.

"So far, BSA has stayed alive because it's the place people go for in-depth secrets about the big names. They watch my cousin because he brings stars down to earth. Famous people turn human in his limelight.

"But what if it worked the other way around? What if people watched to see *themselves* turn into *stars* for an evening, instead? We'd still do the celebrity features, but we'd space them out more. We'd add a new spot, something like ... Everyday Heroes ... no, that's been done ... you get the idea ... I'd bring on perfectly normal folks and tell their stories, *elevate* them, show how even the least of us can *rise above*. That's what we'd call it. Rise Above.

"Take Leigh here. Not a lot of people know it, but she's a vet. I'd bring her on..."

"A veterinarian?" said Carmody.

"A *veteran*. Saved twenty kids in an Afghan orphanage. She doesn't talk about it, but she's got PTSD and an honorable discharge to her name. Some nights, she wakes up—"

Manny slammed Carmody with his coffee cup, first in the wrists, then in the skull. Carmody screamed, and the gun flew loose. Leigh snatched it. After a moment's hesitation, she gripped it in both hands and pointed. Carmody screamed again as Virginia swung her own mug, shattering it across his nose. Then Manny, Leigh, and Virginia fled the house to call the police, leaving a bleeding, scalded Carmody behind.

La Soupçon Finale

"A veteran? Twenty kids in an Afghan orphanage?" said Leigh several hours later.

"Sorry. I was getting into the role too much." They were at Manny and Leigh's house now, hoping for a phone call. They were all still on edge, though L.E. Carmody had been arrested when he took his facial blisters and broken nose to an emergency room. "The part about me getting inside my characters was true."

"I've never seen you work up close like that. I didn't realize what you were doing until you started spewing nonsense about Leigh," said Manny. "We were *all* hypnotized."

"Why do you think I hit the table? I was afraid I'd startle him into firing, but I had to get one of you to pay attention *somehow*. I was running out of saleable clichés."

"I hoped he was right and you'd tripped an alarm in the doorway," said Leigh.

"No. I'd have needed to be at an exit to do that. I loosened my shoe. If Manny hadn't pounded him with the coffee cup, I was going to try the point of the heel."

"And you think he killed Kevin," Manny said. "It seems to me like he had a pretty good reason *not* to."

"He absolutely killed Kevin. The reason was a fabrication."

Leigh shifted closer to her husband. "Why murder the host who's keeping your network alive?"

"I don't think he meant to. Carmody's an angry man, but squeamish. You saw how he preferred shooting furniture to bodies in my living room. I think he dropped in on Kev and tried to manipulate him while Kevin worked around him in the kitchen. Kevin pushes ... pushed Mother's buttons all the time by acting like she wasn't talking. But Carmody's fury turned violent."

"But *why?*" Leigh repeated.

"This was Kevin's last season," said Virginia. "I doubt Carmody knows that's information I'm privy to, though. Kev was sick of keeping BSA afloat for that creep and wanted to go out on a high note, while he was still popular. I had no idea how bad it was at the network, or I'd have suspected Carmody sooner.

Kevin was going to get into films. Mother eavesdropped and found out, and that's what had her so jealous. But she didn't hear everything. Kevin and I only told Carolyn that he wasn't going in on the acting side."

"What do you mean?" Manny asked.

"He and I wrote a script together," said Virginia. "It got optioned last year, and it's beginning to look like it will really be produced. Kevin wasn't going to *overshadow* me. He *never* overshadowed me. We'd have been a stronger team than we ever were. I'm sure Mother went over to badger him and found Carmody there already. Or maybe she invited Carmody herself. I wouldn't put it past her."

"And then she watched him ..." Leigh didn't finish her sentence.

"Maybe. Or maybe she arrived when it was all over, and it was as easy for Carmody to get inside *her* hysteria as it was for *me* to get inside *his*. He could have convinced her to swipe one of Aunt Cressida's wigs and pose as her sister long enough to meet Carolyn at some halfway point."

"And you think Carolyn's still alive."

"I hope so. I hope he was too prudent to kill except in anger. Besides that, Mother obviously thought Carolyn would make a nice scapegoat, and I don't think she's had the wrong pills in that bottle for more than a couple of weeks. They'd be handy to dope someone up. She's been floating those outlandish theories at me. I thought it was her paranoia, but maybe she's really been looking for something people would *believe* when Carolyn turned up. I hope Carolyn's mother..."

The phone in Virginia's hand rang, and she answered. A few seconds later, she burst into tears. "Oh thank God," she said. "I was afraid he'd .... well, you know ... before he came to my house. Especially after Mother ... yes ... thank you, Mrs. Routledge. Please, give her my love."

"You were right?" said Leigh.

"Yes. They found her. She's alive."

"How did you *know?*" Manny asked.

"They'd have gotten to her eventually, now that they've arrested Carmody."

"But how did you *know* she was in his wine cellar?" Manny repeated.

"Mother as much as said it at Aunt Cress and Uncle Derek's night before last. She guaranteed Carolyn was holed up in a cellar somewhere. Then there was that nonsense about the port-wine blouse, and she was muttering about port wine again before she passed out at the funeral.

"She'd only have said 'port-wine' about a *stain*, though. She would have used 'royal purple' to describe her own clothing. I was trying to figure out what had gotten the name of a *sweet* wine stuck in her head, and something clicked when I realized Carmody had drunk a bottle of her sauvignon blanc.

"You saw how he reacted when I offered him a port. He got *scared*. It was enough to make me hope Mother had helped him stash Carolyn, and her port obsession stemmed from something she saw then. She may be out of her mind, but she's still a wine snob. She *hates* sweet reds and can't *abide* ports. She'd consider it far more gauche to *own* a port-wine blouse than to *lose* one."

      "And Demelda is *never* unfashionable in her own mind," said Leigh.

      "No," Manny agreed. "She's so fashion forward that the rest of us may never catch up."

      "Kevin won't, anyhow," said Virginia. "And it's a shame, because this was going to be his year. He had a god-awful gold lamé suit, and he was so looking forward to outshining her at his wedding."

EXCERPT

The Marriage At the Rue Morgue

"Powell (*Divorce: A Love Story,* 2011) bounces from arch humor to tragedy and back again. Lovably eccentric characters maintain a s light edge over sentimentality in what is most likely the finest simian cozy to date." — Kirkus Reviews.

"This intriguing whodunit is an appealing read." -- Publishers Weekly

Chapter 1

Lance Lakeland dodged as a well-aimed fecal mass sailed past him.

"Thanks for the warning, Noel," he called as he headed towards me. "Integration not going so well?"

"Slow." I had been toting breakfast to the enclosures before I stopped to check in on our newest monkey. The pungent smell of overripe fruit mingled with the earthy scent of Ohio forest as I leaned across the chow bucket and Lance bent down so I could peck his cheek. "Anyway," I asked, "what's up?"

Lance's hairy right hand crept up to the top of his head. Though I couldn't see it from my own height of barely over five feet, I knew he was scratching his bald spot. His left thumb started drumming on the dial of his two-way radio, and he hunched in what I called his gorilla pose. "Bub got in," he finally said.

"What?" My sympathy for his stress faded fast. "I thought your brother wasn't coming!" I thumped down the chow again, primates temporarily forgotten in light of this new personal crisis. "What are we going to do with him?"

"I don't know," Lance said. But he did know. We both knew. His right hand moved down to the back of his neck, and he looked at the bucket of food like maybe the answer was fermenting in the mangos and bananas.

Around us, the din of primate chatter edged up a notch. The animals were restless, perhaps keying off of their caretakers' moods, or maybe reacting to the distant racket of mall construction. In one enclosure, chimpanzees emitted their characteristic high-pitched screeches with lower huffing-hooting accompaniment. In another, the red-ruffed lemurs' chatter periodically erupted into chirps and croaks. In front of me, the rhesus macaque screamed bloody murder. It didn't seem at all repentant about throwing its excrement at my fiancé.

Above the animal ruckus, a car honked. The animals increased their volume. "Wonder who that is," Lance said. "We're not expecting anybody at the visitors' gate, are we?"

"No."

We looked at each other. I said, "That better not be your brother."

Simultaneously, Lance said, "If that's Bub, I swear I'll kill him."

"Tell me you didn't invite him to stay with us."

"No, no!" Lance held out his arms, palms open. "I told him you and I would have to discuss it."

"Making *me*, of course, the bad guy if we say no." I trained my glower over his shoulder and tried not to be angry. The anger boiled down to stress and the fact that we should have listened and taken the entire day before our wedding off work.

The horn blared again. I looked towards the barn. "Art will get it," Lance said. "He was sitting up there fiddling with paperwork when I left him. Give him something to do."

Thinking about Lance's brother again, I said, "I love you." But I was thinking *Perspective, perspective, perspective* to keep myself from shouting.

"Good thing," Lance replied. He lowered his eyes to the bucket between us.

Since Lance was taken up with scrutinizing the meal, I turned my attention to the monkey. Although he looked starved, his real problem was an inappropriate diet. He smelled better now that we had regulated his insulin levels and gotten his kidneys under control, but his body still showed signs of his former circumstances. Most of all, the neglect could be seen in his face, where his prominent nose seemed too close to his sunken eyes.

This knowledge didn't fix the problem of my future brother-in-law. At forty-two, I was far from the typical first-time bride. It was difficult enough getting around the fact that Lance's brother Alex was very much a volatile ex-boyfriend of mine, without dealing with the landmine of my future mother-in-law's fury should she feel I had denied Alex hospitality. She already considered me monstrous for leaving one brother for the other, never mind that it happened ten years ago and I had good reason.

Sophia's willingness to make herself comfortable in Lance's and my guest room in the days leading up to the wedding had initially given me hopes for a less tense relationship. But my hopes of her acceptance faded considerably when the first words out of her mouth off the plane last week were, "He's finally gotten you to change your name, has he?" Nor had she been happy to learn that even after my title became "Mrs.", my name would still be Noel Rue. I had not reached middle age without becoming firmly attached to my own identity, and I didn't plan to change the paperwork on everything from my driver's license to a bevy of graduate degrees.

Lance clearly hadn't thought of who would be portrayed how and in whose eyes, should Alex be consigned to a hotel. In fact, it was doubtful he had thought of seriously turning his brother down at all. More than likely, he had said anything to get his younger, more athletic, more financially successful sibling off the phone so he could come break the news of the arrival to me.

"Where is he now?" I asked. "How long do we have to come up with something?" It was always possible he had flown in at the more distant Dayton, or even Cincinnati, airport, not up the road in Columbus.

This time, Lance didn't say anything. He looked around me. Then his hands went down to his sides and our eyes finally met.

"He called you from our house, didn't he?" I asked.

Lance nodded once, an infinitesimal slump of the head, and then he resumed his examination of the food bucket.

"Which means," I went on, "it's a good bet that whatever we say, your mother has already counteracted it." We'd invited Alex to the wedding as a courtesy to Lance's parents, and now that he had accepted our grudging offer at the last possible moment, I wanted to move back in time and rescind the invitation.

Now, Lance put his hands in his pockets and nodded.

I blew out a loud breath, trying to decide if anything could be done. Nothing came quickly to mind, and instead I looked over at the monkey I was trying to socialize. Maybe he had some ideas.

Darting glances at the humans, the rhesus crept over to the food I had so recently delivered to his bowl. Out of the corner of my eye, I watched as he slid a hand into the mix. He checked again to make sure neither of us planned to snatch his selection back. Lance assumed the same nonchalant pose that I had suddenly adopted, pretending to look at everything *but* the monkey. It scurried over to the cage's far corner to eat, and I tried to think rationally about my future in-laws.

"If Alex contributed to this guy's normalization, I might be willing to forgive him quite a lot," I finally said. "Maybe I could stay the night with my folks."

Lance sagged in total defeat. "Maybe that would be best," he said quietly. Then his shoulders came up again. He said, "If you do, I think I'll come with you." It was the first time since I'd seen him coming down from the barn that he'd looked even remotely happy.

"Seriously?" I asked.

I had hoped my question contained a hint of *are you crazy?* But Lance missed my tone or chose not to hear it. "It's perfect!" he said. "Mom hasn't spent a night in the same house as Bub since he left for college. We'll leave the two of them alone and see who comes out alive."

I hissed, then picked up my bucket and headed towards the other cages, where hungry primates hooted and warbled in anticipation of their meals.

Behind me, Lance continued, "Maybe she'll . . . ." He trailed off, seeming to realize I'd walked away.

I called back, "Great. That's going to fix everything."

The squirrel monkeys twittered and scolded while I filled their bowls and shook some crickets on top. If we didn't mix their diet up on a regular basis, they would get bored and stop eating.

Lance caught up to me and said, "It's not like he'd seriously hurt his own mother. Bub isn't the same guy we used to know."

"I don't want to hear it. Don't you *dare* tell me how fabulous he suddenly is." Now I felt as frustrated as Lance had looked when he first arrived beside the rhesus' cage.

We stared at each other across the squirrel monkey feed for a few more moments. I picked the bucket up, but Lance took it out of my hand. He set it down behind him, out of my reach. "It's all going to be finished tomorrow," he said. And then he kissed me.

I had seen the kiss coming, but I still nearly lost my balance when he pulled me towards him. He's quite a bit taller than I am, and his arms encircled my shoulders as he drew me in close. I wrapped my own arms around his waist and felt my initial flush of surprise turn into one of desire. A lot of our friends seemed startled when we opted for a ceremony to formalize the union we had known was permanent for a very long time. But when I imagined kissing Lance like this, in front of our assembled relatives, colleagues, and comrades, I knew it was exactly the right thing for us.

When we finally broke apart, Lance said, "Allow me, madam," as he bowed down to collect my bucket for me.

"Oh!" we both said.

Lance had put the bucket entirely too close to the spider monkey enclosure. Although none of them could reach it with their arms or legs, a very determined tail had crept down to wind around the bucket's handle. The little animal was now straining mightily to lift the prize it felt it had won. Lance deftly unwound the tail and pulled the food out of reach. I rewarded the intrepid explorer by feeding that group next. Then, Lance still carrying my bucket, we headed over to the colobus area.

Before we could deliver to that group of primates, Art came on the radio. "Sally, Lance, Noel, Trudy, Gary, Janie, Allen, Pat, Linda, all of you, whoever's here today, get up to the entrance fast."

"Art," Lance said, "what's wrong? You're paging last spring's interns. And Sally and Gary both graduated!"

"Never mind that!" Art shouted. His voice breathy, and urgent, he went on, "There's an orangutan up here!"

EXCERPT

The Case of the Red-handed Rhesus

The Case of the Red-handed
Rhesus leaves you
"expecting either a family
drama or a whimsical
whodunit" —Kirkus
Reviews

Chapter 1

Natasha's cell vibrated on
the counter, but I ignored it. She often forgot to turn it off when she
surrendered it to my care at 10 pm. It was well past midnight now,
and I was busy unpacking. The move into Ironweed had been
sudden, though anything but impulsive, and my husband and I were
busy with the kitchen boxes tonight.

Tasha's phone stopped buzzing as Lance lifted a stack of
plates and set them on the counter. "I hate all this waste," he
complained, unwrapping the dishes and putting them in the cabinet

above the sink. "Will you be able to reach these if I put them on the lowest shelf, Noel?"

"Try not to think about the waste." I sliced open a box, revealing our stemware, then stretched my arms into the cabinet. Since I top out at at five feet, day to day items are best stored in easy reach. "As long as the plates are in front, I should be okay."

The phone buzzed again. Lance groaned. Since she came to live with us, our fifteen-year-old foster daughter had blossomed socially. So much so that we found it necessary to place limits on everything from the internet, to outings with friends, to the aforementioned cell.

We had also been forced to adapt our views of what it meant to be a teen, which had heretofore been shaped by our contact with my sister's children. Natasha was nothing like the college bound Rachel or Rachel's fifteen-year-old sister, Brenda. For that matter, I doubted Tasha would have much resembled ten-year-old Poppy at the same age. Perhaps when she was eight. Maybe when she was my nephew Bryce's age, she had seemed like a child. But right now, she was more like a badly confused adult in an underage body.

In fact, Natasha was a large part of the reason for this move. Lance and I used to pride ourselves on our economical lives in our small house, but that home had what Natasha called "one *bedroom* and one *room with a bed*." It was all we could afford while trying to run the financially strapped Midwest Primate Sanctuary that was our passion as well as our profession.

Natasha's grandfather Stan, a wealthy man who donated to all of Ironweed's foundations, had made three bedside calls and purchased this home behind our backs. Then he sold it to us for a dollar. When I told him, "You can't buy us a house like that, Stan!" he smiled and went mute, as if the pneumonia he had developed in the hospital had suddenly stolen his vocal cords.

What I wanted to tell him, "You can't buy back Natasha's mental health," didn't need to be spoken. He knew it. And it hurt him as badly as his broken bones.

On the way home from the hospital, Natasha wept, "This is my fault. I told him I got scared at night out there." She took a veritable pharmacy of anti–anxiety medications to get through each day. And our old backyard had too many dark shadows.

"None of this is your fault, Tasha," I told her. "He's He's assuaging guilt. , He also blames himself for Art's death and everything you've been through." It didn't matter to Stan that until he and Gert finalized her adoption, Stan had been her step-grandfather. She was his only grandchild, and he and Gert were *her* only grandparents She was the most precious thing in their worlds. Art wasn't only dear to Stan. He was our good friend, too. He had been killed by Natasha's cousin, the same man who injured Stan, Gert, and Natasha herself.

When we realized how badly injured Gert and Stan were, and that Natasha had nowhere to go with her grandparents disabled, we impulsively invited her to stay with us. I had no doubt that even from what had nearly been his deathbed, Natasha's grandfather had greased the social services wheel to speed the foster-care process. Somehow, our home study was already in progress while we completed the six weeks of parenting classes, even though the classes should have come first.

Thus, what should have been a three- to six-month delay to formalize Natasha's durability as our guest wound up only taking eight weeks. We might not have needed to go through the formality at all if our connection to Stan and Gert hadn't been so tangential or if Natasha's former situation hadn't been so dire.

I thought Lance was motivated purely by sympathy. But it was more personal for me. I knew a little more about what she had been through, having been once sucked into an abusive relationship myself, and I hoped I could reach her where another might not be able to do so.

In the end, Lance and I rented a truck, packed up our things, and moved into the town of Ironweed. However, now that we had done it and were preparing to rent out the old place, I felt less sure of the decision. I wanted my small home back.

As we placed the last of the plates and silverware, the phone once again ceased to rattle. Lance picked up another box. "That thing makes the whole counter shake."

"It doesn't." I started working on the pots and pans.

Yet again, the cell on the counter vibrated. "Gah! If that thing goes off again, I'm turning it *off*." Lance banged the spice box too hard, and I was momentarily grateful for the wasted paper and over-packing.

"If it rings again, I'm answering it. These kids can't keep calling here at all hours." In fact, I was delighted to have those kids calling late at night. Not that I was planning to let Natasha stay on the phone after ten, but it meant she had friends to call.

When she came to us in June, she was friendless. Partially, this was because she was still grieving for her mother. Partially, it was because she had finally passed the seventh grade the day after her fifteenth birthday. But much of Natasha's condition resulted from her inability to accept that she was a victim rather than a perpetrator. She still apologized out loud to her grandparents in her sleep and took responsibility for everything that went wrong in her vicinity.

Her therapist had been helping to ease her fears of socialization with amazing speed. She *wanted* friends, after all, and her sweet personality made it easy for her to keep them. But she hadn't known how to make them.

Again, the phone stopped. "Dr. Rue," Lance said to me, "I believe we are moved in."

"Dr. Lakeland, I think you're right." Other than the detritus of boxes scattered around the living room and the trash can full of pizza boxes and paper plates, we had now unpacked everything. It helped to live so economically.

"A celebration!" He reached for the stemware I'd so recently put away and I went for the bottle of champagne that was the only alcohol in the house.

"A toast!" I held up my glass and looked around our new home, with its four bedrooms and basement of unseemly proportions. "To excess and holding down two jobs to achieve the American Dream." Not that we were technically carrying a mortgage, but we had agreed between ourselves to set aside money as if we were, so we could argue appropriateness with Stan at a more suitable time.

"May our return to teaching this semester be as simple as hiring graduate students to move our boxes proved to be." We toasted and drank, but didn't get to enjoy so much as an entire glass of the bubbly.

On the counter, the phone buzzed again. "Really?" I sipped my champagne and picked up the offending device.

"Turn it off." Lance flopped on the couch with an arm crooked for me to sit in. "Her friends need to learn to call at reasonable hours."

No name displayed with the number on the caller ID panel. "It's not in her contacts list. And it's a Columbus number. Six-one-four area code."

"Lance sat up and lowered his arm. Columbus could mean bad things for Tasha's grandparents or bad things from her past. If it were the grandparents, someone would have been trying to reach *us*, not her. Which meant this might be the other.

"Hello?" I used my 'Dr. Rue' voice, the one I had been practicing to use on undergraduates. The one I used setting limits with my foster teen.

"I thought I was calling Natasha Oeschle." It was a woman on the other end of the line. An adult, not a kid, and she sounded breathless.

I kept my tone professorial. "Who's calling, please?"

"You must be her foster mother. I'm Nelly Penobscott. Tasha fostered with me when she was twelve, and we've always kept in touch."

"I see." When she was twelve, Natasha had been making skin flicks for two years. Her mother's drug issues meant she *had* briefly been in the care of the state, but I didn't trust this caller. Lance had moved to stand behind me, and I twisted the phone so he could hear, too.

"Yes. I don't have much time. I know what she's been through, and I'm glad you're protective of her. I have a message, and you can deliver it or not."

"And what message is that?" I had dropped from professor to ice queen.

"When she was here, there were these twins, Sara and William. They went to live with an aunt and uncle in Muscogen County about the same time as Tasha went to her grandparents out there. Only now they're back in care, and the little boy's gone missing. They're mounting a house-to-house search, and I thought maybe Tasha would want to help. They've bumped into her a couple of times. William knows her, and maybe he'd come out for her. If he's only hiding. He's *got to be* only hiding." Her voice shook, as if she was begging me to make this missing child be a hidden one, not something worse. "You can call the sheriff's department if you think I'm lying."

I didn't speak. Not initially. My recent experience with liars and deception was too raw to accept her words at face value. And yet, the conversation was punctuated by bursts of another voice in the background, like she was being hurried along to come help with something. Her urgency seemed so real. "I'll talk to Natasha," I finally said, "and I'll call the sheriff's department. *They* will be able to tell us where to meet." *If this is real. If you aren't calling from some rented phone trying to lure my foster daughter into danger herself, under the pretext of a rescue mission. If June isn't about to come back around and bite us in August.*

I hung up the phone. "What do you want to do?" I asked Lance.

"You wake up Natasha," he said. "I'll wake up Officer Carmichael."

Over the course of the investigation in June, we had become friends with a deputy, a junior detective, at the county sheriff's office, and he could be trusted to give us honest information, even if we dragged him out of bed from a sound sleep.

Lance got out his own phone and started dialing while I walked down to Natasha's room. As soon as I said Nelly Penobscott's name, she leapt out of bed and started pacing. "Why didn't you let me talk to her?"

"For all I know, she's one of those crazy people." I didn't finish the thought. I didn't need to.

"Let me see the number. She's in my book."

I handed Natasha the phone. "This one came up without a name."

Natasha studied her call history. "If it's really Mrs. P," she finally said, "she's calling from someone else's house."

"Agreed."

"But she knew so *much*! I saw Will and Sara at the pizza place yesterday and again earlier this afternoon. Sara was the little girl talking my ear off while we waited in line. You might have noticed her, but Will's quiet. He doesn't talk much. He'll wander off where nobody can find him. Wait! Did Mrs. P. say kindergarten? Anywhere in the conversation, did she use that word?"

"No-o-o, why?"

"It's our safe word. So I'll know it's her. But if she was upset, and confused because you answered, she might not have remembered."

Lance poked his head into the room. "Be right back," he said.

"Why? Where are you going?"

"Drew says it's all legit. I want to check out the place where the volunteers are gathering."

"Don't go." Natasha, who had blazed at me for withholding her phone call, sounded frightened. "Let me call Mrs. P back first."

"If it's not . . ."

"She didn't say kindergarten. If it's her, *somebody* is going to answer at either this number or the one in my book. And then we'll know at least one thing."

Natasha's wariness since June was equivalent to that of a jealous spouse. And she was right. A call to a trusted number could at least establish some things. "Use your contacts first," I advised her.

She shifted the phone from hand to hand after she dialed. From the look on her face at the answer, something was wrong. She handed me her handset and buried her head in her pillow. "This is all my *fault!*"

"I . . . uh . . . kindergarten . . .", I blurted out.

The woman who answered had obviously been asleep. "Natasha? Honey, it's the middle of the night," she said.

"I'd better call Drew back," Lance said. "I'm going to bet that kid didn't wander off." He snorted. "It's like one of those problems in your mother's advice column. 'Dear Nora: Stalkers keep trying to lure my teen into danger. Please help or send thread."

I appreciated my husband's stab at humor, but I doubted we would be seeing my mother tackle this issue in "What's Next Nora?". I briefly outlined the situation for the real Nelly Penobscott, but hurried her off the phone. I needed to make another call, this one to a federal agent. And I needed to see about getting Natasha a new cell phone, one with a better protected number.

Interview

Michael Guillebeau: What kind of reader should give your stuff a shot?

Jessie Bishop Powell: My writing appeals primarily to youngish, middle-aged dowagers with crumbling finances, trust funds, and purse poodles. Also cat ladies.

Seriously, though, I write cozy noir mysteries. My subgenre barely exists. Cozy noir stories have the humorous elements of cozies, but they also dip into some of the more intense ideas that are verboten in straight-up lighthearted fiction.

The Rue and Lakeland series is set in a rural area, and a primate sanctuary features heavily in all the storylines. There is guaranteed monkey mayhem. But my main character, Noel Rue, was a battered woman, and that shapes her perceptions. Both the humor of the sanctuary and the seriousness of Noel's past are necessary for the books to work. Other elements of the novels play off each other in a similar way.

I would recommend myself to those who like a good laugh but don't require the whole story to hinge on the humor. Parnell Hall, Mary Daheim, and Joan Hess fans should give me a whirl.

MG: What do you want the world of your stories to feel like? Sad? Warm? Funny? Dark?

JP: You're asking about mood. Let me answer you in a roundabout way. As a reader, I'm incapable of suspending disbelief. But it's a mistake and an oversimplification to think one must believe something in order to believe *in* it. I always believe *in* the stories I enjoy. And I want to create worlds that make others feel the same.

The stories I believe in most are the ones that show multiple moods. Cozy Noir really does combine two extreme opposites in the mystery genre. Cozies are lighthearted and humorous. There's often romance, and the main characters have new high jinks in every chapter. Noir is dark. It features hard-nosed sleuths and hard-edged crime. So my worlds, in order to be plausible, have to offer strong middle ground for readers. When I'm world building, I incorporate details I feel readers can identify with, anchors to hold onto when the roller coaster starts to fly on the hills.

MG: What's the significance of your online handle, Jester Queen?

JP: Let me first say that it has *nothing* to do with *Yu-Gi-Oh*. I was slightly familiar with the card game and cartoon, but my son was five before I realized it had a Jester Queen. I'm nothing like her.

For me, the name Jester Queen means three things. First, it relates to my ability to write both hilarious and dark fiction. People think of the court jester as the funnyman, the clown, the guy who amused the nobility. But in reality, the jester often used humor as a means of getting at the realities people didn't want to face. He was the one person who could be totally honest. Sometimes, he got strung up by the toenails anyway. But if anyone in the court could speak truth to the king, it was the fool.

Second, the Jester Queen was a character in a story I wrote when I was seventeen. I submitted the piece to a magazine, and it was rejected, as everything I submitted at age seventeen was. But my pages were returned with a note scrawled on the front. "Not for us. Try my friend X at this other magazine."

I didn't understand editor-speak. All I saw was the rejection. It was years before I realized the guy seriously meant I should have submitted it to his friend at the other magazine. I might have published that story, if I'd paid attention, and it was one of my favorite pieces.

Looking back, I'm glad it never saw print. I'm touchy about my errors, and it has more than a few "I can't believe I wrote that" moments. If I ever publish it, I'll revise heavily. But at seventeen, I *should have* sent that story out again. I was devastated by the rejection. I should have been elated by the advice. So using the Jester Queen handle is also a reminder to myself that I'll always be out-of-step with the world, but that's actually a good thing and no reason to hold back.

Finally, my husband's last name is Merriman. The name Merriman is derived for another title of the court jester, the court merry man. (And you'll see the name spelled Merryman in some places.) It seems only appropriate that the Merriman should be married to the Jester Queen.

MG: What writing advice do you have for other aspiring authors?

JP: This advice isn't original to me, but it's useful. Drop the word "aspiring" from your vocabulary. There isn't a mystical line between "aspiring" and "real" writers. An aspiring author is the person you meet at the office Christmas party who plans to write a book one of these days, but who has not taken steps towards doing so. That's someone who *wants* to write, who aspires to it.

That's not an accurate depiction of a person who has actually written something with the intent of developing a story, poem, or song out of it. It isn't appropriate to substitute "aspiring" for "inexperienced" or "unpublished". Once a person begins to write, the term "aspiring" no longer applies. Unpublished authors deserve validation

Writing doesn't necessarily come with an apprenticeship program, and there are multiple paths to success in this field. Even with two published novels and a third nearing release, I find myself plagued by fears that I'm a fraud, because I need income from another source. In fact, I teach college English full time, and that's where I actually earn money. Am I *really* a professional writer? I hope so.

So my advice for unpublished writers is this: Believe in yourself. Shut down the internal jerk who questions every little detail in a piece. Let that voice help in editing, but don't let it shape self-perception. If you believe in your writing, you can learn to make others do the same.

LARISSA REINHART

Larissa considers herself lucky to have taught English in Japan, escaped a ferocious monkey in Thailand, studied archaeology in Egypt, and survived teaching high school history in the US. However, adopting her daughters from China has been her most rewarding experience. After moving around the Midwest, the South and Japan, her home address is Peachtree City, Georgia.

In June 2015, she and her husband, daughters, and Biscuit, a Cairn Terrier, moved back to Nagoya, Japan, where she'll continue to write about Southern characters, although some might find their way to the Land of the Rising Sun.

She loves small town characters with big attitudes, particularly sassy women with a penchant for trouble. The Cherry Tucker Mystery series with Henery Press begins with **Portrait of a Dead Guy** (August 28, 2012), a 2012 Daphne du Maurier finalist, a 2012 The Emily finalist, and a 2011 Dixie Kane Memorial winner. Following *Portrait* are **Still Life in Brunswick Stew** (May 21, 2013), the 2014 Georgia Author of the Year and Silver Falchion nominee, **Hijack in Abstract** (November 5, 2013), and **Death in Perspective** (June 24, 2014), the 2015 Georgia Author of the Year finalist for Best Mystery. The Cherry Tucker novella, **Quick Sketch**, in the mystery anthology The **Heartache Motel** (December 10, 2013) is a prequel to *Portrait*. The fifth Cherry Tucker mystery, **The Body in the Landscape,** will launch December 15, 2015.

EXCERPT

Portrait Of A Dead Guy

Praise for Portrait of a Dead Guy

"Portrait of a Dead Guy is an entertaining mystery full of quirky characters and solid plotting. Larissa Reinhart writes with panache and flair, her colorful details and vibrant descriptions painting a vivid, engaging picture of a small Southern town...Highly recommended for anyone who likes their mysteries strong and their mint juleps stronger!"

Jennie Bentley,

NY Times Bestselling Author of Flipped Out

"The story moves at a rapid pace taking you on a curvy road with a disastrous funeral, crazy ex-boyfriends, and illegal high stakes gambling...Portrait of a Dead Guy is pure enjoyment, a laugh out loud mystery with some Southern romance thrown in. Five stars out of five."

—Lynn Farris,

National Mystery Review Examiner at Examiner.com

"Laugh-out-loud funny and as Southern as sweet tea and cheese grits, Larissa Reinhart's masterfully crafted whodunit, Portrait of a Dead Guy, provides high-octane action with quirky, down-home characters and a trouble-magnet heroine who'll steal readers' hearts..."

—Debby Giusti,

Author of The Captain's Mission and The Colonel's Daughter

"A fun, fast-paced read and a rollicking start to her Cherry Tucker Mystery Series. If you like your stories southern-fried with a side of romance, this book's for you!"

—Leslie Tentler,

Author of Midnight Caller"

one

In a small town, there is a thin gray line between personal freedom
and public ruin. Everyone knows your business without even trying.
Folks act polite all the while remembering every stupid thing you've
done in your life. Not to mention getting tied to all the dumbass
stuff your relations — even those dead or gone — have done. We
forgive but don't forget.

I thought the name Cherry Tucker carried some
respectability as an artist in my hometown of Halo. I actually chose
to live in rural Georgia. I could have sought a loft apartment in
Atlanta where people appreciate your talent to paint nudes in
classical poses, but I like my town and most of the three thousand or
so people that live in it. Even though most of Halo wouldn't know a
Picasso from a plate of spaghetti. Still, it's a nice town full of nice
people and a lot cheaper to live in than Atlanta.

Halo citizens might buy their living room art from the guy
who hawks motel overstock in front of the Winn-Dixie, but they also
love personalized mementos. Portraits of their kids and their dogs,
architectural photos of their homes and gardens, poster-size photos
of their trips to Daytona and Disney World. God bless them. That's
my specialty, portraits. But at this point, I'd paint the side of a barn

to make some money. I'm this close from working the night shift at the Waffle House. And if I had to wear one of those starchy, brown uniforms day after day, a little part of my soul would die.

Actually a big part of my soul would die, because I'd shoot myself first.

When I heard the highfalutin Bransons wanted to commission a portrait of Dustin, their recently deceased thug son, I hightailed it to Cooper's Funeral Home. I assumed they hadn't called me for the commission yet because the shock of Dustin's murder rendered them senseless. After all, what kind of crazy called for a portrait of their murdered boy? But then, important members of a small community could get away with little eccentricities. I was in no position to judge. I needed the money.

After Dustin's death made the paper three days ago, there'd been a lot of teeth sucking and head shaking in town, but no surprise at Dustin's untimely demise from questionable circumstances. It was going to be that or the State Pen. Dustin had been a criminal in the making for twenty-seven years.

Not that I'd share my observations with the Bransons. Good customer service is important for starving artists if we want to get over that whole starving thing.

As if to remind me, my stomach responded with a sound similar to a lawnmower hitting a chunk of wood. Luckily, the metallic

knocking in the long-suffering Datsun engine of my pickup
drowned out the hunger rumblings of my tummy. My poor truck
shuddered into Cooper's Funeral Home parking lot in a flurry of
flaking yellow paint, jerking and gasping in what sounded like a
death rattle. However, I needed her to hang on. After a couple big
commissions, hopefully the Datsun could go to the big junkyard in
the sky. My little yellow workhorse deserved to rest in peace.

I entered the Victorian monstrosity that is Cooper's, leaving
my portfolio case in the truck. I made a quick scan of the lobby and
headed toward the first viewing room on the right. A sizable group
of Bransons huddled in a corner. Sporadic groupings of flower
arrangements sat around the narrow room, though the viewing didn't
actually start until tomorrow.

A plump woman in her early fifties, hair colored and
highlighted sunshine blonde, spun around in kitten heel mules and
pulled me into her considerable soft chest. Wanda Branson,
stepmother to the deceased, was a hugger. As a kid, I spent many a
Sunday School smothered in Miss Wanda's loving arms.

"Cherry!" She rocked me into a deeper hug. "What are you
doing here? It's so nice to see you. You can't believe how hard these
past few days have been for us."

Wanda began sobbing. I continued to rock with her, patting
her back while I eased my face out of the ample bosom.

"I'm glad I can help." The turquoise and salmon print silk top muffled my voice. I extricated myself and patted her arm. "It was a shock to hear about Dustin's passing. I remember him from high school."

I remembered him, all right. I remembered hiding from the already notorious Dustin as a freshman and all through high school. Of course, that's water under the bridge now, since he's dead and all.

"It's so sweet of you to come."

"Now Miss Wanda, why don't we find you a place to sit? You tell me exactly what you want, and I'll take notes. How about the lobby? There are some chairs out there. Or outside? It's a beautiful morning and the fresh air might be nice."

"I'm not sure what you mean," said Wanda. "Tell you what I want?"

"For the portrait. Dustin's portrait."

"Is there a problem?" An older gentleman in a golf shirt and khaki slacks eyed me while running a hand through his thinning salt and pepper hair. John Branson, locally known as JB, strode to his wife's side. "You're Cherry Tucker, Ed Ballard's granddaughter, right?"

I nodded, whipping out a business card. He glanced at it and looked me over. I had the feeling JB wasn't expecting this little bitty girl with flyaway blonde hair and cornflower blue eyes. My local customers find my appearance disappointing. I think they expected me to return from art school looking as if I walked out of 1920s' Bohemian Paris wearing black, slouchy clothes and a ridiculous beret. I like color and a little bling myself. However, I toned it down for this occasion and chose jeans and a soft orange tee with sequins circling the collar.

"Yes sir," I said, shaking his hand. "I got here as soon soon as I could. I'm sorry about Dustin."

"Why exactly did you come?" JB spoke calmly but with distaste, as if he held something bitter on his tongue. Probably the idea of me painting his dead son.

"To do the portrait, of course. I figured the sooner I got here, the sooner I could get started. I am pretty fast. You probably heard about my time in high school as a Six Flags Quick Sketch artist. But time is money, the way I look at it. You'll want your painting sooner than later."

"Cherry, honey, I think there's been some kind of misunderstanding." Wanda looped her arm around JB's elbow. "JB's niece Shawna is doing the painting."

"Shawna Branson?" I would have keeled over if I hadn't been at Cooper's and worried someone might pop me in a coffin. Shawna was a smooth-talking Amazonian poacher who wrestled me for the last piece of cake at a church picnic some fifteen years ago. Although she was three heads taller, my scrappy tenacity and love of sugar helped me win. Shawna marked that day as a challenge to defeat me at every turn. In high school, she stole my leather jacket, slept with my boyfriend, and brown-nosed my teachers. She didn't even go to my school. And now she was after my commission.

"She's driving over from Line Creek today," Wanda said. "You know, she got her degree from Georgia Southern and started a business. She's very busy, but she thinks she can make the time for us."

"I've seen her work," I said. "Lots of hearts, polka dots, and those curlicue letters you monogram on everything."

"Oh yes," said Wanda, showing her fondness for curlicue letters. "She's very talented."

"But ma'am. Can she paint a portrait? I have credentials. I'm a graduate of SCAD, Savannah College of Art and Design. I'm formally trained on mixing color, using light, creating perspective, not to mention the hours spent with live models. I can do curlicue. But don't you want more than curlicue?"

Wanda relaxed her grip on JB's arm. Her eyes wandered to the floral arrangements, considering.

"I have the skill and the eye for portraiture," I continued. "And this is Dustin's final portrait. Don't you want an expert to handle his precious memory?"

"She does have a point, JB," Wanda conceded.

JB grunted. "The whole idea is damn foolish."

Wanda blushed and fidgeted with JB's sleeve.

"The Victorians used to wear a cameo pin with a lock of their deceased's hair in it," I said, glad to reference my last minute research as I defended her. "It was considered a memorial. When photography became popular, some propped up the dead for one last picture."

"Exactly. Besides, this is a painting not a photograph," said Wanda. "It's been harder as Dustin got older. I wanted to be closer to him. JB did, too, in his way. And then Dustin was taken before his time."

I detected an eye roll from JB. Money wasn't the issue. Propriety needled him. Wanda loved to spend JB's money, and he encouraged her. JB's problem wasn't that Wanda was flashy; she just shopped above her raising. Which can have unfortunate results. Like hiring someone to paint her dead stepson.

"A somber representation of your son could be comforting," I said. Not that I believed it for a minute.

"Do you need the work, honey?" Wanda asked. "I want to do a memory box. You know, pick up one of those frames at the Crafty Corner for his mementos. You could do that."

"I'll do the memory box," I said. "I've done some flag cases, so a memory box will be no problem. But I really think you should reconsider Shawna for the painting."

"Now lookee here," said JB. "Shawna's my niece."

"Let me get my portfolio," I said. Pictures speak louder than words, and it looked like JB needed more convincing.

I dashed out of the viewing room and took a deep breath to regain some composure. I couldn't let Shawna Branson steal my commission. The Bransons needed this portrait done right. Who knows what kind of paint slaughter Shawna would commit. As far as I was concerned, she could keep her curlicue business as long as she left the real art to me.

*****

My bright yellow pickup glowed like a radiant beacon in the sea of black, silver, and white cars. I opened the driver door with a yank, cursing a patch of rust growing around the lock. Standing on my toes, I reached for the portfolio bag on the passenger side. The stretch tipped me off my toes and splayed me flat across the bench.

"I recognize this truck." A lazy voice floated behind me. "And the view. Doesn't look like much's changed either way in ten years."

I gasped and crawled out.

Luke Harper, Dustin's stepbrother.

I had forgotten that twig on the Branson family tree. More like snapped it from my memory. His lanky stance blocked the open truck door. One hand splayed against my side window. His other wrist lay propped over the top of my door. Within the cage of Luke's arms, we examined each other. Fondness didn't dwell in my eyes. I'm never sure what dwelled in his.

Luke drove me crazy in ways I didn't appreciate. He knew how to push buttons that switched me from tough to soft, smart to dumb. Beautiful men were my kryptonite. Local gossip said my mother had the same problem. My poor sister, Casey, was just as inflicted. We would have been better off inheriting a squinty eye or a duck walk.

"Hello, Luke Harper." I tried not to sound snide. Drawing up to my fullest five foot and a half inches, I cocked a hip in casual belligerence.

"How's it going, Cherry?" A glint of light sparked his smoky eyes, and I expected it corresponded with a certain memory of a nineteen-year-old me wearing a pair of red cowboy boots and not much else. "You hanging out at funeral homes now? Never took you for a necrophiliac."

This time I gave Luke my best what-the-hell redneck glare. Crossing my arms, I took a tiny step forward in the trapped space. He stared at me with a faint smile tugging the corners of his mouth. If I could paint those gorgeous curls and long sideburns — which will never happen, by the way — I would use a rich, raw umber with burnt sienna highlights. For his eyes, I'd mix Prussian blue and a teensy Napthal red. However, he would call his hair "plain old dark brown" and eyes "gray." But, what does he know? Not much about art, I can tell you that.

"I thought you were in Afghanistan or Alabama," I said. "What are you doing back?"

"Discharged. You still mad at me? It's been a while."

"Mad? I barely remember the last time I saw you." I wasn't really lying. My last memory wasn't of seeing him, but seeing the piece of trash in his truck. And by piece of trash, I mean the kind with boobs.

"You were pretty mad at the time. And I know you and your grudges."

"I've got more to do than think about something that happened when I was barely out of high school."

"Are you going to hold my youthful indiscretions against me now?" He smiled. "I'm only in town for a short time. You know I can only take Halo in small doses."

"If you're not sticking around, I can't see how my opinion of you matters. Not like you asked me about your sudden decision to join the Army and clear out of Dodge."

"That's what you're mad about?"

Dear God, men are clueless. Why He didn't sharpen them up a bit has to be one of life's greatest mysteries.

"There are a number of things you did. But I'm not about to print you out a list."

"We had some good times, too."

"Which you sabotaged with your idiocy."

"You're one to talk," he mumbled.

I took another step forward, but Luke didn't move. His eyes roamed from my face to my boots. My irritation grew.

"Do you mind? I need to get back to Cooper's. I'm working."

I shoved him out of the way, dragging my unwieldy portfolio bag behind me.

"Just trying to put my finger on what about you changed."

I clamped my mouth shut as an unwelcome blush crept up the back of my neck.

"I know," he continued. "Your boots are plain old brown. Where're those red cowboy boots?"

I stomped toward the funeral home. "At home with my Backstreet Boys albums. I don't have time to play catch up with you. I've got stuff to do."

"How about playing catch up later, then?" I glanced back to see a glimmer of a smile. "Don't you think it'd be fun to stroll down memory lane? Does everybody still hang out at Red's?" The sunlight played with the auburn highlights in his dark curls and the tips of his long, black eyelashes.

Lord, why does he have to be so good looking? It was incredibly unfair how easily beauty weakened me. Gave suffering for art a whole new meaning.

"It was seven years ago," I said before I could stop myself.

"What?"

"Not ten years," I corrected. "But a lot has happened in seven."

"I bet."

*****

I found Wanda shredding a tissue in the viewing room, watching JB bark orders at the assorted non-nuclear Bransons who then cowed and scurried as if he were the king of Forks County. He owned many businesses that supported most of the Branson clan, including the big Ford dealership, but he had actually inherited the Branson patrilineal power seat. Ironically, the two Bransons who never bowed to JB were his son, Dustin, and stepson, Luke. And that was where the similarities between Dustin and Luke stopped.

Luke and Dustin were never close. Luke loved his mother and put up with Dustin when she remarried. However, Luke got out of Halo as soon as possible. Couldn't blame him, with a cold stepfather and a mother pouring her attention into rehabilitating an emerging sociopath. But poor Wanda had her hands full.

Made me wonder, though. With Dustin out of the picture, was there now more room for Luke? Interesting that Luke left the Army right when his stepbrother got offed.

Hating that ugly thought, I hurried over to Wanda. "I just ran into Luke," I said, giving her shoulder a quick hug. "I'm glad to see he's here to help you through this."

"Yes, it is a blessing. Served his time, you know, and of course, he won't tell me his plans yet. But that's Luke. Doesn't like to worry me."

"Keeps his cards pretty close to his chest, does he?"

"Look at him." Wanda waved at her son. "I've never been able to tell what he's thinking. Just like his father, God bless him. Maybe it was losing his daddy so young. He just keeps everything clammed up inside."

Spotting his mother's wave, Luke wandered into the viewing room. He had always been a wiry guy, displaying his strength in high school on the wrestling team and fighting behind the Highway 19 Quik Stop with the other boys carrying boulder-size chips on their shoulder. He still seemed dangerous, yet more settled and confident. There was no softness about him. Luke was all hard edges.

"Oh, I don't know," I murmured. "I lost my daddy young, too, but I've always been an open book."

"Well, boys and girls are different," said Wanda.

"Don't I know it." I swung one palm to my hip but waved my other in casual deference to Luke's arrival. "Let's go sit, and you can take a look at my portfolio. While you're looking at my samples, I'll sketch some ideas I have for Dustin."

"What's this?" Luke asked. "Ideas for Dustin?"

"I'm having Dustin's portrait done," Wanda explained. "I'll hang it next to the painting of him as a child. That one's thirty-by-forty. I'd like them to be the same size."

Holy cow, that's a big picture of a dead guy, I thought, but nodded my head as if it was the most reasonable idea in the world.

"That's downright morbid." Although he directed the statement to his mother, the accusation lay at my feet. "I swear you haven't changed Cherry, with all the nutty art stuff."

I felt like telling Luke, this is your mother's crazy notion, not mine. Instead I responded in my most proper aren't-you-an-idiot drawl, "Your momma is just dealing with this horrible tragedy the best she can, God bless her. It's a memorial."

"A memorial for Dustin? You don't know what Dustin was mixed up in, Mom. Death doesn't turn a sinner into a saint. God knows you tried your best. More than his own father."

"Come on, Miss Wanda," I tugged on her arm. Between Luke and Shawna, I was going to lose this commission. "I'll get you a cup of tea and you can look at my paintings. It'll get your mind off things for a minute, anyway. I've got a real cute one of Snug, Terrell Jacob's Coonhound."

Wanda beckoned JB and they conferred for a moment. With a shrug he followed her out of the viewing room.

Luke shoved his hands in his pockets. "You spent all that money on art school to paint pictures of dogs?"

"I spent all that money on art school to become a professional artist," I said. "It's early days yet. For now, I take what I can get."

"Including painting the departed?"

"You ever heard of a still life?" I shot back and stalked out of the viewing room, swinging my portfolio bag behind me.

I followed Wanda and JB into a little room crowded with a table and chairs. Unzipping the large bag, I pulled out a binder of photographs of my college works and a sheaf of plastic-encased photos of my newer stuff. Snug the dog, a horse named Conquering Hero, and a half-dozen kid portraits. I much preferred animals to children as subjects, something you don't learn in school. Getting a four-year-old to sit still is damn near impossible. However, you take a well-trained dog in the right pose, and you've got the perfect model.

Snug the Coonhound sat better than most people. We had an easy working relationship, what with Snug's deferential silence.

No need for forced conversation with that subject. Of course with this job, I couldn't expect any conversation either. I could make do with photographs.

But first I needed to get the job.

"I don't know why you're wasting my time looking at pictures," said JB. He tossed the portraits of Snug and Hero on the table.

"This one is just beautiful, Cherry," said Wanda, holding up a Sargent inspired painting. The model wore a sheet draped like a toga, but the effect was tasteful with wonderful folds to show depth and shadow.

"I'm glad you pointed out that one. Don't you love the light on her face? You might not be able to tell, but that's not an oil painting. I had a tight schedule, so I used acrylics. They dry quickly and I didn't have to varnish the painting immediately. Someone mentioned you displaying the portrait at the funeral service? Oils wouldn't dry fast enough to get the painting done without messing up the color."

"I was fixing on making a photo display for the service when I realized we didn't have many of Dustin after he passed a certain age." Wanda's face colored and she cast her eyes away from JB. "I've just been in a tizzy, not knowing what to do with myself and not sleeping. That's when I got the idea for the memory box. Started gathering stuff Dustin left in his old room. Then I remembered the family portraits we had done at our wedding and thought maybe a new painting would be a nice tribute."

"Let her have what she needs," said JB. "A picture's not bringing him back, but if it makes Wanda feel better, she can have it."

"I totally agree, sir," I said. "That's why you should let me have the honor of painting this portrait. You can see what quality I can produce. You don't want a final memorial done by an amateur."

"What about Shawna?" he said, eyeing me. "Although Shawna did set a pretty hefty price for painting my son."

I squirmed, caught between a rock and a rattlesnake. JB would sell out his niece for a cheaper price. But probably wouldn't help me underbid her, either.

"A portrait lasts for generations." I began with my salesman pitch. "My paintings are heirloom quality and will be around long after..." Since the subject was dead, I stopped before my mouth ate my foot. "Anyway, a portrait is priceless."

"Priceless? You talking free?" JB leaned back in his chair.

"Of course a professional artist would base the price on other features. Number of people. Intricacy of the clothing, jewelry and props. Complexity of the background. And of course, the size." I could not get over the size.

"How complex is a coffin?" He steepled his hands under his chin. "And we don't need background details."

"JB, don't be cheap," said Wanda. "Like Cherry said, we're talking heirloom quality."

"Who in the hell wants to inherit a picture of Dustin in a coffin, Wanda?" JB said. "Even if little Dustins start crawling out of the woodwork, and God help us if that happens, I'm sure none of them will want this painting. We can cut some corners, here."

"Coffin portrait?" I said, swallowing hard. My mouth went dry, and I had trouble getting my tongue to form intelligible words. "I thought you'd want me to work from snapshots or something. Dustin standing in a field, looking off to heaven, that sort of thing."

"Oh no," said Wanda. "That would be phony. Dustin never would have stood in a field unless he was hunting, and I doubt he thought about heaven much." She cast a quick look at her husband. "I want him as he is now. And realistic. None of that abstract stuff."

I gulped. "As he is now." The man was murdered. An abstract would be easier to stomach. Not like anyone would enjoy looking at David's "The Death of Marat" in their TV room. "All right. Uh, do you want me to create a pose, or do you want the whole, um, coffin?"

"Could you paint it like we were looking down at Dustin? Like angels gazing?" Wanda's moist blue eyes stared off into the distance and I shivered.

I grabbed my notebook and made a quick sketch. "Something like this?" I showed her the rough illustration of my idea.

"Oh, it's just perfect," she said, grabbing the sketchbook to shove at JB. "Let's give Cherry a chance, honey. I really want this view. Shawna said she has an allergy to formaldehyde so she couldn't paint Dustin this way."

"Tell you what." JB leaned forward, hands flat on the table. "I'll give you a shot. I want Wanda to be happy after what all she's endured with Dustin. He was my son and I owe her that."

"Yes, sir," I said, although my skin still prickled from the word formaldehyde.

"But," he said, "you got to have the painting done for the funeral. The whole she-bang. Wanda can choose between you and Shawna, so you better make it good. She likes quality. After the funeral, I'm done. Wanda can hang up his picture and look at it all she wants, but I'm putting this whole blasted deal out of my mind.

I'm paying off his creditors right and left, dealing with folks' complaints, and living through the embarrassment of the way he went. Do you know what they are saying about him?"

I knew, but I sure wasn't going to say. Folks thought a bad drug deal or payback from a robbery ring. Or someone just got tired of Dustin's mouth and went postal on him. Hard to say with Dustin. There were so many crimes to choose from.

"I'll work up a contract," I said. "Thank you for this opportunity. I'll get cracking right away and I'll also do the memory box."

"We'll have Cooper set out the body for you then." JB didn't smile but I did see a flash of teeth. "Got to admire your tenacity, Cherry. I hate to say it, but stories I heard about your family made me question your reliability."

A shot of heat worked its way from my toes to my scalp. People always bring up my family's history over the years, but it never got any easier.

"My reputation is important to me. I am judged by my own actions as well as those that surround me. You know how people like to talk."

"Yes, sir."

He looked at me evenly. "I'm glad we agree on this issue. As a businesswoman, you have your own reputation to protect and a lot of history to overcome.

A million comebacks crossed my mind, but none were appropriate for a bereaved father sitting in a funeral home with a large check that could have my name on it. I swallowed my pride and tried not to choke. "I'll bring that contract by tomorrow."

He had better keep his end of the bargain, because after that humiliation, I sure as hell wasn't working for free.

two

I hustled out of the cramped conference room to find Cooper. Walking down the dim hallway, I glanced in the first room on the right. The wooden door rested open showing an office filled with oversized mahogany furniture and misty paintings of sunrises or sunsets. I'm never sure which they're supposed to be.

I waved at Cooper who chatted with Will Thompson, our county coroner and sheriff, and one of my favorite men on the planet. But that's a pretty short list.

"How are you, girl?" Will was a good friend of my grandpa. Will was about thirty years younger, a hundred pounds heavier, and a million times nicer than Grandpa, but they paired up better than sausage and biscuits.

"Hey, Uncle Will. How are you, Mr. Cooper?" I waltzed into his serenity-blue office to give Will a hug.

"What are you doing here, Cherry?" asked Cooper. "Get a time wrong for a visitation?"

"I'm here for the Bransons. And I need a favor. Did you hear about the painting they want?"

Cooper nodded. Will leaned back in a well-padded armchair and settled folded hands over the mounded expanse of his belly. Will had been a tackle for Georgia back in his prime. It worked to his advantage as sheriff, but I knew him as a big teddy bear.

"Did the Bransons talk to you about making the body available?" I asked.

Cooper pursed his lips. He almost perfected the art of masking his emotions except for the occasional tic that managed to escape.

"Why would the Bransons need the body available today?" Will questioned Cooper while watching me. "Visitation is tomorrow, isn't it? Is your girl even done making him up?"

"She is," said Cooper. "Originally, I assumed they wanted to spend extra time with the body. Happens occasionally. Then they started talking about having a," Cooper coughed quietly into his hand, "memorial painting made."

"Memorial painting?" said Will.

"Portrait of Dustin," I said. "In his coffin."

Bug-eyed, Will turned from Cooper to me. I rocked back on my heels, doing my best to keep a straight face. It wouldn't do to have a Branson walk into the office with us hooting about their strange choice of commemorating their son.

Will pulled himself together, but for a half a second I was sure he was going to fall out of his chair. "Good Lord."

"Mr. Cooper. How's this going to work? Please tell me I don't have to visit your basement. I'm still shaking with the heebie jeebies as it is."

"I can bring Dustin upstairs," said Cooper. "His room is ready. But, honey, I thought some Branson was coming to do his picture."

"I convinced Wanda and JB to let me try." I couldn't help a little smirk at competing for the job with Shawna. She was going to throw a big hissy. And I hoped I got to see it.

"Well, if you say so." Creaking, Cooper rose from his wooden desk chair. "It's your funeral." He dry heaved a few chuckles. "That's a little mortuary humor, hon."

A whoop of laughter burst from Will.

"Good one," I said and pulled the curl out of my lip.

Cooper ambled out the office, heading for the basement morgue.

"You best get yourself together, Sheriff Thompson," I said to Will and made a quick pivot to speed out of the office.

"Hang on a minute." Will swung his considerable body around to face me. "Where you going?"

"I've got some sketching supplies in my truck."

"I'll walk with you. Let's go out the back door."

He rose, towering over me, and placed a large hand on the back of my neck. Like a dog on a leash, Will guided me through the hallway until we reached an arched doorway. After a glance down the hall, he hustled me through the door and into a kitchen. I shook free of his grip and crossed the room. Leaning my back against a Formica counter, I waited for Will to say his piece.

"Just spit it out, Uncle Will," I said. "I'm not walking clear around this house looking like you're ready to shove me into a police car. Obviously, you got something to tell me."

"You doing all right?"

"I'm okay. What's going on?" I crossed my arms and met his look. Will didn't usually worry about me. My siblings, Casey and Cody, were a whole different kettle of fish, though. Some days it felt like their good decisions were the exception to a lifetime of dumb moments.

"I mean for money." Will shoved his hands into his pockets. "Why are you taking a crazy gig like this? Miss Wanda is a nice woman, but she has some different ideas about decorating. Did you hear about her having all those bushes cut like animals?"

"That's topiary. What's the big deal about that?"

"She had clothes made for them, too. What kind of woman dresses up hollies?"

"Don't worry about me." I relaxed off my previous attitude. "But every dollar helps. Art school wasn't cheap. Although I'm glad to not live at the farm, Great-Gam's house is a money pit. Today I found something oozing through the plaster in the living room wall. And you know about my truck. Besides, this portrait means doing what I really love, painting pictures of people. Even if the guy's not breathing."

"I'd help you if you'd let me."

"Thank you, but I'm plenty old enough to take care of myself." And if Casey and Cody heard I borrowed money from Will, they would forever be knocking at his door looking for handouts. "Grandpa didn't raise me to take charity."

Will grunted in affirmation.

"Now tell me about the murder." I spied an electric kettle and a box of tea bags on the countertop. "You want some tea? It'll take Cooper a minute to bring up Dustin."

"No thanks, hon." Will ran a hand over his thick salty-brown buzz. "I'm leading the investigation, of course. Still don't have a number on what happened to him. That's between you and me, now."

"You got some suspects? Murder weapon?"

He stared at me stone-faced.

"Come on, Uncle Will. Give me something."

"Girl, you know better than to mix our personal relations with my job."

"That's no fun." I twisted around to lean over the counter, hunting for a mug in the cupboards. "For once, I'd love to be the first one to report some exciting news to Grandpa."

"By news you mean gossip." He reached over my head, snatched the mug on a shelf just out of my reach, and slid it onto the counter. "You kids are getting a little old to compete for Ed's attention like that."

I shrugged and dropped a tea bag into the mug. "Speaking of gossip, what's the deal with Dustin's stepbrother coming back in town?"

"Who, Luke Harper? You sound like it's unreasonable for him to come to a family funeral." He eyed my fake nonchalance. "What's wrong with you?"

"Me?" I turned my back to Will and checked the kettle. "I'm just asking. He hasn't been home in seven years. I'm just wondering what you heard about his plans now that he's out of the Army."

"Luke Harper's plans?" Will chewed on that idea for a moment. "I know what this is about. It's his looks, isn't it?"

"Good Lord, I'm not a boy crazy teenager anymore." I spun around, color rising in my cheeks. "Give me some credit. I used to know him. I just wondered is all."

"You lost your credit with that fiasco in Vegas." Will winked, referring to my dumbest moment in twenty-six years.

"Todd cannot keep his mouth shut," I muttered. "We did not get married. I don't care what he says. And why would anyone believe him over me? I've had more intelligent conversations with Snug the Coonhound than Todd McIntosh."

"Thereby proving my point. All I'm saying is know your weaknesses and avoid them."

"Man. You can't get away with anything in this town."

"Remember that. It'll keep you in line." Will squeezed my shoulder as the steam blew. "There's your kettle. You best get your skinny behind to work. If something's oozing through your walls, that'd be a plumbing issue. You want to get rich, marry a plumber."

"I'll work on that."

"I'd rather you work on marrying a plumber than doing crazy jobs like painting Dustin Branson's picture." He faked a shudder to accompany his wink. "Just thinking about painting a guy in a funeral home is enough to give me the willies."

*****

I threaded my way through the back maze of Cooper's to the front lobby, intent on grabbing my sketching supplies from my truck bed. Now that I competed for the commission with Shawna, I realized the craziness of the situation. Wanda and JB compartmentalized their feelings like crime scene veterans. Of course, I wasn't privy to the private goings-on of the Bransons. There was probably some perfectly good psychological explanation for wanting a coffin portrait of a son you didn't seem to like very much.

I had bigger things to worry about. Like spending some quality time with a dead guy.

And avoiding Luke, I thought, as Wanda flagged me down. Luke hovered next to her. The portfolio case I had snagged from the conference room bumped against my back, keeping time with my steps. As I threw him an eye roll, my toe hit a seam in the carpet and I stumbled. The long case strap twisted beneath my arm and the oversized bag flipped forward. A hard corner smacked me in the gut. With a mostly silent grunt, I fixed the strap, flipped the case back, and looked up.

A dimple glimmered in Luke's cheek and went out.

"Cherry, where did you get to?" asked Wanda. She pointed to a large red shopping bag at her feet. "I've got Dustin's mementos here for you. I had them in my car in case I got a chance to pass by Crafty Corner."

"Great." I slung the portfolio bag onto my back, picked up the bag, and supported the sagging weight under one hand.

Luke's dimple, hovering somewhere beneath his hardened jaw, threatened to emerge as he watched my struggle.

"I'd get the door for you," he said, "but I'm sure you'll be fine seeing as how you're a businesswoman and all. You probably got used to getting your own doors in the last seven years. I was raised a gentleman, but I'm not going to tread on your independence."

Wanda nudged him. "Honey, you help Cherry. Stop teasing her. She might not know what a joker you are."

"Don't worry, ma'am," I said. "I find it hard to take him seriously."

"Give me the bag," he said.

I eyed Miss Wanda and heaved a big sigh. Considering my overburdened arms and my rush to get started, my protests would seem ridiculous.

"Fine." I set the bag on the floor and yanked off my portfolio case. "Take this to the viewing room. I'll be back in a minute with my sketching stuff." I didn't want to chance getting stuck in my truck with him. Memories of Luke and my truck were starting to trickle back. Although they weren't as bad as memories of Luke and his truck. His truck had been much more comfortable than mine.

I jettisoned to the Datsun and back to find Dustin ready and waiting in the viewing room. JB's minions had cleared out. Wanda and JB had also disappeared, although their Lincoln MKT still sat in the parking lot. So did a black Ford Raptor pickup. Someone with a stepdad in the auto industry had recently received a shiny new truck. The man with the penchant for black pickups had dropped the portfolio case on a chair in the viewing room and disappeared. I blew a sigh of relief and used the solitude to get accustomed to my first literal still life.

"Hey Dustin," I whispered. "I'm sorry about your passing. At least the way you went. No one deserves to have their life taken from them like that."

Footsteps approached the doorway, and I realized the family probably hadn't spent time with Dustin yet. I grabbed my sketchbook and slid to a back corner chair, where a grouping of floral arrangements kept my presence unobtrusive. Luke, Wanda, and JB strolled in with Cooper.

"Oh my," said Wanda, walking directly to the coffin. She closed her eyes in prayer for a moment. "You did a good job, Cooper."

"I got a new girl," said Cooper, "she's pretty good. Keeps forgetting her keys, though, and leaving them in the kitchen."

"Hard to train new staff," said JB gruffly. He and Luke hung back and stood at right angles to the casket. "The coffin turned out real nice. I didn't think we needed top of the line, but a lot of people are going to see it, I suspect."

From behind a palm frond, I watched Cooper nod. "You should have a good turnout for the visitation and the funeral. I've been taking calls all day."

"Heard from Virginia yet, JB?" Luke asked.

"Surprisingly, no," said JB. "Any normal woman would have scooted up here as soon as she heard her son was dead." He ran a hand through his thinning hair. "As if I could take any more embarrassment over this fiasco. Now I'll have my crazy ex-wife up here stirring up trouble. She's probably postponing the visit on purpose."

"What purpose?" Switching his stance to face JB, Luke placed himself in line with me. I hunkered over the sketchbook, pretending to draw, and prayed the Bransons would be too preoccupied to notice me. I didn't want to lose the commission over something as dumb as being in the wrong place at the wrong time. Shawna would love that.

"Who knows with Virginia?" JB uttered a disgusted grunt. "Probably trying to figure out how to get some money out of this. You know she tried to sue me for child support after she abandoned her own kid?"

"She didn't abandon Dustin," Wanda said.

"I don't know what else you call leaving a kid to run around like a cat in heat." JB turned his back on the coffin.

"Not like you were a saint at the time," Luke said. "I wonder if Daddy Branson hadn't told you to straighten up or lose the family business, you might still be carousing with Virginia. Were you ever going to do the same with Dustin? Call him on the floor before delivering the empire?"

"Luke," Wanda said, hurrying to JB's side. "Don't talk to JB like that."

"It's the truth, Mom." He crossed his arms and stole a glance at Cooper. "Sorry, Cooper. Don't mean to air the Branson dirty laundry in front of you."

Cooper gave a noncommittal cough and shuffled to the casket, putting some space between him and the family.

"I'd say I've had enough time in here," said JB. "Come on, Wanda."

"We should go over the service if you're ready," said Cooper. He patted the casket and faced the Bransons. "We can go to the conference room or my office."

"Let's get it done," said JB. "I want to get to the office and check a few things."

"Can't you get Ronny to do that for you?" Wanda tucked her arm inside JB's, slowing his pace to exit the room. "We're expecting more people today."

Cooper trudged after them, looking like he barely survived World War III. Which for Cooper meant a couple extra lines furrowing his brow.

"Did you get all that?"

I looked up from the little dog I doodled in my notebook. Luke stood facing me, his stance wide and arms crossed. Scrambling up from the chair, I scooted around a flower arrangement.

"I was already in here and didn't want to disturb you," I said. "But yeah, I heard. We all got some skeletons in our closets. No big deal."

Luke scowled. "Knowing I'm going to encounter Virginia always puts me in a bad mood. She's a couple fries short of a Happy Meal. Dustin didn't have much of a chance with that DNA combination."

"Well, I know something about mothers who choose a love life over their kids."

"Yeah," Luke wandered over to my pile of supplies and picked up a portable easel, "me, too."

There wasn't much more to say unless someone started handing out shots of Jack with a Loretta Lynn song on the jukebox. I let Luke futz around with my easel while I took another tour of Dustin. There was no "angel viewing" angle with my height. Cooper

had the coffin jacked up unnecessarily high. I held my sketchpad
under one arm and stood on my toes peering over the coffin. Dustin
looked pretty good. The police hadn't revealed how he had been
killed, but there was no obvious injury to his face, thank the Lord.

"I could lift you up so you can see more than the coffin
handles," said the soft baritone hovering above my head.

"That's original. A joke about my height." I resisted the urge
to turn around. "You want to give me a little space? I don't know
Dustin well enough to get this friendly with him."

Luke stepped back but shifted to my side instead of leaving.
His hands dropped to rest on the coffin's edge. "He would have liked
to know you're hanging all over him now. Harassing his parents to
get a chance to spend time with him."

"Wasn't going to happen while he was alive, so I guess I can
give him some attention now."

Luke tried to crack a smile, but you could have bounced a
penny off those tight shoulders.

"Do you know how he died?" I asked.

"Somebody smacked the back of his skull with something
heavy." Luke stared at his stepbrother. "Probably walked up to him
and beamed him in one blow."

"How could someone do that?"

"Easy. I could've knocked you a good one. Hidden something in my pocket or picked something up in the room. You knew I was in the room and didn't turn around. I stood right..."

The hair rose on the back of my neck. "Yeah, I know where you were standing, and you've done it a few too many times today." I looked at him askance. "I don't like my personal space violated."

"That's not what I remember..."

"You can stop right there, Hugh Hefner. Let's get something straight. I'm all grown up. I'm not, nor was I ever, some piece of trash you could get drunk on Boone's Farm, have your way with in your truck, and leave at the Waffle House with an unpaid check."

"Man, that was a long time ago. You really do hold a grudge."

"You did it more than once!" I tossed my sketchbook to the floor. Placing my hands on my hips, I took a step closer and flung my chin up.

"Hell, you're just mad because you wanted me so bad, you let me get away with it."

"You want to try that again?"

"You know I'm right."

"You are a..." I struggled for appropriate words to use in a funeral home. "Pig! I've news for you, Luke Harper."

He edged closer. I resisted retreat and took another step forward until we stood inches away. I glowered and poked a finger into his chest.

"You start messing with me, you're gonna end up with an ass full of buckshot. Not only do I still have that piece of crap yellow truck, I also have my daddy's shotgun, and I know how to use it."

Snatching my hand, he folded the offending finger to rest within his palm. "And if you don't keep your fingers to yourself, you're going to lose one." He released my hand.

I stepped back and retrieved my sketchbook from the floor. "It's time I got back to work. Now that I'm done with SCAD, I've crazy student loans to pay off, not to mention a few other bills. Make yourself useful. Ask Cooper how to lower this table so I can get a good view."

He stared at me a beat, then left the room.

I scrambled through my tackle box looking for a good piece of charcoal. Quality art supplies were expensive, and I tried to balance the line between conservation and cheapskate. I opened a larger sketchpad of heavier bond, luxuriating in the feel of the soft, bumpy surface on my fingers. Flipping through the pages, I found a blank sheet, set the sketchpad on the easel with the charcoal, and waited for the return of Luke with Cooper.

No Luke or Cooper.

I eyed the oak-paneled casket. As usual, a discussion with Luke spun me away from reality. Had we just gone another round while a dead body lay before us like a pitcher of beer and plate of nachos? I needed to refocus on the reason I stood in a funeral home with a sketchbook and empty pockets. This time when I peered over the side of the oak paneling, I wanted to see Dustin as his mother would. Or stepmother, in this case.

Dustin usually had stringy blonde hair, worn long and unkempt, but Cooper had his beautician brush and trim it. Now the smooth, blonde locks fell gently, pillowing his head. Death softened his face, hiding the angry lines that held a scowl and a scornful set to the eyes. Dark eyebrows relaxed above blonde eyelashes tipped in brown, permanently closed. I sighed, trying to imagine Dustin singing with angels. Too hard. More than likely a giant pitchfork poked him right about now.

My eyes drifted over the blue suit to the clasped hands. The long fingers had beautiful shape and an undisclosed strength. I'd be willing to bet they would have been skilled at fine arts and crafts. Such a waste to have those beautiful hands and not the mind to match them. I wanted to capture the slight turns and creases of the knuckles, the long digits that portrayed an artistic suppleness. Even the nails appeared smoothly squared and buffed.

Of course, the nails looked nice. He just had the manicure to end all manicures. Literally.

I took a deep breath and gave myself a mental shaking. I had my focal point. No need to get all artsy-fartsy.

I turned away from Dustin and walked to the doorway in search of living beings. Glancing around the empty reception area, I took a right down the hallway. Voices murmured from the kitchen. I quick-stepped through the hall and stopped in the archway.

Intent on their heated discussion, Luke and Uncle Will didn't notice me. Their voices remained low and tense. Will used his bulk to tower over Luke. He gestured with one hand, the other rested on his holster. Luke stood ramrod straight with arms crossed and chin high.

I didn't guess they were arguing about baseball since the Braves only had a few games under their belt. The Bulldogs still had about four months until their first game. NASCAR wasn't that controversial. That left me out of ideas. I backed out of the doorway and got my nose out of their business.

Interview

Michael Guillebeau: Introduce us to your series protagonist, Cherry Tucker. What is it about her that appeals to you as a writer?

Larissa Reinhart: Cherry Tucker is a short and sassy spitfire living in small town Georgia. She's a bit of a redneck but also a classically trained artist. Her family dysfunction is something from a Jerry Springer episode, but she was raised on a farm by her traditional grandparents. I love paradoxical characters. There's a lot of room for humor when you have contradictory characteristics.

MG: How would you categorize your mysteries? Do you find there are advantages/disadvantages to labeling it as such?

LR: The Cherry Tucker books are considered cozy mysteries. I'd call them humorous mysteries. Readers know what to expect from a cozy. Not a lot of language, sex, or violence. Generally small town humor. It's something I think about as I'm writing, because I don't want to let down my readers.

MG: How much of you or your experience is in your book/series?

LR: My wheelhouse for the Cherry Tucker series are small towns and art. I try not to use any people I know as characters—that's a sure way to tick someone off—but I'll compile character traits from certain types of people. In her fifth book, *The Body in the Landscape*, I did get my idea for setting a murder mystery at a Hogzilla hunt based on a remark at a wedding from a cousin who has a ranch and who had a certain celebrity visit his property for a wild hog hunt. Wild hogs are tearing up farm land all over the U.S, but particularly the South. It seemed like a good place for someone to get killed on purpose.

MG: Describe your writing environment.

LR: I write at home in a mid-century, Danish wingback chair with a matching stool we inherited from my husband's grandparents. They brought it home from Europe after the war. It's very comfortable. I sit with my laptop in my lap and a notebook and pencil at my side. I can't write sitting up at a desk because my ADD kicks in and I squirm more than I think.

MG: Besides writing do you have any other creative pursuits to cross-train your brain?

LR: I live in Japan, so every day is a cross-training pursuit in communication. I love to binge read novels and binge watch Netflix. On the weekends, we do a lot of travel and sightseeing. I love spending my weekends exploring Japan with my family.

MG: When did you first know you were a writer?

LR: I don't really think of myself as a writer. It's how I introduce myself but I always feel self-conscious doing that. I've always liked writing, starting at age four by making lists of words. That's pretty much what I still do except my vocabulary, thankfully, has expanded a bit.

MG: What aspect of writing do you consider your super power and what do you consider your kryptonite?

LR: Wow. Super power? Hicklit. I'm good at expressing hick speak. Kryptonite would be love scenes. If you notice, in my books strange things happen when the Barry White soundtrack starts playing.

MG: Lastly, leave us with a quote by one of your characters?

LR: "Sometimes it takes a person a few minutes to adjust to my creative ingenuity."— Cherry Tucker

JADEN TERRELL

Jaden Terrell is a Shamus Award finalist and the author of a Nashville-based private detective series featuring natural horseman and former homicide detective Jared McKean. Terrell is a contributor to the *Killer Nashville Noir, Cold-Blooded* short story anthology and to *Now Write! Mysteries*, a collection of exercises published by Tarcher/Penguin for writers of crime fiction. Terrell is Special Programs Coordinator for the Killer Nashville Crime Literature Conference and has served on the National Board of Mystery Writers of America and as president of the Middle Tennessee Chapter of Sisters in Crime. She's also a member of International Thriller Writers and Private Eye Writers of America. The former special education teacher has a red belt in Tae Kwan Do, loves ballroom dancing, and is certified in Equine Sports Massage, which she practices on her two special-needs horses. Website: www.JadenTerrell.com.

SHORT STORY

Rhapsody In Red

The foyer of the apartment building where the dead hooker had lived was dank and smelled sour, a blend of unwashed bodies, stale cigarettes, and rancid cooking odors underlaid with a faint hint of urine. A yellowed sign taped to the elevator doors said, "Out of Order. Please Use Stairs."

Detective Thomas Booker looked from the sign to the narrow, impossibly steep steps, and swallowed a curse. His partner, Ray Coppinger, tapped two fingers against the sign. "Figures."

Booker didn't answer. The victim's apartment was on the fourth floor, and he needed to save his strength. Besides, he didn't care for Coppinger. Booker was a methodical investigator, and Coppinger a wham-bam-thank-you-ma'am kind of guy, a description that characterized both his personal life and his investigative style.

Coppinger rolled his shoulders, flexing muscles so toned they made a carapace across his back. "Okay, Padre. Let's go catch us some bad guys. See if we can wrap this up before the Super Bowl."

Booker ignored the nickname and did the computation. "The Super Bowl is four months away."

"I've seen you work. You think I'm bein' optimistic?"

"Let's just go." Booker stepped aside to let his partner pass.

Coppinger kicked a crumpled beer can out of the way and started up the steps. Booker sucked in a deep breath and plodded after his partner, distracting himself from the climb with thoughts of the case. Coppinger might be right about this one. A dead hooker. How long could it take? Nine times out of ten, a case like this, you'd nail the victim's pimp or drug dealer within a few hours. They'd work the scene, he'd fill out the paperwork—somehow Booker always ended up doing the paperwork—then maybe drop by Waffle House on the way home, see if Jen was working the counter. It beat fried bologna sandwiches and reruns of *Masterpiece Theater*.

By the time they reached the fourth floor, Booker was wheezing. Coppinger shot him a contemptuous look and ducked under the yellow crime scene tape stretched across the doorway of the victim's apartment.

4-C, Booker noted, through sweat-stung eyes.

C is for coronary.

He had to work out more, that was all there was to it. Lift some weights, dig the running shoes out of the bottom of the closet. Coppinger ran six miles a day, and look at him. Not a hint of a flush or a drop of sweat. Booker, on the other hand, was drenched to the bone.

He paused to catch his breath, swiped the sleeve of his coat across his forehead, and edged into the knot of people gathered around the body. Against all odds, the medical examiner was already there, along with the uniforms who'd answered the 911 call and a clot of forensic technicians taking photographs and sliding plastic baggies over the dead woman's hands.

The woman's body sprawled at an unnatural angle, a puddle of blood congealing around her head. He took in the curve of her jaw, the sprinkle of freckles across the bridge of her nose, the smear of mascara beneath each eye. Sallow complexion, scabs on her cheeks, the rotting teeth and bleeding gums narc cops called Meth Mouth. Her eyes were open, the color of peridot.

He jerked his gaze away from her face. His chest felt tight, and he wondered if this was what a heart attack felt like.

Then Coppinger elbowed him in the gut and said, "What's the matter, Padre? You look like you've seen a ghost."

*****

Her name was Giselle Braun, and it had been almost a decade since she'd walked out of Booker's life. He could still conjure the look on her face the day they'd met. She sat alone at a window table in his favorite Armenian restaurant, a little crease forming between her eyebrows as she frowned into the pages of a slender, leather-bound book. In her silk skirt and embroidered blouse, she looked like an Impressionist painting.

She was out of his league, but she glanced up as he passed her table, and he felt heat in his cheeks. His gaze dropped, and he noticed the title of her book. *Metamorphosis.*

"Kafka," he blurted, surprised. "That was my favorite book when I was in high school."

"Really." She smiled and placed her fork carefully on the edge of her plate. "Interesting choice for a teenage boy."

His laugh was a nervous bark. "I suppose I had father issues."

"A man with baggage. Just what every woman wants."

He turned away, embarrassed, then paused, stopped by the touch of her hand on his sleeve.

"Wait," she said. Her smile was a brilliant flash. "Let's see if your baggage likes my baggage."

Three days later, she moved into his apartment.

Three and a half years later, she moved out.

And in between?

He closed his eyes and drew in a long breath. He couldn't think about that yet. Not with her lying in a pool of her own blood, the soft flesh of her inner arm scarred with needle tracks and a network of collapsed veins.

He turned away and had to do a little hopping maneuver to avoid stepping on a broken picture frame. He recognized it, burnished silver with a treble clef symbol etched into one corner. He'd given it to her himself. The frame was bent, the glass shattered. Whatever had been in it was gone.

His eyes burned, and the pain in his chest sharpened. He made a small, broken sound.

"You know her?" asked Coppinger. His smirk made Booker want to put a hollow point through it. "I didn't know you had it in you, Padre."

Booker cleared his throat. "I've seen her around."

The body had been discovered by the victim's eight-year-old daughter, Ariana, who had been at a friend's house for a sleepover the night before. The girl had found the door unlocked and come in to find her mother's body sprawled across the floor of their ransacked apartment. The child had the presence of mind to run to a neighbor's and dial 911.

A daughter, thought Booker. He tried to picture Giselle with a child. Couldn't quite manage it.

Coppinger slapped Booker lightly on the shoulder. "Sounds like a job for you, Padre. Why don't you interview the kid while I canvass the building?"

Booker knew what Coppinger hoped. That in the course of his interviews, he might happen across a youngish woman, not too fat and not too skanky, who might find it exciting—or useful—to make the beast with two backs with a cop.

"Fine." Booker cast a final, despairing glance at the body and turned toward the door, jamming his hands into his pockets. "Don't be all night."

A harried DCS social worker with a bulging briefcase met him in the hall. She was in her mid-forties, built like a wombat and wearing a matching skirt and blazer with a pair of Mennonite-sensible shoes. "You're looking for the little girl?" she asked. "Ariana?"

At his nod, she jerked her head toward the apartment behind her. "The neighbor's willing to keep her for a couple of days. Until we can find a better placement."

"No father?"

She made a dismissive gesture. "Not in the picture."

"Same old, same old."

"Ain't that the truth?" She brushed a strand of mud brown hair away from her forehead. "The neighbor's name is Gleason. Peggy Gleason. Widowed. Place smells like cabbage." She brushed past him, nose wrinkled, as if she carried the stench in her nostrils.

Booker watched her disappear into the stairwell, then rapped twice on the door to Peggy Gleason's apartment. He heard shuffling footsteps. Then the door opened a crack and the stink of the aforementioned cabbage hit him. A wrinkled face glowered at him from behind the chain. Peggy Gleason, he presumed. She had a scowl like Ma Barker's.

He flashed his badge. "Detective Booker. I'd like to speak with Ariana."

"Don't know why you bother," she grumbled. "Like you care about some dead whore."

"I'm not the one who murdered her," he said, more roughly than he'd intended. "So how about cutting me a little slack?"

The door closed, and a moment later, the chain rattled as she slipped it from the lock. She swung the door open and waved toward the living area, where the child sat on a dingy green sofa, drawing something in a cheap newsprint tablet. Her dark hair had fallen across her face, and when he called her name, she looked up and swept back her bangs in a graceful gesture so like Giselle's it almost broke his heart.

Eight years old, pale and slender, with her mother's fine features and the same pale green eyes. He looked for some trace of himself in her, found none. Did the math. Close, but not close enough. He felt a pang of jealousy. This should have been his child.

He sauntered past the widow Gleason and perched on the arm of the couch beside the child. "You like to draw?"

The girl shrugged and nibbled at the tip of her eraser. "I guess."

"May I see?"

She handed him the picture, a woman with long dark curls playing the piano. He didn't know much about children, but he thought it was very good.

He looked at it too long and handed it back reluctantly. "That's your mother. But I didn't see a piano in your apartment."

"She sold it."

The thought of Giselle, bereft of her music, made his chest ache. "She must have really needed the money."

"We always need money." She ducked her head, and the dark hair fell across her face again.

"She was a beautiful woman, your mother," said Booker. "Talented. Smart."

Beneath the curtain of hair, Ariana nodded.

"But she had a problem. And she knew a lot of other people who had problems. And sometimes they might need money, too."

She didn't answer, but there was another slight nod, and he knew she was listening. He went on. "Sometimes they take things that don't belong to them, and sometimes they hurt other people when they do it. Can you tell me if your mother had anything somebody else might have wanted?"

She lifted her head and shook back her hair. "She had some jewelry. Nice jewelry. From her boyfriends."

Boyfriends.

Grimacing, he reached into his pocket for a palm-sized steno tablet and dutifully scrawled the child's descriptions of the jewelry—a pair of diamond earrings, a moonstone necklace, a sapphire and diamond ring he recognized as one he had given Giselle on the anniversary of their first meeting. According to the child, there had been other pieces over the years, but Giselle had eventually sold or pawned them. In addition to the jewelry, she had a wad of cash in an oatmeal canister—two hundred dollars or so. For heroin and groceries, Booker suspected, and just enough rent to keep from being evicted.

He got a name and a description of Giselle's dealer, a jittery, wall-eyed black man who answered to the name of Goose.

"Does he come to your house a lot?" Booker asked the girl. "If he'd knocked, would she have let him in?"

"I guess so. Is that what happened? She let somebody in?"

"The lock wasn't broken, so yeah, it looks that way." He pinched the bridge of his nose and said, "Anybody else she might have let in?"

The girl gnawed at her lower lip. "I have a lot of uncles," she said finally, and counted on her fingers. "Uncle Trey, Uncle Beau, Uncle Jim, Uncle Mack, Uncle Bobby."

"These uncles..."

"They aren't really uncles," she said.

Booker winced at the knowledge in the girl's voice. She described the uncles in a flat, dull tone too old for her years. Uncle Trey was the married CEO of an investment company. Uncle Beau was an architect, Uncle Jim a computer programmer, Uncle Mack the manager of a local Food Mart. Uncle Mack was Ariana's favorite; he brought her drawing pads and colored pencils and talked to her like she was a real person. Uncle Bobby was a studio musician who supplemented his income by writing and composing advertising jingles.

"Would you like to hear one?" she asked. At his nod, she clasped her hands in her lap and sang:

"If sleepless nights have got you down,
And all you do is toss around,
Just take a swig of Rest-in-Ease
And wake refreshed as a cool breeze."

The laugh burst out of him without warning. "God. That's dreadful."

"It is!" She seemed pleased with his assessment. "But he thinks he's wonderful. Do you want me to sing another one?"

She was on the third jingle when there was another knock at the door, and Coppinger burst in, grinning like he'd won the lottery. "Say goodbye to the kid and get your coat, Padre. I just solved this one."

"What do you mean, you solved it?" asked Booker. "Just like that?"

"Nothing to it." Coppinger jammed his hands in his pockets and put on his *aw-shucks* look. "Lady upstairs was bringing in her groceries when this junkie whore runs past her covered in blood and carrying a pillowcase."

Beside Booker, Ariana gasped and pressed her hand to her mouth. Booker patted her knee and gave her what he hoped was a reassuring smile. To Coppinger, he said, "Why wait until now to say anything? Why didn't she call the police then?"

"Around here? You got sunstroke, Padre? Or, the way you were huffing and puffing all the way up here, maybe just a stroke."

Booker ignored the insult. Coppinger was right about one thing, anyway. This was the kind of neighborhood where nobody ever saw anything. "This junkie. She got a name?"

"LeVeaux. Shiraine LeVeaux."

"No," the girl said. "Shiraine wouldn't hurt Mom. She sleeps on our couch sometimes, when her boyfriend beats her up."

Coppinger shrugged. "You never know, with junkies. Come on, Booker. I want to put this thing to bed before midnight."

"Just one more thing." Booker turned back to the girl. "There was a silver picture frame on the floor beside—" He caught himself. "A silver frame. The picture inside was missing. Can you tell me what was in it?"

"Music," she said, bending over her drawing. "Like this."

Her pencil flew across the page, a storm of musical notes with sharp, dagger-like tails. With a final flourish, she held it up to him, and the title she had scrawled across the page struck him like an arrow.

"Rhapsody in Red," it said. Giselle's most prized—and macabre—possession. And he had given her that, too.

"You know what this is?" he asked the girl.

Her nod was solemn. "It belonged to her music teacher. The one who got murdered."

In October of their final year together, Giselle's mentor and former professor, a well-known composer and pianist named Walter Koresky, had been bludgeoned to death in his Belle Meade mansion. DNA tests indicated two blood types, the professor's and— presumably—his killer's. Among the pieces of evidence admitted was a blood-spattered folder filled with sheet music, including two pages of a new composition, "Rhapsody in Red."

The irony of the title was lost on no one.

Booker shook his head, started to ask another question.

In the doorway, Coppinger shifted his weight impatiently. "Come on, Padre. We're burnin' daylight."

*****

They found the hooker—Shiraine, Booker reminded himself—sprawled across the sofa, glassy-eyed. On the coffee table in front of her lay a syringe, a plastic bag of whitish powder, and a pawn shop receipt for a pair of diamond earrings, a necklace, and a sapphire and diamond tea ring.

"Got something," he said, as Coppinger poked his head into the kitchen.

"Got something here, too," said Coppinger, from the next room. "Jeans and a sweatshirt soaking in the sink. And that ain't rust in the water."

*****

"I ain't killed nobody." Shiraine, crashing and cranky, slapped her palms on the table and flipped her long blond cornrows over her shoulder. "She was dead when I got there."

"Sure she was," said Coppinger. "And I got a nice little statue in New York harbor I can sell you real cheap."

Booker shot Coppinger a look, and Coppinger crumpled his empty coffee cup in his fist and stalked from the room. "I'll watch through the two-way," he said, and slammed the door behind him.

Booker turned his attention back to Shiraine. "If she was dead when you got there," he said, "why were you covered in her blood?"

"I was tryin' to see was she still alive. She was my best friend, case you didn't catch that part of it."

"We caught it," said Booker. "We just didn't get the part about why, when you found your best friend lying on her floor in a pool of her own blood, your first instinct was to steal her blind."

"She didn't need that stuff no more."

"Did you ever think to leave it for that little girl?"

She looked away, eyes red and watery. "She was gonna be rich. That's what Giselle said. Gonna be set for life."

"Really."

"Said she knew some things worth big bucks. Secrets."

"Whose secrets?"

She shrugged. "We was friends, not business partners."

Booker said, "What happened to the music?"

She cocked her head, brow furrowed. "What music?"

"In her picture frame. It was just a piece of paper with some music notes on it. It wasn't in your apartment, and it wasn't listed on the pawn receipt, so where is it?"

She gave a sharp little laugh. "What the hell I want with that shit? You can't eat it, can't sell it, you can't even get high on it. So what the hell good is it to me?"

"True enough," Booker said, through clenched teeth. "One more question. Why didn't you try to save her?"

"I did try to save her," said Shiraine. "How you think I got her blood all over me?"

*****

"She's telling the truth," said Booker, when Shiraine had been returned to her cell. "She doesn't know about the music."

Coppinger blew out an exasperated breath. "You got a junkie whore running from the scene, covered in blood, carrying a pillowcase full of the victim's jewelry, and you want to fuck up a slam-dunk case because of a scrap of paper with little black scribbles on it?"

"She didn't do it. Don't you think we ought to find out who did?"

Coppinger threw up his hands. "You want to play Nancy Drew? Fine. Play away. But I'm going home to my wife, my kids, and my big screen TV, and come Monday, I'm filing my report. And if you don't have anything more to go on than some crazy idea about sheet music, we're closing the case. The vic is nobody, Padre. Just some dead hooker."

Booker looked down at his hands, but he kept his mouth shut, because a day ago, he might have been the one closing the file on Nobody. A schizophrenic homeless man doused in gasoline and set on fire by a couple of kids from good neighborhoods. A used-up prostitute slashed by her pimp and left in a dumpster.

They were all Giselles to someone. And if they weren't, they should be.

He sighed and picked up the file. He needed sleep, but what was it Hamlet had said? *To sleep, perchance to dream...Aye, there's the rub.* He didn't think his dreams tonight would be the pleasant kind.

At one o'clock, Jen called. "I just got off and tried your place. Since you didn't answer, I thought you might be working late. Tough day?"

"You could say that."

"I'll be up for a while," she said. "There's beer in the fridge."

"Rain check, okay?"

"Okay. But if you change your mind, you know where I keep the key."

"I'll probably end up working most of the night. I'm sorry."

"It's okay. What you're doing, it's important."

Giselle had thought so too, at first. He could still feel the warmth of her fingers as she smoothed the front of his shirt and called him her hero. Then, somehow, things changed. He'd come home late, exhausted by death and bleary from lack of sleep, and she'd meet him at the door—drunk or high, or maybe just crazy—pounding at his chest and flailing at him with fists and nails. "You stupid son of a bitch. Running yourself ragged for the cost of a PB&J? Who do you think you are, some kind of fucking white knight?"

He'd hold her wrists and absorb her fury, his tongue like stone in his mouth.

Yes, he thought but did not say. *Yes*.

*****

He said goodbye to Jen and hung up, wondering why he'd blown her off like that. Jen was a good kid, but hell, she thought Camus was the name of the killer whale at Sea World. He wished that didn't bother him.

God—almost a decade, and he still missed those long, intense discussions with Giselle, the ones that started with a glass of

wine on the sofa and ended up with the two of them in bed,
drunk with alcohol and ideas, consumed by literature and lust.
Dostoevsky and the Russian masters, Renaissance art, Schopenhauer,
a priori knowledge and Immanuel Kant.

He pushed the thought away and picked up the file again.
Made himself pore over every photograph, every interview.

The super had seen a man in a knit scarf, ski mask, and
hooded jacket go upstairs maybe a half an hour before Giselle was
killed. Maybe that meant something, maybe it didn't—the wind had
been bitter that day, and a lot of people were wearing scarves and ski
masks.

He closed the file and sat there for a long time, thinking.
Always before, he'd known she was out there, somewhere. Now the
world felt suddenly empty. *He* felt empty.

He thought of the picture frame, and his throat closed.
Giselle had wanted to play classical piano, not the generic dreck that
passed for music these days, and Booker was happy to pull in the
paycheck while she attended classes and played her music. If their
living conditions were modest, he hardly noticed. He was a man of
few needs.

He failed to see—or maybe didn't want to see—the dilated
pupils, the insomnia, the wild fluctuations between mania and
depression. She stopped taking studio gigs, mainly because she'd
stopped getting offers. Her talent was prodigious, but not even
beauty and talent could compensate for her erratic behavior. If she
showed up at all, she was just as likely to call the featured artist a

cocksucking bastard as to shake his hand, as likely to stalk out of
the session as sit down at the keyboard.

She would come home an hour before dawn, reeking of
liquor and sex, sobbing hysterically and begging him to forgive her.
And because of the other times—times spent watching her long
fingers fly over the piano keys, feeding her strawberries on the back
porch of his parents' house, kissing her eyelids after a long night of
lovemaking—he always did.

Maybe she could have pulled herself together, gotten
counseling, gone into rehab. Maybe he could have pulled some
strings, gotten her into a good program. Then Professor Koresky was
murdered.

Giselle took it hard. Her career was in shards, her friend
and mentor murdered, and to top it all off, on that very same night,
another friend and former classmate had been mugged and robbed,
his eyes blacked and his nose broken. Giselle met him for lunch the
next day and, later, lay in Booker's arms and sobbed. "Poor RJ. He
looked like he'd been smashed in the face with a shovel. What the
hell is wrong with the world?"

While the folder languished in the evidence room,
Koresky's widow found the first page of "Rhapsody in Red" in her
husband's composition book. It was recorded as "Unfinished
Rhapsody" and hailed as the composer's most brilliant work.

A few days later, a young Kurdish man with a history of
petty crimes was arrested for Koresky's murder. The boy was
convicted—despite a shortage of evidence and a prosecution case a

six-year-old could have punched holes in—and sentenced to sixty years; he'd be an old man by the time he came up for parole. It was a high profile crime, and there was pressure from the top to close the file, and fast.

Booker was grateful the case wasn't his. But when Koresky's widow died of heart failure and the Kurdish boy was shanked in the prison shower, Booker called in a favor and slipped both bloodstained pages of "Rhapsody in Red" out of the evidence room. He mounted them in a brushed silver frame and had a treble clef engraved on it. It was a macabre gift—he knew that—but he also knew Giselle would love it. She was fascinated by such things.

*****

He stopped on the way home for a box of Krispy Kremes, the glazed kind, still warm from the oven. How stereotypical could you get? He was pushing the outer limits of the weight requirement, maybe even crept a few pounds past, but what the hell? He'd go low-carb tomorrow, make up for it.

At home, he dropped the half-empty Krispy Kreme box on the table and headed for the bedroom, tugging off his navy silk tie. He opened the closet door, and a blaze of color greeted him. Silk ties, over a hundred. Salvador Dali's melting watches; Van Gogh's starry night and other famous paintings; a series of wildlife designs; scenes from Casablanca, the Three Stooges, old horror movies; and a slew of Warner Brothers cartoon characters. Giselle, who'd teased him about his staid attire, had given them to him, the first a strip of blue silk emblazoned with scarlet and blue-and-gold macaws.

"I love it," he'd said, and she laughed.

"You'll never wear it."

"I love it anyway."

And he did. Each morning, he took a few minutes to stand in front of the closet and look at his ties. And then, every morning, he reached for the navy.

*****

On Saturday, he got to work early and made some calls to a couple of snitches. By the time his coffee was cold, he'd gotten a lead on Giselle's dealer.

Goose had set up operations in front of a shabby little soul restaurant called *Like Mama's*. A pair of thin wires connected ear buds to an MP3 player clipped to Goose's belt. The dealer's eyes were closed as he bucked and gyrated to imperceptible music.

Booker jerked the buds from Goose's ears. The dealer's eyes snapped open, and he drew back a fist as if to throw a punch.

Booker smiled in a way he knew was not pleasant. "Better watch yourself, friend."

Goose's good eye focused on the badge in Booker's other hand. He dropped his fist to his side. "Shit, man, you gonna give me a heart attack."

"The condition of your heart doesn't concern me, Goose."

The dealer fluttered his hands in front of his face. "I don't want no trouble."

"Then we should get along just fine. You deal to a woman named Giselle? You'd remember her—looks like a Bouguereau angel."

"What are you, some kind of professor?" Goose tipped his head so that his wall eye faced Booker. "Cause you sure don't talk like a cop."

"But I am a cop. So I suggest you answer my question. Do you sell to a woman named Giselle?"

Goose chewed at his lower lip. Booker could see him weighing his options. Booker knew he didn't look like much, a little bit balding, a little bit overweight, but he had the badge, and the bulge of his Glock was visible beneath his jacket.

Goose sighed and shuffled his feet. "Hey, man, she gonna get it somewhere. I don't give it to her, she just gonna get it somewhere else. Maybe somebody worse than me, somebody treat her bad."

"She's dead, you dumbass. Can't get much worse than that."

"Dead!" Goose looked genuinely surprised. "Since when?"

"Since yesterday."

"Huh. Can't put this on me, then. I was in jail yesterday. Just got kicked this morning."

Booker's stomach sank. "You know I'll check."

"You do that."

Booker would have liked nothing better than to kick the wall-eyed bastard's scrawny ass all the way to Brushy Mountain, so he was both angry and depressed when Goose's alibi panned out.

By Saturday afternoon, he'd tracked down and interviewed the Uncles. Uncle Trey, concerned primarily with the fear that his wife might discover his indiscretion, kept Booker shivering on the porch while he fetched hotel receipts and airline ticket stubs to prove he'd been at a business conference in Las Vegas. Bobby, the jingle writer, invited Booker in and showed him ticket stubs and a program for a symphony matinee. While Bobby rummaged through his desk drawer for the tickets, Booker plinked a tune on a Steinway upright piano.

Bobby looked up, program and tickets in hand. "Giselle used to play that song."

"A lot better than this, I assume."

"You assume right, man. She was a great talent."

Jim the computer programmer and Beau the architect also had alibis—a handball game and a dozen witnesses at the office, respectively—and Mack was too genuinely distraught to have been anything but innocent.

"What happens to Ariana?" Mack asked, when he could finally speak.

"We don't know that yet," said Booker.

"I could take her in," said Mack. At Booker's hard look, he hastened to add, "Or maybe my sister could. She has two girls of her own."

Mack remembered the framed sheet music, but shook his head in genuine bewilderment when asked if he knew of anyone who might have wanted to steal it. As for secrets, you could never tell, but

Booker would have bet money that the only secret Mack had ever had was Giselle herself.

*****

Booker liked to think that, even without the baby, he would have asked Giselle to marry him. The pink line of the pregnancy test had simply pushed his timeline forward. But when he presented her with the ring, she stared at it dumbly and then pushed it away.

"What's the matter?" he said. "We're good together."

"That's no reason."

"I love you," he said. "How's that for a reason?"

Her hands balled into fists. "What kind of world is this to bring a baby into? Look what happened to Professor K. And to RJ. You know what it's like. You see it every day."

"So we make it better."

"And what about my career? I'm not giving everything up for a thing the size of a jellybean."

He wanted to say she didn't have a career, that she had thrown it away for a fleeting high, but he didn't want to fight with her. Fighting never helped with Giselle. Instead, he said, "Honey, it's just seven more months. Then we can look into day care. Or we could scrimp a little, hire an *au pair*."

Her laugh was derisive. "You. An *au pair*. And what will you pay her with? Your bright and shining armor?"

Five weeks later, he came home to find her huddled beneath a crocheted afghan, her knees drawn up to her chest, her eyes swollen and rimmed with red.

He bent down and pressed his lips to her forehead. "Hard day?"

She nodded, almost imperceptibly.

"How's our jellybean?"

A tear trickled down her cheek. "There is no jellybean."

"What?"

"There. Is. No. Jellybean," she repeated. "No baby. I got it taken care of."

Taken care of. For a moment, the air seemed to have been sucked from the room. "You didn't even talk to me about it?"

She picked at a fingernail, flaked off a chip of cherry red polish and flicked it away. "It wasn't your decision."

"It was my child too."

"It wasn't a child," she said. "It wasn't anything. A tiny blob of cells."

But he knew better. At thirteen weeks, it had a heartbeat of its own, a nervous system, brain waves. At thirteen weeks, it could feel pain.

More than that, it had been his chance to toss a ball around in the backyard, build a tree-fort, take his son—or daughter—to a Titans game. All the things he'd never done with his own father but might have done with his child. And she had robbed him of them.

Through sheer force of will, they kept their relationship together for six more months. He found himself thinking of the child. Would it have been a boy or a girl? Would it have had her eyes? His hair? He imagined himself reading his daughter a bedtime story, taking his son fishing, though he had never been fishing a day in his life.

Lovemaking was perfunctory. A few bitter couplings. The last time, he'd rolled out of bed and gone for a walk. When he came home, she was gone.

He wished he'd gone after her. He wished a lot of things. He only heard from her one time after that, and he remembered that late-night call with shame. The phone rang and rang, as he lay on the couch and let the machine pick up. "Hey, Booker. I wondered if...um...I thought you might want to...that maybe we could..." There were tears in her voice. He thought he might die if she kept on.

And then he was on his feet, reaching for the phone, and she was saying, "Oh hell, never mind," and he was left holding the receiver, tears streaming down his face as he listened to the dial tone.

*****

Two days ago, if anyone had asked Booker what his greatest strength was, he would have said patience. Methodical and plodding, as ordinary as dirt, he had always identified with the cartoon turtle who always somehow beat the hare: *I may be suh-low, but I'm sure.*

Today, though, he felt anything but patient. He forced himself to take his time, review the file again, do detailed background checks on each of Ariana's Uncles.

A dull throb began at his temples, and he swallowed two aspirins dry and chased them with a cream cheese Danish from the vending machine. He rummaged through his desk and found a CD

Giselle had made for him a thousand years ago, leaned back in his chair and listened to her playing Mozart's "Piano Sonata No. 11" and Liszt's "Dream Song." Then "Rhapsody in Red" came on, and he closed his eyes and let the music roll over him. He listened to it half a dozen times, then ejected the CD.

The room went suddenly silent. Nothing but tick of the heater and the hum of the lights. Exactly how a world without Giselle should sound.

He turned back to the files.

Just after lunch, he struck, if not gold, at least pyrite. Robert "Bobby" James Glassman, composer of advertising jingles, had once been a student of Walter Koresky.

Booker closed his eyes and called up a memory. Giselle in his arms, sobbing, "Poor RJ. He looked like he'd been smashed in the face with a shovel."

RJ. Robert James.

By three o'clock, he was at the performing arts center, handing a limited warrant to a pert blond behind the information desk.

"Robert James Glassman," he said. "I need to know what seat he was in and if his ticket was redeemed."

She tapped something into her computer. "Just...one...sec. Okaaay. Here it is. F-22. Yes, sir. It looks like he redeemed his ticket."

"Just one ticket?"

"Yes, sir. It looks like he was alone."

"And the people on either side of him?"

"Just a moment, and I'll get you those names."

*****

Two calls, less than five minutes each.

"This is Detective Thomas Booker, homicide."

A few lines of small talk, then, "Do you remember the symphony matinee yesterday?"

"Yes. Of course."

"Seat F-22. Was anyone in it?"

"Oh, yes. But he must have gotten ill, because he left right after the performance started."

"And when did he come back?"

"He never did."

*****

"You can't prove anything," said Bobby Glassman. For the fourth time, he took off his glasses and rubbed them with the tail of his shirt.

"Why? Because you wore gloves and burned the evidence?" Booker waved a music composition tablet at the prisoner. "You forgot to burn this."

"That doesn't mean anything. I compose music. That's what I do."

"You compose drivel," said Booker. "Except for this." He flipped through the tablet until he found a familiar composition. "You left off the name, but this is 'Rhapsody in Red.'"

"Correction. The first page is 'Rhapsody in Red'. The second page is original. I wanted to see if I could finish it."

"I have a recording in my office," said Booker. "It's a recording of Giselle playing both pages of 'Rhapsody in Red.'"

"Both—"

"The page Professor Koresky's widow found, and the second page, the one she never saw because it was locked in the evidence room. Shall we see if Giselle's recording matches your composition?"

Glassman's shoulders slumped. "That won't be necessary."

"Was that how she knew you'd killed Professor Koresky? Because she saw your composition book?"

"Heard me whistling it." Glassman shook his head. "Stupid."

"And then she realized why you said you'd been mugged the night Koresky died. Because the two of you struggled, and he bloodied your nose. Giselle figured it out, tried to blackmail you, so you killed her. But why take the music?"

A vein in Glassman's neck bulged. "Because it was mine!"

"Yours..." Booker bowed his head, understanding.

"It was the best thing I ever wrote. The only decent thing I ever wrote. And that son of a bitch stole it."

"But his widow had the song recorded. You could never claim it again anyway," said Booker. "You killed him for nothing. You killed them both for nothing."

*****

He didn't expect to see Shiraine again, but on Monday morning, there she was, resplendent in a hot pink Spandex mini-dress and four-inch, leopard-print heels. "I got something for you," she said, and tossed an envelope onto his desk. "Giselle said anything ever happened to her, I should look you up and give you this."

He picked the envelope up. Turned it over in his hands. "Thank you."

"That makes us even." She sashayed away, an exaggerated swing in her hips that made him smile in spite of himself.

When she had gone, he took the envelope outside and climbed into his car. It was cold, but he didn't bother with the heat.

Instead, he turned on the radio, found the classical station, and leaned back against the seat. He closed his eyes and let the music fill him.

When he felt calm enough, he opened his eyes.

Then he opened the envelope.

Inside was Giselle's diploma from the music academy, a valentine Booker had given her, a homemade CD of her music, and a birth certificate.

"Ariana Nicole Braun," it said.

He looked at the next line.

Father, it said. *Thomas Booker.*

He looked at it for a long time. Did the math again, and came to the same conclusion.

Then he drove home in a haze and made another call.

*****

For the second time that weekend, Booker rapped on Peggy Gleason's door.

He tugged at the macaw tie, which seemed conspicuously bright.

Inside, Giselle's daughter sat on the sofa, hands clasped in her lap, a scuffed duffel bag at her feet. She looked like she'd been waiting for a long time.

He pushed aside the coffee table and knelt beside the couch. "Ariana," he said. "I'm your . . ." He stopped. He could lie to the case worker—and would, if it came to that—but he couldn't lie to the girl.

But was it a lie? Wasn't a father more than blood and DNA?

"I know who you are," she said. She touched a finger to the bright strip of color at his chest and said, "I like this tie."

"I like it too," he said, and held out his hand.

EXCERPT

River of Glass

"This third Jared McKean mystery is a worthy successor to *Racing the Devil* and *A Cup Full of Midnight*...with a tough yet sympathetic protagonist who goes to all ends for friends and family. Solid plotting and well-drawn characters make this a series to add to any hardboiled-mystery reader's list." — **Michele Leber, Booklist**

"Even at close to 300 pages, this book was one of those rare novels that are fast-paced and moved so smoothly I read it in one sitting. The reader is pulled into the story from the first page, and the author keeps you spellbound to the last exciting page. I loved it. Highly recommended." **—Tom Johnson, Detective Mystery Stories and Pulp Den**

The storm blew itself out around midnight, and by dawn, a new bank of clouds had rolled in. They filled the sky from horizon to horizon, gray and roiling, swollen with rain. A few scattered drops fell throughout the day, as if God were spitting on us.

That afternoon, I put on my father's leather bomber jacket, locked my elderly quarter horse in the paddock, saddled my Tennessee Walker, and rode out into the woods behind the house. The air was cool and damp, thick with the smells of mud and moss, the mulchy scent of deadwood, and the occasional far-off whiff of skunk. The trail twisted like a copperhead, littered with broken branches and mottled with gray light.

The wind rose and rattled the leaves. Crockett tossed his head and picked up his pace, hoof beats muted by the rain-softened earth. When I gave him his head, he slipped into a running walk, hips lifting and falling as his hind legs stretched beneath him in a smooth, ground-covering gait.

He faltered at a side trail, turned his head toward it. The underbrush made the trail seem darker there, the air somehow less clean. Crockett drifted toward it, but I'd had my fill of darkness. I nudged him forward and past, into a band of sunlight.

Somewhere to my right, the wheeze of Frank Campanella's Crown Vic broke the stillness like a chainsaw in the wilderness. I knew it was Frank, even without benefit of sight. He'd had the Vic long before he and I had worked homicides for Metro Nashville's now-defunct Murder Squad, probably before I'd graduated from the academy at nineteen, possibly since before I was born.

A thousand scenarios flashed through my mind—car crashes and drownings and God-knew-what-else involving my son, my ex-wife, my nieces, my brother and his estranged wife . . . Frank was my friend, but there was no good reason for him to show up at my home unannounced.

Dread closing my throat, I turned my horse and urged him toward the house.

When I rode out of the woods, Frank was on the porch, a glass of lemonade in his hand, my friend and housemate, Jay Renfield, hovering anxiously beside him. I'd known Jay since kindergarten, and our friendship had survived both his revelation that he was gay and his ongoing struggle with AIDS.

Frank looked up as I bent to open the pasture gate. He said something to Jay, set his glass down on the porch railing, and started down the steps. By the time I led Crockett across the pasture and into the barn, Frank was waiting for me.

He was a cinder block of a man, shoulders straining against his regulation suit. Square jaw, bristling eyebrows, silvering hair. He ran a hand through it, leaving a ruffled patch above one ear. Then he gave me an awkward man hug and said, "How you doing, Cowboy?"

I gave his back a thump and turned back to loosen the latigo of Crockett's saddle. "You didn't come here to ask me how I'm doing."

"No, but now that I'm here, the question has crossed my mind."

"I'm fine," I said. "Or was, until you stopped by."

"I'll try not to take that personally."

"It's not personal. You know what they say about shooting the messenger. You have your bad news face on."

"I have a bad news face?"

"It's like your regular face, but squintier."

He let that pass. "Did you go to the office today?"

"What are you, the office police?" I tugged the cinch loose and lifted the saddle and pad from Crockett's back. There was a saddle-shaped patch of sweat beneath. I ran my hand over it, checking for tenderness, and found none. "I did a skip trace and a couple of background checks. Nothing I couldn't do from here."

He cocked his head. Gave me a narrow look. "Skip traces. Background checks."

"It's honest work. Pays well. Plus, I can do it from my couch."

"You're wasted on it." He jammed his hands into his pockets, pretended to study Crockett's saddle. "Jared, what happened to Josh wasn't your fault."

A vision of my nephew lying limp in a tub of bloody water shot a sharp pain through my temples. If I'd done things differently . . .

"I know that," I said. "But you didn't come here to tell me that, either."

He looked pained, but let it pass. "A situation's come up. Malone asked me to come by and ask you to take a look at a crime scene. A courtesy."

"From me to her, or from her to me?"

"From the department to you," he said. "And vice versa."

"Paul has a Cub Scout meeting tonight." I slung the saddle over the saddle rack and looked pointedly at my watch. "I'm just about to go pick him up."

Frank shook his head, his lips pressed tight.

"Aw, shit," I said.

He held out a clear plastic evidence bag, and in it was a sepia-toned Vietnam-era photo of a young guy in fatigues, a small Asian girl on his shoulders and an infant in his arms. The photo was creased, as if it had been crumpled in a fist, and there was a rust-colored stain on one corner. He flipped it over, and I saw another stain, like a bloody thumbprint, across the back. Scrawled in pencil beneath the thumbprint was a phone number and address. My office number and address.

"What's this?" I said.

"You know who this is?"

"Of course I know who it is." The crooked grin, the shock of buckskin-colored hair, the slant of the jaw . . . I saw them every day in the photo on my bedside table, saw similar features in the mirror every morning. So like him, my mother used to say, and trace my cheekbones with her thumbs.

I reached for the bag, as if a closer look might prove me wrong, and after a moment he handed it over.

"You know the routine," he said. "Don't open it."

I knew the routine. I looked at the picture, smoothing the plastic over the photo with my thumb to reduce the glare.

"Where'd you get it?"

"We got a call, one of those Strip-o-Gram girls works downstairs in your building."

I worked out of an office on the top floor of a former boarding house. One of the downstairs offices belonged to a grandmotherly type who ran a call-out strip business. Bachelor parties. Birthday parties. Boys' nights at the office.

"They prefer to be called women now," I said, because I couldn't think of anything else to say. "Or so I'm told."

"This one looked like a girl," Frank said. "Eighteen, nineteen, maybe. But then, they all look young to me these days. She went out to toss a trash bag in the dumpster—guy who works on the second floor carried it out for her—and when they opened it, there was a dead woman inside. Asian." He nodded toward the photo in the evidence bag. "That was in her hand."

"That's not possible."

"And yet, there it is. So what we need to know—what I came here to ask you—is why there's a dead girl in your dumpster with a picture of your father in her hand?"

Michael Guillebeau: We've tried to put together a wide variety of stories in this collection. What kind of reader should give your stuff a shot?

Jaden Terrell: I'd say my work appeals to readers who like their stories dark but not bleak. Narayan Radhakrishnan, of *New Mystery Review*, said of my first novel, "The book is not noir, but it has a noir feel," while Sheila Deeth, who reviews for Café Libre and is an excellent author in her own right, called the series "the perfect combination of noir and human hope." The world can be dark at times, but as human beings, we have the ability to make it better.

MG: Tell us a little about how your writing has evolved?

JT: I started as a fantasy writer, but while I was still learning the craft, I fell in love with Jared McKean, the hero of my private detective novels. That was the series that attracted interest from agents and publishers, so the fantasy went on the back burner. My first attempt at *Racing the Devil* was abysmal. I was lucky enough to get an agent right away and some very encouraging rejections because I was strong enough at character development to obscure the fact that there was hardly any plot. It was just a coat hanger to put this elaborate character sketch on. But since I believed in the story and the characters, I kept revising it, adding scenes and distilling the character development until eventually, the Permanent Press picked it up. It was short-listed for a Shamus award, which was extremely validating, considering how far it had come.

I think I've gotten better at the craft as a whole over the years. At least, I hope I have. Writing is one of those things where there's always more to learn. Every book has a different challenge. In *A Cup Full of Midnight*, which was inspired by the "vampire" murders in Kentucky several years ago, the challenge was dealing with intensely emotional situations while weaving together the main plot and several subplots that echo the main themes. The next book, *River of Glass*, is about human trafficking. Two of the biggest challenges in that one were building the relationship between Jared and his newly discovered half-sister and keeping the tension high as they pursue inevitable dead ends. It's the first book that has scenes from a point of view other than Jared's, to show the perspective of the young woman being held captive.

MG: Which writers inspire you? Which writers do you think your books are like? Who do you wish they were like?

JT: Readers who like Robert Crais, Steven Womack, Dennis Lehane (especially his Kenzie and Gennaro novels), and Jonathan Kellerman would probably enjoy mine, even though I don't claim to be as good as those guys, who are all favorites and inspirations to me. I wish I could use description and characterization as well as S.J. Rozan,

Michael Connelly, Lawrence Block, William Kent Krueger and
Timothy Hallinan. John Connolly's prose is so lyrical sometimes it
just makes me want to weep because I know I'll never be that good.
For dialogue, action, and stripped-down, punchy prose, I love Lee
Child. And J.K. Rowling's Robert Galbraith books have rich and
beautiful characterizations. I go back to all these authors again and
again to see how they handle transitions, how they use dialogue, how
they weave in interior monologue, and so on. I read their books once
for pleasure and then over and over again to try and parse out how
they make the magic.

I read outside the genre as well—J.R.R. Tolkien, George
R.R. Martin, and J.V. Jones, just to name a few. I try to learn from
everybody.

MG: Why do you write the kind of stories you write?

JT: I think we often write about what we love, what we fear, and what
we don't understand. When I was 18, my father was killed. At the
time, we thought it was suicide, but we learned later that it was more
likely murder. We never got a definitive answer about what happened
or why, and at this point, we never will. Real life is messy that way,
but in fiction, you always know. The bad guys get caught, and the
world is put right. You can explore the *why*. Of course, Dad's death
isn't the only reason I write what I do. The high-stakes situations
intensify a character's emotions and make the genre a perfect vehicle

for exploring what people become when everything they love is at risk.

MG: What is your best marketing tip?

JT: Try only to do things you would be glad to have done, even if they didn't result in a single sale.

MG: What are you working on now? What is your next project?

JT: It's the fourth book in the Jared McKean series. It's called *A Taste of Blood and Ashes*, and it's about the Tennessee Walking Horse soring controversy.

MG: If you were a super hero, what would your name be? What costume would you wear? What would your superpower be?

JT: My super hero name would be Swan Song. I'd wear either all black or all white, with a flowing cape of feathers (only molted feathers; no swans would actually be hurt in the making of this costume). I'd be able to sing magic, especially healing and protective magic.

MG: Do you dream? Do you have any recurring dreams/nightmares?

JT: I have spectacularly vivid dreams, but I'm rarely in them. There's usually a point-of-view character who acts as a protagonist, and I understand that I'm this person, but watching the action from outside, like a movie. Some of them are fully formed stories, and I give them titles, like "The Polar Bear King," in which two children go to the Winter World to ask the Polar Bear King to put the world in balance by making it snow in Africa or "God's Shadow," in which a community's faith makes them invisible to an invading army of barbarians. I rarely have nightmares, and when I do, they often turn into something else. "Cloudy with a Chance of Zombies" started as a horror story about zombies attacking humans and ended with a musical montage in which humans and zombies lived together in peace. I don't know what they did about their need for brains, but somehow it all worked out.

LISA WYSOCKY

It is obvious that Lisa Wysocky loves both books and horses! As an author and motivational speaker who trains horses for and consults with therapeutic riding programs, she stays really busy, but wouldn't have it any other way.

Her debut mystery, *The Opium Equation*, is an equestrian cozy mystery set near Nashville, Tennessee and features an unlikely cast of characters including a (possibly) psychic horse. The book won four awards, including a Mom's Choice award for fiction. The sequel, *The Magnum Equation*, won Best Equine-related Book from the American Horse Publications, the first time a fiction book had been awarded such an honor.

Lisa is a PATH International therapeutic riding instructor and has been chosen as one of the country's Top 50 riding instructors by ARIA. Her book *Therapy Horse Selection* helps horse owners who are considering donating their horse to a therapy program understand what kind of horse a therapeutic riding center might need, and also helps centers find horses for their programs.

SHORT STORY

Searching for Bubba

"Cat?" Darcy's voice at the end of the barn aisle was dead calm, and that alone made my insides crawl. One of my top riding students, Darcy was usually a high-strung and excitable high school senior.

"In here," I said. I was in a stall untangling the tail of Sally Blue, a young Appaloosa mare who some people claimed was psychic.

"Frog Berry just called my cell. He saw Bubba."

This was the news we had been waiting for, but I tried not to get too excited. At sixteen, Frog Berry had been in jail more often than he'd been home. He also has a thing for Darcy and thought his missing front tooth and spiky, multi-colored Mohawk were sexy. In my book, for those reasons alone, he couldn't be trusted. I glanced at Sally to see if she had any psychic reaction to this news, but she just blinked.

Darcy anticipated my question. "Frog saw him this morning, near the Walmart in West Nashville."

Our eleven-year-old neighbor, Bubba Henley, had run away from home for what must have been the ba-zillionth time. Considering the kind of person his dad was, I couldn't say I blamed him, but an eleven-year-old did not need to be out on the street. I really did hope that Frog had seen Bubba, but past experience made me dubious. "Was Frog sure?"

"Very sure. Remember that Frog and Bubba are friends. Well, sort of. But Frog certainly knows what Bubba looks like." Darcy paused. "You think Frog was lying?" she asked.

I gave her a look.

"Like I know Frog maybe just wants attention, but he gave me a lot of detail that he's not smart enough to make up on his own."

"Such as?" I untangled the last few strands of Sally's tail, gave her a pat, and closed the stall door.

"Frog said Bubba was behind that pizza place next to Walmart and he was talking to a thin, blond girl wearing a torn, brown hoodie."

A cold spear of ice ran through me. That area housed a number of homeless men and women. Most were peaceful, down-on-their-luck people, but some had been known to be dangerous.

"What was Frog doing in West Nashville?" I asked.

"Driving through with his dad on his way to court. He saw Bubba from the road. Cat, can you go get him? Bubba annoys me, but he's just a kid."

Darcy had recently moved in with me. Her mother lived overseas and her dad ran a huge Internet publishing business. With only Ruby the housekeeper at home most days, Darcy must have thought I was better company. I was surprised that I didn't mind having her in my extra bedroom. Usually, I was a solitary sort.

"You know the Nashville cops won't go look just on Frog's word," said Darcy. "And even if they did, by the time they got out there he could be all the way across town."

Darcy was right. Plus, I knew that kids grew up fast when they were homeless. I didn't want Bubba to have that kind of education.

"Yes," I said, putting my arm around her as we headed down the aisle. "I'll look for him."

*****

Bubba's dad was Hill Henley, a no-account, white trash trainer of Tennessee Walking Horses who lived two farms away. Bubba's mother had run off a number of years ago, and Hill often left Bubba alone in their aging double-wide, which was decorated in a tattered Confederate flag motif. Knowing Hill, life was probably better for Bubba when Hill wasn't there.

I thought of the irony. Bubba had risked his life to save mine earlier in the year. Now maybe it was my turn to save his, although I hoped there wouldn't be much risk involved. I had a boyfriend who frowned on that sort of thing. Then I sighed. Because of a stray kid, I'd have to cancel a rare lunch date with said boyfriend, who was a very nice veterinarian named Brent. He took the news a little too well, which put me in a bad mood, so I was short with Jon Gardner, my barn manager and all-around right arm when he asked if I could pick up some Epsom salts before I left Walmart. We soaked horse's feet in the salts whenever they got an abscess, which was rare, but it sometimes happened.

The area around Walmart was not as crowded as I had expected, even though it was coming up on the noon hour on a breezy Tuesday. In addition to the breeze, there was an autumn chill in the air, which was odd for us this early in September. The shoppers I passed in the parking lot moved quickly, eager to find the bright warmth of the mega-store.

After I made a quick scan of the parking lots of the little strip mall where Bubba had been seen, as well as the parking areas for Walmart and its neighboring big box, Lowe's, I parked my truck behind the strip mall. Before I left the farm, Darcy had printed off a few copies of the only photo I had of Bubba. It was a great likeness of him in happier times sitting on our champion Appaloosa gelding, Hillbilly Bob.

I showed the photo to two ragged and bearded men who were sitting on top of a low pile of pallets that someone had left behind one of the stores. They passed a half-empty bottle between them as they looked at the photo. The picture drew a shake of the older man's head, but the younger, a man who had introduced himself as Jay, suggested I try to find someone they called The General. This man, apparently, was the head homeless person in the area and knew everything that was going on.

"Where should I look for him?" I asked.

"No looking involved," Jay said, swiping a dirt-stained hand across his lips. "Just hang around the stores and parking lots. He'll find you."

"If anyone's seen your boy, The General will know about it," said the older man, speaking for the first time. "Watch it, though. He's a little crazy."

Oh, goodie.

I moved my search into the stores. Bubba had been missing for nearly a week, as far as we could tell. Hill hadn't been home when Bubba had taken off, so the actual date and time of the departure were unknown. Bubba was resourceful, and had some street skills from his earlier runaways. But, he previously had either gone to Frog's house, or into Ashland City. This was the first time I knew of that he had headed toward Nashville.

In each store, I looked at the face of every stocky, five-foot tall person that I saw, but none of them were Bubba. As I was exiting Lowe's, a large man dressed in a striped poncho, pink sweat pants and a battered cowboy hat that long ago had lost any color that it might have had, stood on the sidewalk smack in front of me. It was like he had appeared out of thin air.

Instinctively, I pulled away and was about ready to scream when he saluted me. Then he took off his hat to reveal a few wisps or gray hair, and bowed.

"The General is at your service, ma'am."

Before I could say a word, the man beckoned, and then limped off toward the woods behind the store. I hesitated, then sent texts to Jon, Darcy, and Martin Giles, a young Cheatham County deputy who happened to be the brother of the veterinarian I should have had lunch with. My nature was to be impulsive, but even I wasn't going to skip off into the woods with a crazy homeless man without telling people where I was going.

The General looked back and eagerly waved me to the edge of the woods with his right arm. I put my cell into the pocket of my jeans, then stuck my hand into my purse and got a firm grip on the can of pepper spray I had started to carry after I got kidnapped last February.

I glanced around, still not sure this was what I needed to be doing, then I thought of Bubba. The General was an older man, and not in great shape from the way he walked. I had pepper spray and I could always clock him with my heavy purse if the need arose. I was also pretty fit from riding horses six to eight hours most days. I gave one last look around the parking lot, and then stepped into the woods with The General.

We traveled down a dry, narrow path that paralleled the Cumberland River, which ran behind Lowe's. After what must have been the equivalent of a long block, we entered a clearing that had been made for a monster of a utility tower. Large cables ran through the many, long arms of the silver tower, and I was sure I could feel the electric current vibrating through my body as we passed underneath it. Or, maybe my insides were just shaking with fear. The General led me into more woods on the other side of the clearing and we walked another hundred yards to a second open area. In the center were five blue sleeping tents, each identical and standing about five feet in height.

My mouth gaped open. I had heard of homeless camps, but had never before seen one. A lot of trash was strewn about, mostly plastic shopping bags and crushed beer cans. A clothesline hung from two tall Sycamore trees on the left side of the camp, and two sleeping bags were draped to air out over the line.

Three or four people in unkempt attire milled about. Two sat on rickety lawn chairs, and one tended a campfire. Homelessness is hard on a person's body, so it was hard to tell the age of any of the people, but they certainly did not look young. I wondered if Bubba was hiding in one of the tents, or if any of the other people were crazy, like The General.

The General saluted me again as I sat at a table near the campfire, then proceeded to take off all of his clothes, except his underwear. I had never been so grateful to see undergarments in all my life. As The General wiggled his dirty toes in front of the fire, I declined the bottle of water that an older woman offered.

The photo of Bubba didn't look familiar to anyone in the camp, even though I explained that he had been seen near here. I scanned each of the faces. I believed they all were telling me the truth. My heart both leapt and sank. While I didn't want Bubba to have experienced life in this camp, I had also desperately hoped he'd be here, so I could take him home.

"Where would someone like Bubba go?" I asked the group.

"Lots of places," the older woman, Mary, said. "There's another camp on the hill behind the pizza store. Just look for the path and start climbing up. You'll see it."

"Pete and Jay's camp," said The General.

I was pretty sure those were the two men I had met behind the store.

"We'd know if he was hanging with them, though," said The General.

I nodded and asked about the woman Frog had seen Bubba with.

"Sounds like Maxi," said Mary. "She's been off her meds lately. Sweet kid. She's not dangerous, just thinks she's John Lennon."

I could relate. I had a growing feeling that I was Alice in Wonderland and had just dropped down the rabbit hole.

"Then there's the abandoned Howard Johnson's across the freeway," said The General. "That's a bad, bad place." He grabbed my arm, hard. "Do. Not. Go. There. If your boy is there, there is no saving him."

The General had a look in his eye that frightened me and my hand tightened on the can of pepper spray in my purse. Mary noticed my unease and shook her head. "Not a good thought, is it, to have a child out on the streets like we are?"

"He's been missing about a week now," I said, "and I don't think he had much money to start with. I just don't know where to go next."

"Talk to the people in the stores," Mary said. "Look at everyone who walks by, and look in every car. Someone has seen him."

I left The General singing marching songs at the camp and wound my way back to Lowe's. At the back of the store an older teen swept the loading dock. There was something about the sullen way that he looked at me, so I walked up to the dock and sweetly handed the photo of Bubba up to him. Sullenness brings out the worst in me, and causes me to be intentionally irritating

"Hi," said with my perkiest smile. I couldn't help myself. "Have you seen this boy?"

"Nope."

He hadn't even looked at the picture, so I put my hands on my hips and used the calm but commanding voice that made silly horses stop and take notice. "Stop sweeping," I said. "A kid is missing."

He glanced at Bubba's image and shook his head.

My Irish intuition told me he was lying and suddenly I wished that Sally Blue were here. Agnes, her owner, swore up and down that Sally gave clues through her odd behavior and through the way she positioned her body.

"You work here every day?" I asked.

"Most days." He paused to consider me. "Why do you want to find this guy?"

"I'm a friend. A neighbor. I want to help him."

"You're not the law? Not social services?"

I shook my head, then he reached for Bubba's picture. "Okay. He stayed here a few nights, on top of that pile of pallets." He pointed behind him. "He was gone when I came in yesterday."

"How did he seem?"

"He was tired and hungry. I slipped him a few candy bars."

"I'm sure Bubba appreciated that . . ."

"Chip."

"Let me ask you, Chip. Where would he go?"

He thought. "There's a little service station across Charlotte Avenue. Some homeless hang out there. Sometimes the owner lets them stay in a storage room."

As Chip talked, I noticed that my urge to be irritating decreased in direct proportion to his willingness to help. I thanked him, flashed him another smile (this time it was genuine), and headed to the service station. On the way I called Jon.

"I'm making headway, but haven't found him yet," I explained. "Can you feed for me this afternoon?" Jon was feeding mornings and I in the afternoons this week. Jon agreed and I also asked if he could take a look at Sally Blue, to see what she was doing.

"You're not buying into the psychic thing are you?" he asked. I heard the smile in his voice.

"No . . . well maybe."

I heard Jon walk to Sally's stall at the end of the barn, then say, "She's got her eyes closed and is swinging her head back and forth as she stumbles around her stall."

"Hmm. That's going to require some thinking. Thanks, Jon."

"No trouble." He paused. "Cat, I hope you find Bubba soon. If I can help, let me know."

"You just did, you and Sally."

The service station was a single-bay affair with a tiny waiting room. Faded yellow linoleum cling limply to the floor, and a dusty display case held half a dozen candy bars and what possibly could have once been a granola bar. A grimy, white door opened onto the filthiest bathroom in modern history. Again, I both wanted Bubba to have used it and hoped that he hadn't been within half a mile of it.

A heavy, lumpy man with a shiny, bald head sat behind the counter smoking a cigar. The name embroidered on his blue work shirt read STICKS. A former drummer, maybe. I tried not to breathe in cigar fumes when I showed Bubba's picture to him, but quickly realized the smoke was so think that I must be absorbing an alarming amount of toxins through my skin. Hopefully I would not be there long.

Sticks thought a minute, then stood and yelled over his shoulder, "Maxi."

A wary girl of sixteen or so emerged from a back room that I had not noticed before. Stringy blond hair, waif thin, and a face accented by round John Lennon glasses.

"Maxi don't got nowhere else to go, so I let her stay here," he said to me. Then to her, "Have I seen you with this kid?"

She came to the counter to look. "Sure," she said folding her arms over her thin frame. "That's Bubba."

"Where's he now?" Sticks asked. "This gal here," he pointed at me, "is his friend. She wants to help him."

Maxi shook her head. "I don't know."

There had to be more here, but I couldn't stand another second in the smoky room. "Would you like a cup of coffee?" I asked Maxi. "Something to eat?"

"I could use a burger," she said looking up the road at a Wendy's.

We said our goodbyes to Sticks and I bought us double burgers, large fries and Sprites. After we found a booth, she began to wolf her food down, only stopping for huge gulps of her Sprite. I waited for her to finish, then asked, "When did you meet Bubba?"

"Four or five days ago. He was looking through the dumpster behind Walmart." My heart ached for Bubba.

"Then you and he hung out together?"

"Yeah. We wandered around, mostly. Once, a lady came around and gave all the homeless bus passes, so we rode into Nashville and scored some food on Music Row, just sat down at an outdoor table and finished off some food that people had left behind. It's amazing the amount of food people waste." This last was said with the first sense of animation that I had seen in her.

"Did he say why he ran away?"

"Because of the kids at school." Maxi was eying the rest of my food so I pushed my tray toward her. She made short work of the remains of my hamburger. When she had finished she said, "Bubba told me he and his dad were poor, and there were times when he didn't have decent clothes or any food."

"I'm sorry to say that he's right."

"Kids today make it hard when you're different," Maxi said, dipping into my left over fries. "If you're different they don't want to have anything to do with you. Bubba was bullied at school, and bullied at home. Sounds like his dad is a real loser."

"So Bubba decided he'd had enough, and left," I said.

Maxi nodded glumly, the realities of the world etched into her young face.

"I can help him," I said to Maxi. "I can talk to his dad, call the school to let them know what is going on. It won't be great, but I will make sure life is better for Bubba when he gets home." I was a little surprised at the intensity of the words that poured out of my mouth, but I realized that I meant them. "When did you last see Bubba?"

"This morning. We both spent the night in the shop. Then he left. He's out looking for a more permanent place to stay."

What she said brought me to tears. Darcy, Jon, and I had always referred to Bubba as dumb and annoying. My tears were of shame, because I'd not done more to help a young boy get through a difficult childhood.

I thanked Maxi, wished her luck, and went out to search the now darkening streets. I abandoned the Walmart area and headed up Charlotte Avenue toward Nashville, looking in every nook, cranny, dumpster, and wooded area that I could find. As night fell I used the

flashlight app on my phone. Every time I got out of the truck, I
also held on tightly to my can of pepper spray, but by the time I got
back in to drive to the next building I was filled with disappointment.

The search around the Nashville West shopping center
took a long time. There were a number of stores, but other than
dumpsters, the area behind them was clean of pallets and debris. The
stores had closed for the evening, but restaurants in the area were
still busy so I looked carefully in and around each car. There was
absolutely no sign of Bubba.

I read newspapers and watched the news. I knew if Bubba
stayed on the street too much longer, someone would get to him,
someone with bad things on his or her mind. I could not, would not,
let that happen.

I drove back out onto Charlotte and turned into a clearing
where the West Precinct police station used to be. That building had
been torn down and a paved road circled a small log building, a
replica of an early settler's home. The home had recently been
moved, and was set up on a tall pile of cement blocks. The stairs had
not yet been attached back to the porch.

"Bubba?" I called as I had at every other location. "Bubba,
it's Cat. I've come to take you back to my house. Please come. I'll do
my best to make life better."

Without any thought of finding him, I hoisted myself onto
the porch of the two-room cabin. Bubba was in the room on the left,
sitting against the far wall. Even in the dim light of my flashlight, I
could see his tear-streaked face.

I slid down next to him. "Will you come home with me?"

He was quiet for a moment, and then said, "Maybe." We sat in the chilly night in silence for some time before he spoke again. "Why did you come looking for me?" he asked.

Then it was my turn to sit quietly while I thought of the right answer. "Because you once saved my life. Because I care about you. Because Darcy cares about you, too, and demanded that I find you. Because Jon wanted to help, but had to take care of the horses. Because I had a dad who couldn't be responsible enough to be a dad and I know what it's like. And because Sally Blue was worried about you."

"How do you know that?"

"I called Jon to ask him to check on her, to see if she could tell us where you were. She was walking around her stall with her eyes closed, weaving her head back and forth like a blind person moves a walking stick," I said.

Bubba almost laughed, but caught himself just in time.

"I didn't understand it then, but I now think it means one of two things," I said. "Sally either had dust in her eyes and was looking for her water bucket . . ."

"Or?" Bubba asked.

"Or she knew you were in a dark place and were having trouble seeing."

"And here I am in the dark and it's hard to see!" said Bubba, who had always been on the side of "Sally is psychic."

I paused. "Maxi told me kids are making it hard for you at school."

Tears leaked from Bubba's eyes, then he turned to me and sobbed as I wrapped my arms around him.

"Did you mean it," he finally asked, "About going home with you?"

"I did. For tonight, and maybe tomorrow anyway," I said. "Your dad is going to want you to come home." I felt Bubba stiffen. "But here's what I can do. I'll call Deputy Giles. He will tell your dad that you are safe with me and will bring you back to your house tomorrow. He will also give your dad a good talking to about treating you properly. Then I'll call your school and explain about the other kids. Your job will then be to tell your teachers and me if the kids are still bothering you. Okay?"

I felt Bubba nod in the darkness. Then we both rose, and headed for the dry warmth of the truck.

EXCERPT

The Fame Equation: A Cat Enright Equestrian Mystery

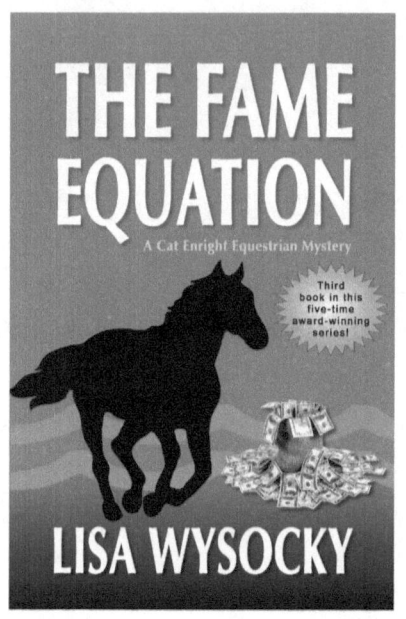

The Fame Equation is the third in the Cat Enright series, which has won Mom's Choice, IBPA Ben Franklin, National Indie Excellence, and American Horse Publications awards, and has been optioned for film and television.

Author's note: This scene takes place a day or so after a funeral for Cat Enright's friend, country music star Melody Cross. Melody came from what we in the South politely call trailer trash. Here, Cat goes to the run-down hotel where Melody's sister and mother, Brandyne and Claudine, are staying until Melody's will is read. At the funeral, Brandyne had attacked Cat, hitting her with her purse and pulling her hair. Later, Cat has a conversation with her trusted barn manager, Jon Gardner, about the (possibly) psychic mare, Sally Blue.

AT THE HOTEL, I PARKED my truck among a series of rusted
out sedans with cracked windshields and duct tape that held heavy
plastic in place instead of glass windows. I looked for a car without a
dent and did not find one. I should have brought Hank the Beagle to
act as a security guard, I thought.

My truck had some tears in and stains on the upholstery,
and it hiccupped going up the occasional hill, but it had over two
hundred thousand miles on it, so it was entitled. Okay, it sometimes
didn't want to start unless I held the driver's side door open, and it
had rust, but you almost couldn't see it unless you knew where to
look. I really wanted to keep it dent-free.

I gave my truck a final glance, found room 217, held my
breath, and knocked on the door. After a moment Brandyne opened
it.

"You," she said.

"May I come in?"

The expression on her face said she'd rather walk barefoot
through a field of doggie doo, but she widened the opening in the
door. Inside, the room was much as I had expected: stained carpet,
dingy bedspread, a wall with streaks running down it from a past
leak, and a smell that made me want to clamp a clothespin over my
nose. There was a dorm sized fridge, and a microwave on top of a
shelf that also held a coffeemaker, which I guessed allowed hotel
management to advertise that their rooms came complete with a
kitchenette. I didn't look into the bathroom. Some things are best left
to the imagination.

Claudine was sitting at a crooked little table near the window smoking a cigarette. She'd been at it a while, because the room was blue with stale smoke. Well that simplified things. My visit would definitely be short.

"Mrs. Potts, Brandyne," I nodded to each of them and decided to ignore the fiasco that had happened at the reception. "I'm Cat Enright. We didn't get to speak properly at the funeral, but I wanted to say how sorry I am about Melody. She was wellliked here in Nashville and had many friends. I was proud to call myself one of them."

A "humpf," was all I got from Claudine. Brandyne stood in the center of the room with her arms folded. I stared at her and finally her posture relaxed.

"Can't say as I agree with you 'bout Raylene havin' all those friends you're talkin' about, as you're the only one's come to call," said Brandyne.

At first I didn't know who she was talking about, then it dawned on me that Melody's family must still have called her by her birth name. Raylene.

"We been sittin' here for two days, waitin' on the will, an' not one person come to say boo to us," she continued.

"Except me," I reminded her. I was trying to hold my breath while I spoke. The smoke in the room was so thick I was certain that I could feel cancer cells multiplying in my lungs.

"'Cept you," she conceded. "Look, I'm sorry about the other day. I was outta my mind with grief. If I ever get my hands on the slimeball who kilt Raylene I'll kick his ass right on into next Tuesday."

"Humpf," commented Claudine.

At least it was better than her wailing.

"Apology accepted," I said. It was another little white lie. By golly I was racking them up. I'm not sure I ever would forgive Brandyne, though. My head still hurt where she had pulled my hair. "Melody was special and I will really miss her."

"I never could cotton to people callin' my baby Melody," Claudine said. "Her name was Raylene Claudette Potts."

"Don't matter what people called her, Momma," said Brandyne. "She's dead."

At that, Claudine started to wail.

"Now look what you gone and done," she said to me.

Me? Brandyne was the passive aggressive one here.

"Thank God this will all be over and done tomorrow and we can get outta Dodge," Brandyne said, offering no comfort whatsoever to her mother. "Soon as we collect our money, we're gone."

I couldn't help myself, even if it meant staying longer so I could grow a few hundred thousand more cancer cells. "What money is that, Brandyne?"

"From Raylene's estate, stupid. My sister was a rich little girl, and we're her family. That money is ours now, mine and Momma's, and brother Bodine's. Well, it'll be Bodine's when he gets outta prison. I'll take care of it for him until then."

I just bet she would. I was just as sure that Bodine would never see a red cent of his sister's estate.

"If she was gonna change her name, why'd she choose somethin' as awful as Melody Cross?" This from Claudine, whose brain was apparently stuck on broken. I looked around and saw a trash can overflowing with beer bottles. Quart sized ones. Ah. That explained it.

"She wanted to get away from us, Momma. To 'distance' herself." Brandyne made quote marks with her fingers when she said "distance." "That's why she changed her name. We weren't good enough for the little princess." This last part Brandyne said with a sneer.

"You know, I probably should go," I said edging my way toward the door. But Claudine got there before me, blocking my way on her unsteady feet.

"I couldn't help it if I wanted to have a little fun, could I?" she asked, waving a cigarette so close to my face I almost gagged. I don't begrudge people the right to smoke. I just normally don't choose to be around them when they do.

"I had them kids, Brandyne and Bodine, when I was just a kid. I was thirty when Raylene came along. Same daddy, in case you're askin.'"

I wasn't.

"By the time Raylene arrived I'd been a momma most half my life. When she got in kindy-garden, I was more than ready to party. This one," she said, now waving her cigarette at Brandyne, "already had two young 'uns of her own by then, and Bodine had got hisself into prison––for the first time. You can't blame me none for wantin' to have a little fun, but I'll never forgive them social service people who came and took my little Raylene from me. Not ever. Look where that got her. My baby's done been kilt."

With that, Claudine wavered, then slumped into a nearby chair. Looked to me as if she'd be out for a while. I should have picked Claudine's burning cigarette up off the floor, but I couldn't quite bring myself to do it. Instead, I said my goodbyes to Brandyne, and got the heck out of there.

I couldn't believe that smart, sweet Melody had come from those people. No wonder she wanted to distance herself. The older church-going couple that had raised her had done an incredible job. I wondered what Melody had been like when they first welcomed her into their home, what she had been like when she was six.

Melody had worked hard to make a better life for herself, and it made me mad all over again to realize that someone had stolen that life from her. Brandyne, I thought, as I got into the truck, could have killed Melody in a heartbeat. There was no love lost there. I wondered where she had been last week. Maybe Martin would know.

Before I started up the truck I texted Jon that I was safe, then rolled down the windows. The smell of Claudine's cigarettes had gotten into my hair and clothes and I couldn't stand to smell myself. First thing on the agenda when I got home was a shower.

*****

I drove back down Old Hickory Boulevard and wove my way up Charlotte Pike and onto River Road. All the time I was trying to come up with a Plan B, just in case Deputy Giles wouldn't let me be his shadow at the will reading the next day. I felt as dumb as Bodine, as I couldn't come up with a thing.

I also wondered about the furniture that Melody had promised me. Not that it was a big deal. Davis, her manager, knew about it, and there was the note Melody had put on the table for the movers. I'd like to have the furniture for the sole reason that the pieces had meant something to my friend.

I kicked myself for not asking Davis about the furniture when I was in his office. But maybe that could be my excuse to pop in at the will reading tomorrow. I could arrive on the pretense of asking about the furniture. I didn't know the time of the reading, but if I parked myself outside the lawyer's office until I saw familiar faces . . . It was weak, I knew, but it was all I had. Hopefully the deputy would agree with my Plan A.

On River Road, with a Keith Carson song blasting through my radio, Jon called.

"You close?" he asked.

"Ten minutes max. What's up?"

"Sally's acting weird again. Or I should say, weirder."

"What now?"

"She was in the pasture and was facing the road, holding her right foreleg in front of her and waving it around."

"Is she lame?"

"Nothing like that. She trotted out fine. I noticed it because Gigi was running circles around Sally while Sally stood with her foreleg like that."

"I guess they should come in, then."

"Already done. Sally walked in just fine."

"I'll be back in a few to do the 'new horse' evaluation on Ringo," I said. "We can watch Sally for colic, but I'm thinking this is just Sally, and that she's not really hurt."

"We might get her a massage, or a chiropractic adjustment," said Jon. "She's been lying in such a strange position that she might have soreness, even though she isn't lame."

I asked Jon to schedule a massage first, and we'd evaluate after. I drove into my driveway a few minutes later and hustled upstairs for a shower. Later, out in the barn, Sally was holding her leg up in her stall. I slid the stall door open and palpated the limb from the top of her shoulder to the sole of her hoof. There was no soreness that I could find. When Jon came by with a flake of hay, Sally put her foot down on the ground and ate like a normal horse. Or, as normal as a horse like Sally could be.

Cat's Horse Tip #11

"Horses easily recognize the emotions of other horses,
as well as the emotions of humans, dogs, cats,
and other animals."

Interview

MG: As a child, what did you want to do when you grew up?

LW: I wanted to be a dump truck driver. That period lasted from the time I was about two until I was in first grade. By that time I knew I wanted to do something with horses.

MG: When did you first realize you wanted to be a writer?

LW: When I was twelve. I was driving my mother nuts one Sunday afternoon and in desperation she handed me a Dick Francis mystery. I was hooked! I was an avid reader even as a child, but until then I had not put together the idea that you could write great mysteries that involved horses. I knew then that someday I would write equestrian mysteries. Getting published just took me a few years longer than I had initially planned.

MG: What do you like to do when you're not writing?

LW: I am a therapeutic riding instructor, so I teach people with life challenges about themselves and about the horse. I also teach horse clinics, and can be seen at some of the horse fairs and expos around the country. When I have time I hike or ride, and I love sitting by a lake or ocean with a good book. Few people are brave enough to play Scrabble with me, but once in a while I find someone who is willing to take the risk!

MG: What was one of the most surprising things you learned in creating your mystery series?

LW: That the characters have such deeply entwined relationships. These characters lived in my head for seventeen years before the first book was published, so I thought I knew who they were. But, they have gone places that I never envisioned in subsequent books. Even I am surprised!

MG: What quirky traits does your protagonist, Cat Enright, have?

LW: As Cat says, she has a "teensy anger management problem." One day she will take care of it, but not today. She is a kind and loyal person who allows frustrating situations and events to build up to the point that all of her emotions explode out of her. Cat thinks hot chocolate should be its own food group, and deals with her damaged past by surrounding herself with an eclectic group of friends who have their own odd pasts to deal with. Other than hot chocolate she can't cook a thing, but she is a heck of a horsewoman.

MG: Why did you set your series in Ashland City, Tennessee?

LW: Many cozies are set in small towns, and as a former newspaper reporter who covered this town, I was familiar with it. Ashland City is rural enough to have some horse farms, yet close enough to Nashville to sometimes bring in elements of the music scene there.

Plus, the geography and terrain of Cheatham County (Ashland City is the county seat) gives me many creative places to hide a body.

MG: What other authors have influenced your writing?

LW: Every author I have read has influenced me in some way. To single out those who have had the most influence, I'd have to start with Dick Francis and his son, Felix, who is doing a fine job of keeping those great stories coming. Sue Grafton, Sara Paretsky, Margaret Maron, Joan Hess, my fellow Nashvillians Steven Womack and J.T. Ellison, Janet Evanovich, Peter Abrahams (Spencer Quinn), Robert B. Parker, John D. McDonald. Robert Crais, Hank Phillippi Ryan, Sue Monk Kidd, Amy Tan, and Rita Mae Brown would be on the list as well. I'm sure I have forgotten to include several dozen other great writers.

MG: What do you think makes a good story?

LW: Engaging characters, a plausible but creative plotline, and a unique setting will hook me every time. I also have to care--about the characters, and about the outcome of the story. Books that keep me up all night are the ones that have me rooting for the main characters from the very first chapter. The writing has to sparkle, as well. There are too many fabulous writers for a reader to spend time with anything other than great writing.

www.ingramcontent.com/pod-product-compliance
Lightning Source LLC
Chambersburg PA
CBHW031149120726
47905CB00006B/1872